Charles W. Upham

Salem Witchcraft and Cotton Mather

SALZWASSER VERLAG

Charles W. Upham

Salem Witchcraft and Cotton Mather

1st Edition | ISBN: 978-3-84605-908-1

Place of Publication: Frankfurt am Main, Germany

Year of Publication: 2020

Salzwasser Verlag GmbH, Germany.

Reprint of the original, first published in 1869.

SALEM WITCHCRAFT

AND

COTTON MATHER.

A REPLY.

BY

CHARLES W. UPHAM,

Member of the Massachusetts Historical Society.

———

MORRISANIA, N. Y.:

1869.

PREFATORY NOTE.

The Editors of the *North American Review* would, under the circumstances, I have no reason to doubt, have opened its columns to a reply to the article that has led to the preparation of the following statement. But its length has forbidden my asking such a favor.

All interested in the department of American literature to which the HISTORICAL MAGAZINE belongs, must appreciate the ability with which it is conducted, and the laborious and indefatigable zeal of its Editor, in collecting and placing on its pages, beyond the reach of oblivion and loss, the scattered and perishing materials necessary to the elucidation of historical and biographical topics, whether relating to particular localities or the country at large; and it was as gratifying as unexpected to receive the proffer, without limitation, of the use of that publication for this occasion.

The spirited discussion, by earnest scholars, of special questions, although occasionally assuming the aspect of controversy, will be not only tolerated but welcomed by liberal minds. Let champions arise, in all sections of the Republic, to defend their respective rightful claims to share in a common glorious inheritance and to inscribe their several records in our Annals. Feeling the deepest interest in the Historical, Antiquarian, and Genealogical Societies of Massachusetts, and yielding to none in keen sensibility to all that concerns the ancient honors of the Old Bay State and New England, generally, I rejoice to witness the spirit of a commemorative age kindling the public mind, every where, in the Middle, Western and Southern States.

The courtesy extended to me is evidence that while, by a jealous scrutiny and, sometimes, perhaps, a sharp conflict, we are reciprocally imposing checks upon loose exaggerations and overweening pretensions, a comprehensive good feeling predominates over all; truth in its purity is getting eliminated; and characters and occurrences, in all parts of the country, brought under the clear light of justice.

The aid I have received, in the following discussion, from the publications and depositories of historical associations and the contributions of individuals, like Mr. Goodell, Doctor Moore, and others, engaged in procuring from the mother country and preserving all original tracts and documents, whenever found, belonging to our Colonial period, demonstrate the importance of such efforts, whether of Societies or single persons. In this way, our history will stand on a solid foundation, and have the lineaments of complete and exact truth.

Notwithstanding the distance from the place of printing, owing to the faithful and intelligent oversight of the superintendent of the press and the vigilant care of the compositors, but few errors, I trust, will be found, beyond what are merely literal, and every reader will unconsciously, or readily, correct for himself.

C. W. U.

SALEM, MASSACHUSETTS.

TABLE OF CONTENTS.

SALEM WITCHCRAFT AND COTTON MATHER.

INTRODUCTION.

An article in *The North American Review*, for April, 1869, is mostly devoted to a notice of the work published by me, in 1867, entitled *Salem Witchcraft, with an account of Salem Village, and a history of opinions on witchcraft and kindred subjects*. If the article had contained criticisms, in the usual style, merely affecting the character of that work, in a literary point of view, no other duty would have devolved upon me, than carefully to consider and respectfully heed its suggestions. But it raises questions of an historical nature that seem to demand a response, either acknowledging the correctness of its statements or vindicating my own.

The character of the Periodical in which it appears; the manner in which it was heralded by rumor, long before its publication; its circulation, since, in a separate pamphlet form; and the extent to which, in certain quarters, its assumptions have been endorsed, make a reply imperative.

The subject to which it relates is of acknowledged interest and importance. The Witchcraft Delusion of 1692 has justly arrested a wider notice, and probably always will, than any other occurrence in the early colonial history of this country. It presents phenomena in the realm of our spiritual nature, belonging to that higher department of physiology, known as Psychology, of the greatest moment; and illustrates the operations of the imagination upon the passions and faculties in immediate connection with it, and the perils to which the soul and society are thereby exposed, in a manner more striking, startling and instructive than is elsewhere to be found. For all reasons, truth and justice require of those who venture to explore and portray it, the utmost efforts to elucidate its passages and delineate correctly its actors.

With these views I hail with satisfaction the criticisms that may be offered upon my book, without regard to their personal character or bearing, as continuing and heightening the interest felt in the subject; and avail myself of the opportunity, tendered to me without solicitation and in a most liberal spirit, by the proprietor of this Magazine, to meet the obligations which historical truth and justice impose.

The principal charge, and it is repeated in innumerable forms through the sixty odd pages of the article in the *North American*, is that I have misrepresented the part borne by Cotton Mather in the proceedings connected with the Witchcraft Delusion and prosecutions, in 1692. Various other complaints are made of inaccuracy and unfairness, particularly in reference to the position of Increase Mather and the course of the Boston Ministers of that period, generally. Although the discussion, to which I now ask attention, may appear, at first view, to relate to questions merely personal, it will be found, I think, to lead to an exploration of the literature and prevalent sentiments, relating to religious and philosophical subjects, of that period; and, also, of an instructive passage in the public history of the Province of Massachusetts Bay.

I now propose to present the subject more fully than was required, or would have been appropriate, in my work on Witchcraft.

I.

THE CONNECTION OF THE MATHERS WITH THE SUPERSTITIONS OF THEIR TIME.

In the first place, I venture to say that it can admit of no doubt, that Increase Mather and his son, Cotton Mather, did more than any other persons to aggravate the tendency of that age to the result reached in the Witchcraft Delusion of 1692. The latter, in the beginning of the Sixth Book of the *Magnalia Christi Americana*, refers to an attempt made, about the year 1658, "among some "divines of no little figure throughout England "and Ireland, for the faithful registering of re- "markable providences. But, alas," he says, "it "came to nothing that was remarkable. The "like holy design," he continues, "was, by the "Reverend Increase Mather, proposed among "the divines of New England, in the year 1681,

"at a general meeting of them; who thereupon
"desired him to begin and publish an Essay;
"which he did in a little while; but there-withal
"declared that he did it only as a specimen of a
"larger volume, in hopes that this work being
"set on foot, posterity would go on with it."
Cotton Mather did go on with it, immediately
upon his entrance to the ministry; and by their
preaching, publications, correspondence at home
and abroad, and the influence of their learning,
talents, industry, and zeal in the work, these two
men promoted the prevalence of a passion for the
marvelous and monstrous, and what was deemed
preternatural, infernal, and diabolical, throughout the whole mass of the people, in England as
well as America. The public mind became infatuated and, drugged with credulity and superstition, was prepared to receive every impulse of
blind fanaticism. The stories, thus collected and
put everywhere in circulation, were of a nature
to terrify the imagination, fill the mind with horrible apprehensions, degrade the general intelligence and taste, and dethrone the reason. They
darken and dishonor the literature of that period.
A rehash of them can be found in the Sixth Book
of the *Magnalia*. The effects of such publications were naturally developed in wide-spread
delusions and universal credulity. They penetrated the whole body of society, and reached all
the inhabitants and families of the land, in the
towns and remotest settlements. In this way, the
Mathers, particularly the younger, made themselves responsible for the diseased and bewildered
state of the public mind, in reference to supernatural and diabolical agencies, which came to a
head in the Witchcraft Delusion. I do not say
that they were culpable. Undoubtedly they
thought they were doing God service. But the
influence they exercised, in this direction, remains
none the less an historical fact.

Increase Mather applied himself, without delay, to the prosecution of the design he had proposed, by writing to persons in all parts of the
country, particularly clergymen, to procure, for
publication, as many marvelous stories as could
be raked up. In the eighth volume of the Fourth
Series of the *Collections of the Massachusetts
Historical Society*, consisting of *The Mather Papers*, the responses of several of his correspondents may be seen. [*Pp. 285, 360, 361. 367, 466,
475, 555, 612.*] He pursued this business with an
industrious and pertinacious zeal, which nothing
could slacken. After the rest of the world had
been shocked out of such mischievous nonsense,
by the horrid results at Salem, on the fifth of
March, 1694, as President of Harvard College, he
issued a Circular to "The Reverend Ministers of
"the Gospel, in the several Churches in New Eng-
"land," signed by himself and seven others, members of the Corporation of that institution, urg-

ing it, as the special duty of Ministers of the
Gospel, to obtain and preserve knowledge of notable occurrences, described under the general
head of "*Remarkables*," and classified as follows:

"The things to be esteemed memorable are,
"especially, all unusual accidents, in the heav-
"en, or earth, or water; all wonderful de-
"liverances of the distressed; mercies to the
"godly; judgments to the wicked; and more
"glorious fulfilments of either the promises or
"the threatenings, in the Scriptures of truth;
"with apparitions, possessions, inchantments,
"and all extraordinary things wherein the exis-
"tence and agency of the invisible world is more
"sensibly demonstrated."—*Magnalia Christi
Americana*. Edit. London, 1702. Book VI, p. 1.

All communications, in answer to this missive
were to be addressed to the "President and Fel-
"lows" of Harvard College.

The first article is as follows: "To observe
"and record the more illustrious discoveries of
"the Divine Providence, in the government of
"the world, is a design so holy, so useful, so
"justly approved, that the too general neglect of
"of it in the Churches of God, is as justly to be
"lamented." It is important to consider this
language in connection with that used by Cotton
Mather, in opening the Sixth Book of the *Magnalia*: "To regard the illustrious displays of that
"Providence, wherewith our Lord Christ gov-
"erns the world, is a work than which there is
"none more needful or useful for a Christian;
"to record them is a work than which none
"more proper for a Minister; and perhaps the
"great Governor of the world will ordinarily do
"the most notable things for those who are most
"ready to take a wise notice of what he does.
"Unaccountable, therefore, and inexcusable, is
"the sleepiness, even upon the most of good
"men throughout the world, which indisposes
"them to observe and, much more, to preserve,
"the remarkable dispensations of Divine Provi-
"dence, towards themselves or others. Never-
"theless there have been raised up, now and then,
"those persons, who have rendered themselves
"worthy of everlasting remembrance, by their
"wakeful zeal to have the memorable providences
"of God remembered through all generations."

These passages from the Mathers, father and
son, embrace, in their bearings, a period, eleven
years before and two years after the Delusion of
1692. They show that the Clergy, generally,
were indifferent to the subject, and required to
be aroused from "neglect" and "sleepiness,"
touching the duty of flooding the public mind
with stories of "wonders" and "remarkables;"
and that the agency of the Mathers, in giving
currency, by means of their ministry and influence, to such ideas, was peculiar and preemin-

ent. However innocent and excusable their motives may have been, the laws of cause and effect remained unbroken; and the result of their actions are, with truth and justice, attributable to them—not necessarily, I repeat, to impeach their honesty and integrity, but their wisdom, taste, judgment, and common sense. Human responsibility is not to be set aside, nor avoided, merely and wholly by good intent. It involves a solemn and fearful obligation to the use of reason, caution, cool deliberation, circumspection, and a most careful calculation of consequences. Error, if innocent and honest, is not punishable by divine, and ought not to be by human, law. It is covered by the mercy of God, and must not be pursued by the animosity of men. But it is, nevertheless, a thing to be dreaded and to be guarded against, with the utmost vigilance. Throughout the melancholy annals of the Church and the world, it has been the fountain of innumerable woes, spreading baleful influences through society, paralysing the energies of reason and conscience, dimming, all but extinguishing, the light of religion, convulsing nations, and desolating the earth. It is the duty of historians to trace it to its source; and, by depicting faithfully the causes that have led to it, prevent its recurrence. With these views, I feel bound, distinctly, to state that the impression given to the popular sentiments of the period, to which I am referring, by certain leading minds, led to, was the efficient cause of, and, in this sense, may be said to have originated, the awful superstitions long prevalent in the old world and the new, and reaching a final catastrophe in 1692; and among these leading minds, aggravating and intensifying, by their writings, this most baleful form of the superstition of the age, Increase and Cotton Mather stand most conspicuous.

This opinion was entertained, at the time, by impartial observers. Francis Hutchinson, D. D. "Chaplain in ordinary to his Majesty, and "Minister of St. James's Parish, in St. Edmund's Bury," in the life-time of both the Mathers, published, in London, an *Historical Essay concerning Witchcraft*, dedicated to the "Lord Chief-justice of England, the Lord Chief-"justice of Common Pleas, and the Lord Chief "Baron of Exchequer." In a Chapter on *The Witchcraft in Salem, Boston, and Andover, in New England*, he attributes it, as will be seen in the course of this article, to the influence of the writings of the Mathers.

In the Preface to the London edition of Cotton Mather's *Memorable Providences*, written by Richard Baxter, in 1690, he ascribes this same prominence to the works of the Mathers. While expressing the great value he attached to writings about Witchcraft, and the importance, in his view, of that department of literature which relates stories about diabolical agency, possessions, apparitions, and the like, he says, "Mr. Increase Mather "hath already published many such histories of "things done in New England; and this great instance published by his son"—that is, the account of the Goodwin children—"cometh with "such full convincing evidence, that he must be a "very obdurate Sadducee that will not believe it. "And his two Sermons, adjoined, are excellently "fitted to the subject and this blinded generation, "and to the use of us all, that are not past our "warfare with Devils." One of the Sermons, which Baxter commends, is on *The Power and Malice of Devils*, and opens with the declaration, that "there is a combination of Devils, which "our air is filled withal:" the other is on *Witchcraft*. Both are replete with the most exciting and vehement enforcements of the superstitions of that age, relating to the Devil and his confederates.

My first position, then, in contravention of that taken by the Reviewer in the *North American*, is that, by stimulating the Clergy over the whole country, to collect and circulate all sorts of marvelous and supposed preternatural occurrences, by giving this direction to the preaching and literature of the times, these two active, zealous, learned, and able Divines, Increase and Cotton Mather, considering the influence they naturally were able to exercise, are, particularly the latter, justly chargeable with, and may be said to have brought about, the extraordinary outbreaks of credulous fanaticism, exhibited in the cases of the Goodwin family and of "the afflicted children," at Salem Village. Robert Calef, writing to the Ministers of the country, March 18, 1694, says: "I having had, not only occasion, but renewed "provocation, to take a view of the mysterious "doctrines, which have of late been so much "contested among us, could not meet with any "that had spoken more, or more plainly, the "sense of those doctrines" [*relating to the Witchcraft*] "than the Reverend Mr. Cotton Mather, "but how clearly and consistent, either with "himself or the truth, I meddle not now to say, "but cannot but suppose his strenuous and zeal-"ous asserting his opinions has been one cause "of the dismal convulsions, we have here lately "fallen into."—*More Wonders of the Invisible World*, by Robert Calef, Merchant of Boston, in New England. Edit. London, 1700, p. 33.

The papers that remain, connected with the Witchcraft Examinations and Trials, at Salem, show the extent to which currency had been given, in the popular mind, to such marvelous and prodigious things as the Mathers had been so long endeavoring to collect and circulate; particularly in the interior, rural settlements. The solemn solitudes of the woods were filled with ghosts, hobgoblins, spectres, evil spirits, and the infernal Prince of them all. Every pathway was infested with their flitting shapes and footprints; and around every hearth-stone, shuddering circles, drawing closer together as the darkness of night thickened and their imaginations became more awed and frightened, listened to tales of diabolical operations: the same effects, in somewhat different forms, pervaded the seaboard settlements and larger towns.

Besides such frightful fancies, other most unhappy influences flowed from the prevalence of the style of literature which the Mathers brought into vogue. Suspicions and accusations of witchcraft were everywhere prevalent; any unusual calamity or misadventure; every instance of real or affected singularity of deportment or behavior—and, in that condition of perverted and distempered public opinion, there would be many such—was attributed to the Devil. Every sufferer who had yielded his mind to what was taught in pulpits or publications, lost sight of the Divine Hand, and could see nothing but devils in his afflictions. Poor John Goodwin, whose trials we are presently to consider, while his children were acting, as the phrase—originating in those days, and still lingering in the lower forms of vulgar speech—has it, "like all possessed," broke forth thus: "I thought of what David said. *2 Samuel*, "xxiv. 14. If he feared so to fall into the hands "of men, oh! then to think of the horrors of "our condition, to be in the hands of Devils and "Witches. Thus, our doleful condition moved "us to call to our friends to have pity on us, for "God's hand hath touched us. I was ready to "say that no one's affliction was like mine. That "my little house, that should be a little Bethel "for God to dwell in, should be made a den for "Devils; that those little Bodies, that should be "Temples for the Holy Ghost to dwell in, should "be thus harrassed and abused by the Devil and "his cursed brood."—*Late Memorable Providences, relating to Witchcraft and Possessions.* By Cotton Mather. Edit. London, 1691.

No wonder that the country was full of the terrors and horrors of diabolical imaginations, when the Devil was kept before the minds of men, by what they constantly read and heard, from their religious teachers! In the Sermons of that day, he was the all-absorbing topic of learning and eloquence. In some of Cotton Mather's, the name, Devil, or its synonyms, is mentioned ten times as often as that of the benign and blessed God.

No wonder that alleged witchcrafts were numerous! Drake, in his *History of Boston*, says there were many cases there, about the year 1688. Only one of them seems to have attracted the kind of notice requisite to preserve it from oblivion—that of the four children of John Goodwin, the eldest, thirteen years of age. The rela-

tion of this case, in my book [*Salem Witchcraft*, i. 454—460] was wholly drawn from the *Memorable Providences* and the *Magnalia*.

II.

THE GOODWIN CHILDREN. SOME GENERAL REMARKS UPON THE CRITICISM OF THE NORTH AMERICAN REVIEW.

The Reviewer charges me with having wronged Cotton Mather, by representing that he "got "up" the whole affair of the Goodwin children. He places the expression within quotation marks, and repeats it, over and over again. In the passage to which he refers—p. 365 of the second volume of my book—I say of Cotton Mather, that he "repeatedly endeavored to get up cases "of the kind in Boston. There is some ground "for suspicion that he was instrumental in origin- "ating the fanaticism in Salem." I am not aware that the expression was used, except in this passage. But, wherever used, it was designed to convey the meaning given to it, by both of our great lexicographers. Worcester defines "to get "up, 'to prepare, to make ready—to get up an "'entertainment;' 'to print and publish, as a "'book.'" Webster defines it, "to prepare "for coming before the public; to bring for- "ward." This is precisely what Mather did, in the case of the Goodwin children, and what Calef put a stop to his doing in the case of Margaret Rule.

In 1831, I published a volume entitled *Lectures on Witchcraft, comprising a history of the Delusion, in Salem, in 1692.* In 1867, I published *Salem Witchcraft, and an account of Salem Village;* and, in the Preface, stated that "the form- "er was prepared under circumstances which pre- "vented a thorough investigation of the subject. "Leisure and freedom from professional duties "have now enabled me to prosecute the research- "es necessary to do justice to it. The *Lectures* "on *Witchcraft* have long been out of print. "Although frequently importuned to prepare a "new edition, I was unwilling to issue, again, "what I had discovered to be an inadequate "presentation of the subject." In the face of this disclaimer of the authoriy of the original work, the Reviewer says: "In this discussion, we "shall treat Mr. Upham's *Lectures* and History "in the same connection, as the latter is an ex- "pansion and defence of the views presented in "the former."

I ask every person of candor and fairness, to consider whether it is just to treat authors in this way? It is but poor encouragement to them to labor to improve their works, for the first critical journal in the country to bring discredit upon their efforts, by still laying to their charge what they have themselves remedied or withdrawn. Yet it is avowedly done in the article which compels me to this vindication.

The *Lectures*, for instance, printed in 1831, contained the following sentence, referring to Cotton Mather's agency, in the Goodwin case, in Boston. "An instance of witchcraft was "brought about, in that place, by his manage- "ment." So it appeared in a reprint of that volume, in 1832. In my recent publication, while transferring a long paragraph from the original work, *I carefully omitted*, from the body of it, the above sentence, fearing that it might lead to misapprehension. For, although I hold that the Mathers are pre-eminently answerable for the witchcraft proceedings in their day, and may be said, justly, to have caused them, of course I did not mean that, by personal instigation on the spot, they started every occurrence that ultimately was made to assume such a character. The Reviewer, with the fact well known to him, that I had suppressed and discarded this clause, flings it against me, repeatedly. He further quotes a portion of the paragraph, in the *Lectures*, in which it occurs, omitting, *without indicating the omission*, certain clauses that would have explained my meaning, *taking care, however, to include the suppressed passage;* and finishes the misrepresentation, by the following declaration, referring to the paragraph in the *Lectures:* "The same state- "ments, in almost the same words, he repro- "duces in his History." This he says, knowing that the particular statement to which he was then taking exception, was not reproduced in my History.

It may be as well here, at this point, as elsewhere, once for all, to dispose of a large portion of the matter contained in the long article in the *North American Review*, now under considera- tion. In preparing any work, particularly in the department of history, it is to be presumed that the explorations of the writer extend far beyond what he may conclude to put into his book. He will find much that is of no account whatever; that would load down his narrative, swell it to inadmissable dimensions, and shed no addition- al light. Collateral and incidental questions cannot be pursued in details. A new law, how- ever, is now given out, that must be followed, hereafter, by all writers—that is, to give not a catalogue merely, but an account of the contents, of every book and tract they have read. It is thus announced by our Reviewer : "We assume "Mr. Upham has not seen this tract, as he neith- "er mentioned it nor made use of its material."

The document here spoken of was designed to give Increase Mather's ideas on the subject of witchcraft trials, written near the close of those in Salem, in 1692. As I had no peculiar interest in determining what his views were—as a careful study of the tract, particularly taken in connec-

tion with its *Postscript*, fails to bring any read- er to a clear conception of them ; and as its whole matter was altogether immaterial to my subject—I did not think it worth while to encum- ber my pages with it. So in respect to many other points, in treating which extended discus- sions might be demanded. If I had been gov- erned by such notions as the Reviewer seems to entertain, my book, which he complains of as too long, would have been lengthened to the di- mensions of a cyclopædia of theology, biography, and philosophy. For keeping to my subject, and not diverting attention to writings of no in- herent value, in any point of view, and which would contribute nothing to the elucidation of my topics, I am charged by this Reviewer, in the baldest terms, with ignorance, on almost every one of his sixty odd pages, and, often, several times on the same page.

All that I say of Cotton Mather, mostly drawn from his own words, does not cover a dozen pages. Exception is taken to some unfavorable judgments, cursorily expressed. This is fair and legitimate, and would justify my being called on to substantiate them. But to assume, and proclaim, that I had not read nor seen tracts or vol- umes that would come under consideration in such a discussion, is as rash as it is offensive ; and, besides, constitutes a charge against which no person of any self respect or common sense can be expected to defend himself. I gave the opinion of Cotton Mather's agency in the Witch- craft of 1692, to which my judgment had been led—whether with sufficient grounds or not will be seen, as I proceed—but did not branch off from my proper subject, into a detail of the sources from which that opinion was derived. If I had done so, in connection with allusions to Mather, upon the same principle it would have been necessary to do it, whenever an opinion was expressed of others, such as Roger Williams, or Hugh Peters, or Richard Baxter. It would de- stroy the interest, and stretch interminably the dimensions, of any book, to break its narrative, abandon its proper subject, and stray aside into such endless collateral matter. But it must be done, if the article in the *North American Re- view*, is to be regarded as an authoritative an- nouncement of a canon of criticism. Lecturers and public speakers, or writers of any kind, must be on their guard. If they should chance, for instance, to speak of Cotton Mather as a pedant, they will have the reviewers after them, belabor- ing them with the charge of "a great lack of "research," in not having "pored over" the "prodigious" manuscript of his unpublished work, in the Library of the Massachusetts Histor- ical Society, the whole of his three hundred and eighty-two printed works, and the huge mass of *Mather Papers*, in the Library of the American

Antiquarian Society; and with never having "read" the *Memorable Providences*, or "seen" the *Wonders of the Invisible World*, or "heard" of the *Magnalia Christi Americana*.

III.

COTTON MATHER AND THE GOODWIN CHILDREN. JOHN BAILY. JOHN HALE. GOODWIN'S CERTIFICATES. MATHER'S IDEA OF WITCHCRAFT AS A WAR WITH THE DEVIL. HIS USE OF PRAYER. CONNECTION BETWEEN THE CASE OF THE GOODWIN CHILDREN AND SALEM WITCHCRAFT.

The Reviewer complains of my manner of treating Cotton Mather's connection with the affair of the Goodwin children. The facts in the case are, that the family, to which they belonged, lived in the South part of Boston. The father, a mason by occupation, was, as Mather informs us, "a sober and pious man." As his church relations were with the congregation in Charlestown, of which Charles Morton was the Pastor, he probably had no particular acquaintance with the Boston Ministers. From a statement made by Mr. Goodwin, some years subsequently, it seems that after one of his children had, for "about a quarter of a year, been laboring un-" "der sad circumstances from the invisible world," he called upon "the four Ministers of Boston, "together with his own Pastor, to keep a day of "prayer at his house. If so deliverance might "be obtained." He says that Cotton Mather, with whom he had no previous acquaintance, was the last of the Ministers that "he spoke to on "that occasion." Mr. Mather did not attend the meeting, but visited the house in the morning of the day, before the other Ministers came; spent a half hour there; and prayed with the family. About three months after, the Ministers held another prayer-meeting there, Mr. Mather being present. He further stated that Mr. Mather never, in any way, suggested his prosecuting the old Irish woman for bewitching his children, nor gave him any advice in reference to the legal proceedings against her; but that "the motion "of going to the authority was made to him by "a Minister of a neighboring town, now depart-"ed."

The Reviewer, in a note to the last item, given above, of Goodwin's statement, says: "Proba-"bly Mr. John Baily." Unless he has some particular evidence, tending to fix this advice upon Baily, the conjecture is objectionable. The name of such a man as Baily appears to have been, ought not, unnecessarily, to be connected with the transaction. It is true that, after the family had become relieved of its "sad circumstances from "the invisible world," Mr. Baily took one of the children to his house, in Watertown; but that is no indication of his having given such advice. The only facts known of him, in connection with

Witchcraft prosecutions, look in the opposite direction. When John Proctor, in his extremity of danger, sought for help, Mr. Baily was one of the Ministers from whom alone he had any ground to indulge a hope for sympathy; and his name is among the fourteen who signed the paper approving of Increase Mather's *Cases of Conscience*. The list comprises all the Ministers known as having shown any friendly feelings towards persons charged with Witchcraft or who had suffered from the prosecutions, such as Hubbard, Allen, Willard, Capen and Wise; but not one who had taken an active part in hurrying on the proceedings of 1692.

If any surmise is justifiable, or worth while, as to the author of the advice to Goodwin—and perhaps it is due to the memory of Baily, whose name has been thus introduced—I should be inclined to suggest that it was John Hale, of Beverly, who, like Baily, was deceased at the date of Goodwin's certificate. He was a Charlestown man, originally of the same religious Society with Goodwin, and had kept up acquaintance with his former townsmen. His course at Salem Village, a few years afterwards, shows that he would have been likely to give such advice; and we may impute it to him without any wrong to his character or reputation. His noble conduct in daring, in the very hour of the extremest fury of the storm, when, as just before the break of day, the darkness was deepest, to denounce the proceedings as wrong; and in doing all that he could to repair that wrong, by writing a book condemning the very things in which he had himself been a chief actor, gives to his name a glory that cannot be dimmed by supposing that, in the period of his former delusion, he was the unfortunate adviser of Goodwin.

When Calef's book reached this country, in 1700, a Committee of seven was raised, at a meeting of the members of the Parish of which the Mathers were Ministers, to protect them against its effects. John Goodwin was a member of it, and contributed the Certificate from which extracts have just been made. It was so worded as to give the impression that Cotton Mather did not take a leading part in the case of Goodwin's children, in 1688. It states, as has been seen, that he "was the last of the Ministers" asked to attend the prayer-meeting; but lets out the fact that he was the first to present himself, going to the house and praying with the family before the rest arrived. Goodwin further states, as follows: "The Ministers would, now and then, come to "visit my distressed family, and pray with and "for them, among which Mr. Cotton Mather "would, now and then, come." The whole document is so framed as to present Mather as playing a secondary part.

In an account, however, of the affair, written by this same John Goodwin, and printed by Mather, in London, ten years before, in *The Memorable Providences relating to Witchcraft and Possessions*, a somewhat different position is assigned to Mather. After saying "the Ministers did of- "ten visit us," he mentions "Mr. Mather particu- "larly." "He took much pains in this great ser- "vice, to pull this child and her brother and sis- "ter, out of the hands of the Devil. Let us now "admire and adore that fountain, the Lord Je- "sus Christ, from whence those streams come. "The Lord himself will requite his labor of "love." In 1690, Mather was willing to have Goodwin place him in the foreground of the picture, representing him as pulling the children out of the hand of the Devil. In 1700, it was expedient to withdraw him into the background: and Goodwin, accordingly, provided the Committee, of which he was a member, with a Certificate of a somewhat different color and tenor.

The execution of the woman, Glover, on the charge of having bewitched these Goodwin children, is one of the most atrocious passages of our history. Hutchinson* says she was one of the "wild Irish," and "appeared to be disordered "in her senses." She was a Roman Catholic, unable to speak the English language, and evidently knew not what to make of the proceedings against her. In her dying hour, she was understood by the interpreter to say, that taking away her life would not have any effect in diminishing the sufferings of the children. The remark, showing more sense than any of the rest of them, had, was made to bear against the poor old creature, as a diabolical imprecation.

Between the time of her condemnation and that of her execution, Cotton Mather took the eldest Goodwin child into his family, and kept her there all winter. He has told the story of her extraordinary doings, in a style of blind and absurd credulity that cannot be surpassed. "Ere "long," says he, "I thought it convenient for "me to entertain my congregation with a Ser- "mon on the memorable providence, wherein "these children had been concerned, (afterwards ".published)."

In this connection, it may be remarked that had it not been for the interference of the Ministers, it is quite likely that "the sad circumstan- "ces from the invisible world," in the Goodwin family, would never have been heard of, beyond the immediate neighborhood. It is quite certain that similar "circumstances," in Mr. Parris's family, in 1692, owed their general publicity

and their awful consequences, to the meetings of Ministers called by him. If the girls, in either case, had been let alone, they would soon have been weary of what one of them called their "sport;" and the whole thing would have been swallowed, with countless stories of haunted houses and second sight, in deep oblivion.

In considering Cotton Mather's connection with the case of the Goodwin children, and that of the accusing girls, at Salem Village, justice to him requires that the statements, in my book, of the then prevalent notions, of the power and pending formidableness of the Kingdom of Darkness, should be borne in mind. It was believed by Divines generally, and by people at large, that here, in the American wilderness, a mighty onslaught upon the Christian settlements was soon to be made, by the Devil and his infernal hosts; and that, on this spot, the final battle between Satan and the Church, was shortly to come off. This belief had taken full possession of Mather's mind, and fired his imagination. In comparison with the approaching contest, all other wars, even that for the recovery of the Holy Sepulchre, paled their light. It was the great crusade, in which hostile powers, Moslem, Papal, and Pagan, of every kind, on earth and from Hell, were to go down; and he aspired to be its St. Bernard. It was because he entertained these ideas, that he was on the watch to hear, and prompt and glad to meet, the first advances of the diabolical legions. This explains his eagerness to take hold of every occurrence that indicated the coming of the Arch Enemy.

And it must further be borne in mind that, up to the time of the case of the Goodwin children, he had entertained the idea that the Devil was to be met and subdued by Prayer. That, and that only, was the weapon with which he girded himself; and with that he hoped and believed to conquer. For this reason, he did not advise Goodwin to go to the law. For this reason, he labored in the distressed household in exercises of prayer, and took the eldest child into his own family, so as to bring the battery of prayer, with a continuous bombardment, upon the Devil by whom she was possessed. For this reason, he persisted in praying in the cell of the old Irish woman, much against her will, for she was a stubborn Catholic. Of course, he could not pray *with* her, for he had no doubt she was a confederate of the Devil; and she had no disposition to join in prayer with one whom, as a heretic, she regarded in no better light; but still he would pray, for which he apologized, when referring to the matter, afterward.

Cotton Mather was always a man of prayer. For this, he deserves to be honored. Prayer, when offered in the spirit, and in accordance with the example, of the Saviour—"not my will but thine

<hr>

"be done," "Your Father knoweth what things
"ye have need of before ye ask him—" is the no-
blest exercise and attitude of the soul. It lifts
it to the highest level to which our faculties can
rise. It

> "opens heaven; lets down a stream
> "Of glory on the consecrated hour
> "Of man, in audience with the Deity."

It was the misfortune of Cotton Mather, that
an original infirmity of judgment, which all the
influences of his life and peculiarities of his
mental character and habits tended to exagger-
ate, led him to pervert the use and operation of
prayer, until it became a mere implement, or dev-
ice, to compass some personal end; to carry a
point in which he was interested, whether relating to private and domestic affairs, or to movements in academical, political, or ecclesiastical
spheres. While according to him entire sincerity
in his devotional exercises, and, I trust, truly re-
vering the character and nature of such expressions of devout sensibility and aspirations to divine communion, it is quite apparent that they
were practiced by him, in modes and to an extent
that cannot be commended, leading to much
self-delusion and to extravagances near akin to
distraction of judgment, and a disordered mental
and moral frame. He would abstain from food—
on one occasion, it is said, for three days together—and spend the time, as he expresses it "in
"knocking at the door of heaven." Leaving his
bed at the dead hours of the night, and retiring
to his study, he would cast himself on the floor,
and "wrestle with the Lord." He kept, usually, one day of each week in such fasting,
sometimes two. In his vigils, very protracted,
he would, in this prostrate position, be bathed in
tears. By such exhausting processes, continued
through days and nights, without food or rest,
his nature failed; he grew faint; physical weakness laid him open to delusions of the imagination; and his nervous system became deranged.
Sometimes, heaven seemed to approach him, and
he was hardly able to bear the ecstasies of divine love: at other times, his soul would be tossed
in the opposite direction: and often, the two
states would follow each other in the same exercise, as described by him in his Diary:*—"Was
"ever man more tempted than the miserable
"Mather? Should I tell in how many forms the
"Devil has assaulted me, and with what subtlety
"and energy his assaults have been carried on, it
"would strike my friends with horror. Some-
"times, temptations to vice, to blasphemy, and
"atheism, and the abandonment of all religion

"as a mere delusion, and sometimes to self-de-
"struction itself. These, even these, do follow
"thee, O miserable Mather, with astonishing fu-
"ry. But I fall down into the dust, on my study
"floor, with tears, before the Lord, and then
"they quickly vanish, and it is fair weather
"again. Lord what wilt thou do with me?"

His prayers and vigils, which often led to such
high wrought and intense experiences, were, not
infrequently, brought down to the level of ordinary sublunary affairs. In his Diary, he says, on
one occasion: "I set apart the day for fasting
"with prayer, and the special intention of the day
"was to obtain deliverance and protection from
"my enemies. I mentioned their names unto the
"Lord, who has promised to be my shield."
The enemies, here referred to, were political opponents—Governor Dudley and the supporters of
his administration.

At another time, he fixed his heart upon some
books offered for sale. Not having the means to
procure them in the ordinary way, he resorted to
prayer: "I could not forbear mentioning my
"wishes in my prayers, before the Lord, that,
"in case it might be of service to his interests,
"he would enable me, in his good Providence,
"to purchase the treasure now before me. But
"I left the matter before him, with the profound-
"est resignation."

The following entry is of a similar character: "This evening, I met with an experience,
"which it may not be unprofitable for me to re-
"member. I had been, for about a fortnight,
"vexed with an extraordinary heart-burn; and
"none of all the common medicines would re-
"move it, though for the present some of them
"would a little relieve it. At last, it grew so
"much upon me, that I was ready to faint un-
"der it. But, under my fainting pain, this re-
"flection came into my mind. There was *this*
"among the sufferings and complaints of my
"Lord Jesus Christ. My heart was like wax
"melted in the middle of my bowels. Hereup-
"on, I begged of the Lord, that, for the sake of
"the heart-burn undergone by my Saviour, I
"might be delivered from the other and lesser
"heart burn wherewith I was now incommoded.
"Immediately it was darted into my mind, that
"I had Sir Philip Paris's plaster in my house,
"which was good for inflammations; and laying
"the plaster on, I was cured of my malady."

These passages indicate a use of prayer, which,
to the extent Mather carried it, would hardly be
practised or approved by enlightened Christians
of this or any age; although our Reviewer fully
endorses it. In reference to Mather's belief in
the power of prayer, he expresses himself with a
bold simplicity, never equalled even by that Divine. After stating that the Almighty Sovereign
was his Father, and had promised to hear and

---

*The passages from Cotton Mather's Diary, used in this
article, are mostly taken from the *Christian Examiner*,
xi. 249; *Proceedings of Massachusetts Historical Society*,
i. 358, and iv. 404; and *Life of Cotton Mather*, by William
B. O. Peabody, in Sparks's *American Biography*, vi. 162.

answer his petitions, he goes on to say: "He "had often tested this promise, and had found "it faithful and sure." One would think, in hearing such a phraseology, he was listening to an agent, vending a patent medicine as an infallible cure, or trying to bring into use a labor-saving machine.

The Reviewer calls me to account for representing "the Goodwin affair" as having had "a "very important relation to the Salem troubles," and attempts to controvert that position.

On this point, Francis Hutchinson, before referred to, gives his views, very decidedly, in the following passages: [*Pp. 95, 96, 101.*] "Mr. Cotton Mather, no longer since than "1690, published the case of one Goodwin's chil- "dren. * * * The book was sent hither to be "printed amongst us, and Mr. Baxter recom- "mended it to our people by a Preface, where- "in he says: 'That man must be a very obdur- "'ate Sadducee that will not believe it.' The "year after, Mr. Baxter, perhaps encouraged "by Mr. Mather's book, published his own *Cer- "tainty of the World of Spirits*, with another "testimony, 'That Mr. Mather's book would Si- "'lence any incredulity that pretended to be "'rational.' And Mr. Mather dispersed Mr. "Baxter's book in New England, with the "character of it, as a book that was ungainsaya- "ble."

Speaking of Mather's book, Doctor Hutchin- son proceeds: "The judgment I made of it was, "that the poor old woman, being an Irish Pa- "pist, and not ready in the signification of Eng- "lish words, had entangled herself by a super- "stitious belief, and doubtful answers about "Saints and Charms; and seeing what advanta- "ges Mr. Mather made of it, I was afraid I saw "part of the reasons that carried the cause "against her. And first it is manifest that Mr. "Mather is magnified, as having great power "over evil spirits. A young man in his family "is represented so holy, that the place of his de- "votions was a certain cure of the young virgin's "fits. Then his grand-father's and father's books "have gained a testimony, that, upon occasion, "may be *improved* one knows not how far. For "amongst the many experiments that were made, "Mr. Mather would bring to this young maid, the "Bible, the *Assembly's Catechism*, his grand- "father Cotton's *Milk for Babes*, his father's "*Remarkable Providences*, and a book to prove "that there were Witches; and when any of these "were offered for her to read in, she would be "struck dead, and fall into convulsions. 'These "'good books,' he says, 'were mortal to her'; "and lest the world should be so dull as not to "take him right, he adds, 'I hope I have not "'spoiled the credit of the books, by telling "'how much the Devil hated them.'"

This language, published by Doctor Hutchin- son, in England, during the life-time of the Mathers, shows how strong was the opinion, at that time, that the writings of those two Divines were designed and used to promote the preva- lence of the Witchcraft superstition, and especi- ly that such was the effect, as well as the pur- pose, of Cotton Mather's publication of the case of the Goodwin children, put into such circula- tion, as it was, by him and Baxter, in both Old and New England. In the same connection, Francis Hutchinson says: "Observe the time of "the publication of that book, and of Mr. Bax- "ter's. Mr. Mather's came out in 1690, and "Mr. Baxter's the year after; and Mr. Mather's "father's *Remarkable Providences* had been out "before that; and, in the year 1692, the frights and "fits of the afflicted, and the imprisonment and "execution of Witches in New England, made "as sad a calamity as a plague or a war. I "know that Mr. Mather, in his late Folio, im- "putes it to the Indian Pawaws sending their "spirits amongst them; but I attribute it to Mr. "Baxter's book, and his, and his father's, and the "false principles, and frightful stories, that filled "the people's minds with great fears and dan- "gerous notions."

Our own Hutchinson, in his *History of Mass- achusetts*, [*II. 25-27.*] alludes to the excitement of the public mind, occasioned by the case of the Goodwin children. "I have often," he says, "heard persons who were of the neighborhood, "speak of the great consternation it occasioned."

In citing this author, in the present discussion, certain facts are always to be borne in mind. One of his sisters was the wife of Cotton Mather's son, towards whom Hutchinson cherished senti- ments appropriate to such a near connection, and of which Samuel Mather was, there is no reason to doubt, worthy. In the Preface to his first vol- ume he speaks thus: "I am obliged to no oth- "er person more than to my friend and brother, "the Reverend Mr. Mather, whose library has "been open to me, as it had been before to the "Reverend Mr. Prince, who has taken from "thence the greatest and most valuable part of "what he had collected."

Moreover, this very library was, it can hardly be questioned, that of Cotton Mather; of which, in his Diary, he speaks as "very great." In an interesting article, to which I may refer again, in the *Collections of the Massachusetts Histori- cal Society*, [*IV. ii. 128*], we are told that, in the inventory of the estate of Cotton Mather, filed by his Administrator, "not a single book is "mentioned among the assets of this eccentric "scholar." He had, it is to be presumed, given them all, in his life-time, to his son, who suc- ceeded to his ministry in the North Church, in 1732.

When the delicacy of his relation to the Mather family and the benefit he was deriving from that library are considered, the avoidance, by Hutchinson, of any unpleasant reference to Cotton Mather, by name, is honorable to his feelings. But he maintained, nevertheless, a faithful allegiance to the truth of history, as the following, as well as many other passages, in his invaluable work, strikingly show. They prove that he regarded Mather's " printed account" of the case of the Goodwin children, as having a very important relation to the immediately subsequent delusion in Salem. "The eldest was taken," he says, " into a Minister's family, where at first " she behaved orderly, but after some time evi- "dently fell into her fits." "The account of her " sufferings is in print ; some things are men- "tioned as extraordinary, which tumblers are " every day taught to perform ; others seem more " than natural ; but it was a time of great cred- "ulity. * * * The printed account was pub- "lished with a Preface by Mr. Baxter. * * * "It obtained credit sufficient, together with oth- "er preparatives, to dispose the whole country "to be easily imposed upon, by the more exten- "sive and more tragical scene, which was pres- "ently after acted at Salem and other parts of "the county of Essex." After mentioning sever- al works published in England, containing "witch- "stories," witch-trials, etc.. he proceeds: "All "these books were in New England, and the con- "formity between the behavior of Goodwin's chil- "dren, and most of the supposed be-witched at "Salem, and the behavior of those in England, "is so exact, as to leave no room to doubt the "stories had been read by the New England "persons themselves, or had been told to them "by others who had read them. Indeed this "conformity, instead of giving suspicion, was "urged in confirmation of the truth of both. "The Old England demons and the New being "so much alike."

It thus appears that the opinion was entertain- ed, in England and this country, that the notorie- ty given to the case of the Goodwin children, es- pecially by Mather's printed account of it, had an efficient influence in bringing on the "trag- "ical scene," shortly afterwards exhibited at Sa- lem. This opinion is shown to have been correct, by the extraordinary similarity between them —the one being patterned after the other. The Salem case, in 1692, was, in fact, a substantial rep- etition of the Boston case, in 1688. On this point, we have the evidence of Cotton Mather himself.

The Rev. John Hale of Beverly, who was as well qualified as any one to compare them, hav- ing lived in Charlestown, which place had been the residence of the Goodwin family, and been active participator in the prosecutions at Sa-

lem, in his book, entitled, *A modest Enquiry into the nature of Witchcraft*, written in 1697, but not printed until 1702, after mentioning the fact that Cotton Mather had published an account of the conduct of the Goodwin children, and brief- ly describing the manifestations and actions of the Salem girls, says: [*p. 24*] "I will not enlarge in "the description of their cruel sufferings, be- "cause they were, in all things, afflicted as bad "as John Goodwin's children at Boston, in the "year 1689, as he, that will read Mr. Mather's "book on *Remarkable Providences*, p. 3. &c., "may read part of what those children, and af- "terwards sundry grown persons, suffered by the "hand of Satan, at Salem Village, and parts ad- "jacent, *Anno 1691–2*, yet there was more in "their sufferings than in those at Boston, by "pins invisibly stuck into their flesh, pricking "with irons (as, in part, published in a book "printed 1693, viz: *The Wonders of the Invis- "ible World.*)" This is proof of the highest authority, that, with the exceptions mentioned, there was a perfect similarity in the details of the two cases. Mr. Hale's book had not the ben- efit of his revision, as it did not pass through the press until two years after his death ; and we thus account for the error as to the date of the Good- win affair.

In making up his *Magnalia*, Mather had the use of Hale's manuscript and transferred from it nearly all that he says, in that work, about Salem Witchcraft. He copies the passage above quoted. The fact, therefore, is sufficiently attested by Mather as well as Hale, that, with the exceptions stated, there was, " in all things," an entire simil- arity between the cases of 1688 and 1692.

Nay. further, in this same way we have the ev- idence of Cotton Mather himself, that his " print- "ed account," of the case of the Goodwin chil- dren, was actually used, as an anthority, by the Court, in the trials at Salem—so that it is clear that the said " account," contributed not only, by its circulation among the people, to bring on the prosecutions of 1692, but to carry them through to their fatal results—Mr. Hale says: [*p. 27.*] "that the Justices, Judges and others con- "cerned," consulted the precedents of former times, and precepts laid down by learned writers about Witchcraft. He goes on to enumerate them, mentioning Keeble, Sir Matthew Hale, Glanvil, Bernard, Baxter and Burton, concluding the list with " Cotton Mather's *Memorable Providences*, "*relating to Witchcraft*, printed, anno 1689." Ma- ther transcribes this also into the *Magnalia*. *The Memorable Providences* is referred to by Hale, in another place, as containing the case of the Good- win children, consisting, in fact mainly of it. [*p. 23*]. Mather, having Hale's book before him, must, therefore be considered as endorsing the opinion for which the Reviewer calls me to account, namely, that "the Goodwin affair had a "very important relation to the Salem troubles." What is sustained touching this point, by both the Hutchinsons, Hale, and Cotton Mather himself, cannot be disturbed in its position, as a truth of History.

The reader will, I trust, excuse me for going into such minute processes of investigation and reasoning, in such comparatively unimportant points. But, as the long-received opinions, in reference to this chapter of our history, have been brought into question in the columns of a journal, justly commanding the public confidence, it is necessary to re-examine the grounds on which they rest. This I propose to do, without regard to labor or space. I shall not rely upon general considerations, but endeavor, in the course of this discussion, to sift every topic on which the Reviewer has struck at the truth of history, fairly and thoroughly. On this particular point, of the relation of these two instances of alleged Witchcraft, in localities so near as Boston and Salem, and with so short an interval of time, general considerations would ordinarily be regarded as sufficient. From the nature of things, the former must have served to bring about the latter. The intercommunication between the places was, even then, so constant, that no important event could happen in one without being known in the other. By the thousand channels of conversation and rumor, and by Mather's printed account, endorsed by Baxter, and put into circulation throughout the country, the details of the alleged sufferings and extraordinary doings of the Goodwin children, must have become well known, in Salem Village. Such a conclusion would be formed, if no particular evidence in support of it could be adduced; but when corroborated by the two Hutchinsons, Mr. Hale, and, in effect, by Mather himself, it cannot be shaken.

As has been stated, Cotton Mather, previous to his experience with those "pests," as the Reviewer happily calls "the Goodwin children," probably believed in the efficacy of prayer, and in that alone, to combat and beat down evil spirits and their infernal Prince: and John Goodwin's declaration, that it was not by his advice that he went to the law, is, therefore, entirely credible in itself. The protracted trial, however, patiently persevered in for several long months, when he had every advantage, in his own house, to pray the devil out of the eldest of the children, resulting in her becoming more and more "saucy," insolent, and outrageous, may have undermined his faith to an extent of which he might not have been wholly conscious. He says, in concluding his story in the *Magnalia*, [*Book vi. p. 75.*] that, after all other methods had failed, "one particular Minister, taking particular "compassion on the family, set himself to serve

"them in the methods prescribed by our Lord "Jesus Christ. Accordingly, the Lord being "besought thrice, in three days of prayer, with "fasting on this occasion, the family then saw "their deliverance perfected."

It is worthy of reflection, whether it was not the fasting, that seems to have been especially enforced "on this occasion," and for "three "days," that cured the girl. A similar application had before operated as a temporary remedy. Mather tells us, in his *Memorable Providences*, [*p. 31*,] referring to a date previous to the "three days" fasting, "Mr. Morton, of "Charlestown, and Mr. Allen, Mr. Moody, Mr. "Willard, and myself, of Boston, with some de- "vout neighbors, kept another day of prayer at "John Goodwin's house; and we had all the "children present with us there. The child- "ren were miserably tortured, while we labored "in our prayers; but our good God was nigh "unto us, in what we called upon him for. "From this day, the power of the enemy was "broken; and the children, though assaults after "this were made upon them, yet were not so "cruelly handled as before."

It must have been a hard day for all concerned. Five Ministers and any number of "good praying people," as Goodwin calls them, together with his whole family, could not but have crowded his small house. The children, on such occasions, often proved very troublesome, as stated above. Goodwin says, "the two "biggest, lying on the bed, one of them would "fain have kicked the good men, while they "were wrestling with God for them, had I not "held him with all my power and might." Fasting was added to the prayers, that were kept up during the whole time, the Ministers relieving each other. If the fasting had been continued three days, it is not unlikely that the cure of the children would, then, have proved effectual and lasting. The account given in the *Memorables* and the *Magnalia*, of the conduct of these children, under the treatment of Mather and the other Ministers, is, indeed, most ludicrous; and no one can be expected to look at it in any other light. He was forewarned that, in printing it, he would expose himself to ridicule. He tells us that the mischievous, but bright and wonderfully gifted, girl, the eldest of the children, getting, at one time, possession of his manuscript, pretended to be, for the moment, incapacitated, by the Devil, for reading it; and he further informs us, "She'd hector me at a "strange rate for the work I was at, and threat- "en me with I know not what mischief for it. "She got a History I was writing of this Witch- "craft; and though she had, before this, read it "over and over, yet now she could not read (I "believe) one entire sentence of it; but she

"made of it the most ridiculous Travesty in the
"world, with such a patness and excess of fan-
"cy, to supply the sense that she put upon it,
"as I was amazed at. And she particularly
"told me, That I should quickly come to dis-
"grace by that History."

It is noticable that the Goodwin children,
like their imitators at Salem Village, the "af-
"flicted," as they were called, were car ful, except in certain cases of emergence, not to have
their night's sleep disturbed, and never lost an
appetite for their regular meals. I cannot but
think that if the Village girls had, once in a
while, like the Goodwin children, been compelled to go for a day or two upon very short allowance, it would have soon brought their
"sport" to an end.

Nothing is more true than that, in estimating
the conduct and character of men, allowance
must be made for the natural, and almost necessary, influence of the opinions and customs of
their times. But this excuse will not wholly
shelter the Mathers. They are answerable, as I
have shown, more than almost any other men
have been, for the opinions of their time.
It was, indeed, a superstitious age; but
made much more so by their operations,
influence, and writings, beginning with Increase Mather's movement, at the assembly of
the Ministers, in 1681, and ending with Cotton
Mather's dealings with the Goodwin children,
and the account thereof which he printed and
circulated, far and wide. For this reason, then,
in the first place, I hold those two men responsible for what is called "Salem Witchcraft."

I have admitted and shown that Cotton Mather originally relied only upon prayer in his combat with Satanic powers. But the time was at
hand, when other weapons than the sword of
the Spirit were to be drawn in that warfare.

THE RELATION OF THE MATHERS TO THE ADMIN-
ISTRATION OF MASSACHUSETTS, IN 1692. THE
NEW CHARTER. THE GOVERNMENT UNDER IT
ARRANGED BY THEM. ARRIVAL OF SIR WIL-
LIAM PHIPPS.

No instance of the responsibility of particular
persons for the acts of a Government, in the
whole range of history, is more decisive or unquestionable, than that of the Mathers, father
and son, for the trials and executions, for the alleged crime of Witchcraft, at Salem, in 1692.

Increase Mather had been in England, as one
of the Agents of the Colony of Massachusetts,
for several years, in the last part of the reign
of James II. and the beginning of that of William and Mary, covering much of the period between the abrogation of the first Charter and
the establishment of the Province under the
second Charter. Circumstances had conspired
to give him great influence in organizing the
Government provided for in the new Charter.
His son describes him as "one that, besides a
"station in the Church of God, as considerable as
"any that his own country can afford, hath for
"divers years come off with honor, in his appli-
"cation to three crowned heads and the chief-
"est nobility of three kingdoms."

Being satisfied that a restoration of the old
Charter could not be obtained, Increase Mather
acquiesced in what he deemed a necessity, and
bent his efforts to have as favorable terms as
possible secured in the new. His colleagues in
the agency, Elisha Cooke and Thomas Oaks, opposed his course—the former, with great deter-
mination, taking the ground of the "old Charter
"or none." This threw them out of all communication with the Home Government, on the subject, and gave to Mr. Mather controlling influence. He was requested by the Ministers of the
Crown to name the officers of the new Government; and, in fact, had the free and sole selec-
tion of them all. Sir William Phips was appointed Governor, at his solicitation; and, in
accordance with earnest recomendations, in a
letter from Cotton Mather, William Stoughton
was appointed Deputy-governor, thereby super-
ceding Danforth, one of the ablest men in
the Province. In fact, every member of the
Council owed his seat to the Mathers, and, politically, was their creature. Great was the ex-
ultation of Cotton Mather, when the intelligence
reached him, thus expressed in his Diary: "The
"time for favor is now come, yea, the set-time
"is come. I am now to receive the answers of
"so many prayers, as have been employed for my
"absent parent, and the deliverance and settle-
"ment of my poor country. We have not the
"former Charter, but we have a better in the
"room of it; one which much better suits our
"circumstances. And, instead of my being
"made a sacrifice to wicked rulers, all the
"Councillors of the Province are of my father's
"nomination; and my father-in-law, with sever-
"al related to me, and several brethren of my
"own Church, are among them. The Governor
"of the Province is not my enemy, but one
"whom I baptized, namely, Sir William Phips,
"and one of my flock, and one of my dearest
"friends."

The whole number of Councillors was twenty-
eight, three of them, at least, being of the Mather Church. John Phillips was Cotton Mather's father-in-law. Two years before, Sir William Phips had been baptized by Cotton Mather, in the presence of the congregation, and received into the Church.

The "set time," so long prayed for, was of brief

duration. The influence of the Mathers over the politics of the Province was limited to the first part of Phips's short administration. At the very next election, in May, 1693, ten of the Councillors were left out; and Elisha Cooke, their great opponent, was chosen to that body, although negatived by Phips, in the exercise of his prerogative, under the Charter.

Increase Mather came over in the same ship with the Governor, the *Nonsuch*, frigate. As Phips was his parishioner, owed to him his office, and was necessarily thrown into close intimacy, during the long voyage, he fell naturally under his influence, which, all things considered, could not have failed to be controlling. The Governor was an illiterate person, but of generous, confiding, and susceptible impulses; and the elder Mather was precisely fitted to acquire an ascendency over such a character. He had been twice abroad, in his early manhood and in his later years, had knowledge of the world, been conversant with learned men in Colleges and among distinguished Divines and Statesmen, and seen much of Courts and the operations of Governments. With a more extended experience and observation than his son, his deportment was more dignified, and his judgment infinitely better; while his talents and acquirements were not far, if at all, inferior. When Phips landed in Boston, it could not, therefore, have been otherwise than that he should pass under the control of the Mathers, the one accompanying, the other meeting him on the shore. They were his religious teachers and guides; by their efficient patronage and exertions he had been placed in his high office. They, his Deputy, Stoughton, and the whole class of persons under their influence, at once gathered about him, gave him his first impressions, and directed his movements. By their talents and position, the Mathers controlled the people, and kept open a channel through which they could reach the ear of Royalty. The Government of the Province was nominally in Phips and his Council, but the Mathers were a power behind the throne greater than the throne itself. The following letter, never before published, for which I am indebted to Abner C. Goodell, Esq., Vice-president of the Essex Institute, shows how they bore themselves before the Legislature, and communicated with the Home Government.

"MY LORD:

"I have only to assure your Lordship, that "the generality of their Majesties subjects (so "far as I can understand) do, with all thank-"fulness, receive the favors, which, by the new "Charter, are granted to them. The last week, "the General Assembly (which, your Lordship "knows, is our New England Parliament) con-"vened at Boston. I did then exhort them to "make an Address of thanks to their Majes-"ties; which, I am since informed, the Assem-"bly have unanimously agreed to do, as in duty "they are bound. I have also acquainted the "whole Assembly, how much, not myself only, "but they, and all this Province, are obliged to "your Lordship in particular, which they have "a grateful sense of, as by letters from them-"selves your Lordship will perceive. If I may, "in any thing, serve their Majesties interest "here, I shall, on that account, think myself "happy, and shall always study to approve my-"self, My Lord,

"Your most humble, thankful
"BOSTON, N. E.   and obedient Servant,
"June 28, 1692.   INCREASE MATHER.
"To the Rt. Honble the EARL OF NOTTINGHAM
"his Maj^ties Principal Secretary of State
"at Whitehall."

While they could thus address the General Assembly, and the Ministers of State, in London, the Government here was, as Hutchinson evidently regarded it, [*i. 365; ii. 69.*] "a MATHER "ADMINISTRATION." It was "short, sharp, and "decisive." It opened in great power; its course was marked with terror and havoc; it ended with mysterious suddenness; and its only monument is Salem Witchcraft—the "*judicial* "*murder*," as the Reviewer calls it, of twenty men and women, as innocent in their lives as they were heroic in their deaths.

The *Nonsuch* arrived in Boston harbor, towards the evening of the fourteenth of May, 1692. Judge Sewall's Diary, now in the possession of the Massachusetts Historical Society, has this entry, at the above date. "Candles are lighted "before he gets into Town House, 8 companies "wait on him to his house, and then on Mr. "Mather to his, made no vollies, because 'twas "Saturday night."

The next day, the Governor attended, we may be sure, public worship with the congregation to which he belonged; and the occasion was undoubtedly duly noticed. After so long an absence, Increase Mather could not have failed to address his people, the son also taking part in the interesting service. The presence, in his pew, of the man who, a short time before, had been regenerated by their preaching, and now re-appeared among them with the title and commission of Governor of New England, added to the previous honors of Knighthood, at once suggested to all, and particularly impressed upon him, an appreciating conviction of the political triumph, as well as clerical achievement, of the associate Ministers of the North Boston Church. From what we know of the state of the public mind at that time, as emphatically described in a document I am presently to produce, there can be no question as to one class of topics and exhortations, wherewithal his Excellency and the crowded congregation were, that day, entertained.

Monday, the sixteenth, was devoted to the ceremonies of the public induction of the new Government. There was a procession to the Town-house, where the Commissions of the Governor and Deputy-governor, with the Charter under which they were appointed, were severally read aloud to the people. A public dinner followed; and, at its close, Sir William was escorted to his residence. At the meeting of the Council, the next day, the seventeenth, the oaths of office having been administered, all round, it was voted "that there be a general "meeting of the Council upon Tuesday next, "the twenty-fourth of May current, in Boston, "at two o'clock, post-meridian, to nominate and "appoint Judges, Justices, and other officers of "the Council and Courts of Justice within this "their Majestie's Province belonging, and that "notice thereof, or summons, be forthwith issued "unto the members of the Council now ab-"sent."

The following letter from Sir William Phips, to the Government at home, recently procured from England by Mr. Goodell, was published in the last volume of the *Collections of the Essex Institute*—Volume IX., Part II. I print it, entire, and request the reader to examine it, carefully, and to refer to it as occasion arises in this discussion, as it is a key to the whole transaction of the Witchcraft trials. Its opening sentence demonstrates the impression made by those who first met and surrounded him, on his excitable nature:

"When I first arrived, I found this Province "miserably harassed with a most horrible "witchcraft or possession of devils, which had "broke in upon several towns, some scores of "poor people were taken with preternatural "torments, some scalded with brimstone, some "had pins stuck in their flesh, others hurried "into the fire and water, and some dragged out "of their houses and carried over the tops of "trees and hills for many miles together; it "hath been represented to me much like that "of Sweden about thirty years ago; and there "were many committed to prison upon suspi-"cion of Witchcraft before my arrival. The "loud cries and clamours of the friends of the "afflicted people, with the advice of the Dep-"uty-governor and many others, prevailed with "me to give a Commission of Oyer and Termi-"ner for discovering what Witchcraft might be "at the bottom, or whether it were not a pos-"session. The chief Judge in this Commission "was the Deputy-governor, and the rest were

"persons of the best prudence and figure that "could then be pitched upon. When the Court "came to sit at Salem, in the County of Essex, "they convicted more than twenty persons be-"ing guilty of witchcraft, some of the con-"victed confessed their guilt; the Court, as I "understand, began their proceedings with the "accusations of afflicted persons; and then went "upon other humane evidences to strengthen "that. I was, almost the whole time of the "proceeding, abroad in the service of their "Majesties, in the Eastern part of the country, "and depended upon the judgment of the Court, "as to a method of proceeding in cases of "witchcraft; but when I came home I found "many persons in a strange ferment of dissat-"isfaction, which was increased by some hot "spirits that blew up the flame; but on inquir-"ing into the matter I found that the Devil "had taken upon him the name and shape of "several persons who were doubtless innocent, "and, to my certain knowledge, of good reputa-"tion; for which cause I have now forbidden "the committing of any more that shall be ac-"cused, without unavoidable necessity, and "those that have been committed I would shel-"ter from any proceedings against them where-"in there may be the least suspicion of any "wrong to be done unto the innocent. I would "also wait for any particular directions or com-"mands, if their Majesties please to give me "any, for the fuller ordering this perplexed "affair.

"I have also put a stop to the printing of any "discourses one way or other, that may increase "the needless disputes of people upon this occa-"sion, because I saw a likelihood of kindling an "inextinguishable flame if I should admit any "public and open contests; and I have grieved "to see that some, who should have done their "Majesties, and this Province, better service, have "so far taken council of passion as to desire the "precipitancy of these matters; these things "have been improved by some to give me many "interruptions in their Majesties service [*which*] "has been her by unhappily clogged, and the "persons, who have made so ill improvement of "these matters here, are seeking to turn it upon "me, but I hereby declare, that as soon as I came "from fighting against their Majesties enemies, "and understood what danger some of their "innocent subjects might be exposed to, if the "evidence of the afflicted persons only did pre-"vail, either to the committing, or trying any of "them, I did, before any application was made "unto me about it, put a stop to the proceed-"ings of the Court and they are now stopped "till their Majesties pleasure be known. Sir, I "beg pardon for giving you all this trouble;

"the reason is because I know my enemies are
"seeking to turn it all upon me. Sir,
 "I am
 "Your most humble Serv'
 "WILLIAM PHIPS.

"Dated at BOSTON IN NEW ENGLAND,
"the 14th of Oct' 1692.

"MEM^DM

"That my Lord President be pleased to ac-
"quaint his Majesty in Council with the ac-
"count received from New England, from Sir
"Wm Phips, the Governor there, touching pro-
"ceedings against several persons for Witch-
"craft, as appears by the Governor's letter con-
"cerning those matters."

The foregoing document, I repeat, indicates
the kind of talk with which Phips was accosted,
when stepping ashore. Exaggerated representations of the astonishing occurrences at Salem Village burst upon him from all, whom he would
have been likely to meet. The manner in which
the Mathers, through him, had got exclusive possession of the Government of the Province, probably kept him from mingling freely among, or having much opportunity to meet, any leading men,
outside of his Council and the party represented.
therein. Writing in the ensuing October, at the
moment when he had made up his mind to break
loose from those who had led him to the hasty
appointment of the Special Court, there is signif-
icance in his language. "I have grieved to see
"that some, who should have done their Majes-
"ties, and the Province, better service, have so
"far taken counsel of passion, as to desire the
"precipitancy of these matters." This refers to,
and amounts to a condemnation of, the advisers
who had influenced him to the rash measures
adopted on his arrival. How rash and precipitate those measures were I now proceed to show.

V

THE SPECIAL COURT OF OYER AND TERMINER.
HOW IT WAS ESTABLISHED. WHO RESPONSIBLE
FOR IT. THE GOVERNMENT OF THE PROVINCE
CONCENTRATED IN ITS CHIEF-JUSTICE.

So great was the pressure made upon Sir
William Phips, by the wild panic to which the
community had been wrought, that he ordered
the persons who had been committed to prison
by the Salem Magistrates, to be put in irons;
but his natural kindness of heart and common
sense led him to relax the unjustifiable severity.
Professor Bowen, in his *Life of Phips*, embraced
in Sparks's *American Biography*, [*vii, 81.*] says:
"Sir William seems not to have been in earnest
"in the proceeding; for the officers were permit-
"ted to evade the order, by putting on the irons
"indeed, but taking them off again, immediately."

On Tuesday, the twenty-fourth of May, the
Council met to consider the matter specially assigned to that day, namely, the nomination and
appointment of Judicial officers.

The Governor gave notice that he had issued
Writs for the election of Representatives to con-
vene in a General Court, to be held on the eighth
of June.

He also laid before the Council, the assigned
business, which was "accordingly attended, and
"divers persons, in the respective Counties were
"named, and left for further consideration."

On the twenty-fifth of May, the Council being
again in session, the record says: "a further
"discourse was had about persons, in the sever-
"al Counties, for Justices and other officers, and
"it was judged advisable to defer the considera-
"tion of fit persons for Judges, until there be
"an establishment of Courts of Justice."

At the next meeting, on the twenty-seventh of
May, it was ordered that the members of the
Council, severally, and their Secretary, should be
Justices of the Peace and Quorum, in the respective Counties where they reside: a long list, besides, was adopted, appointing the persons named
in it Justices, as also Sheriffs and Coroners; and
a SPECIAL COURT OF OYER AND TERMINER was established for the Counties of Suffolk, Essex, and
Middlesex, consisting of William Stoughton,
Chief-justice, John Richards, Nathaniel Saltonstall, Wait Winthrop. Bartholomew Gedney, Samuel Sewall, John Hathorne, Jonathan Corwin,
and Peter Sargent, any five of them to be a quorum (Stoughton, Richards, or Gedney to be one of
the five).

When we consider that the subject had been
specially assigned on the seventeenth, and discussed for two days, on the twenty-fourth and
twenty-fifth, to the conclusion that the appointment of Judges ought to be deferred, "*until*
"*there be an establishment of Courts of Justice*,"—
which, by the Charter, could only be done by the
General Court which was to meet, as the Governor
had notified them, in less than a fortnight—the
establishment of the Court of Oyer and Terminer, on the twenty-seventh. must be regarded as very
extraordinary. It was acknowledged to be an un-
authorized proceeding; the deliberate judgment
of the Council had been expressed against it;
and there was no occasion for such hurry, as the
Legislature was so soon to assemble. There must
have been a strong outside pressure, from some
quarter, to produce such a change of front.
From Wednesday to Friday, some persons of
great influence must have been hard at work. The
reasons assigned, in the record, for this sudden re-
versal, by the Council, of its deliberate decision,
are the great number of criminals waiting trial
the thronged condition of the jails, and "this hot
"season of the year," on the twenty-seventh of May!

It is further stated, "there being no judicatures "or Courts of Justice yet established," that, therefore, such an extraordinary step was necessary. It is, indeed, remarkable, that, in the face of their own recorded convictions of expediency and propriety, and in disregard of the provisions of the Charter which, a few days before, they had been sworn to obey, the Council could have been led to so far "take counsel of passion," as to rush over every barrier to this precipitate measure.

No specific reference is anywhere made, in the Journals, to Witchcraft; but the Court was to act upon all cases of felony and other crimes. The "Council Records" were not obtained from England, until 1846. Writers have generally spoken of the Court as consisting of seven Judges. Saltonstall's resignation does not appear to have led to a new appointment; and, perhaps, Hathorne, who generally acted as an Examining Magistrate, and signed most of the Commitments of the prisoners, did not often, if ever, sit as a Judge. In this way, the Court may have been reduced to seven. Stephen Sewall was appointed Clerk, and George Corwin, High Sheriff.

Thus established and organized, on the twenty-seventh of May, the Court sat, on the second of June, for the trial of Bridget Bishop. Her Death-warrant was signed, on the eighth of June, the very day the Legislature convened; and she was executed on the tenth. This was, indeed, "pre-"cipitancy." Before the General Court had time, possibly, to make "an establishment of "Courts of Justice" in the exercise of the powers bestowed upon it by the Charter, this Special Court—suddenly sprung upon the country, against the deliberate first judgment of the Council itself, and not called for by any emergency of the moment which the General Court, just coming on the stage, could not legally, constitutionally, and adequately, have met—dipped its hands in blood; and an infatuated and appalled people and their representatives allowed the wheels of the Juggernaut to roll on.

The question, who are responsible for the creation, in such hot haste, of this Court, and for its instant entrance upon its ruthless work, may not be fully and specifically answered, with absolute demonstration, but we may approach a satisfactory solution of it. We know that a word from either of the Mathers would have stopped it. Their relations to the Government were, then, controlling. Further, if, at that time, either of the other leading Ministers—Willard or Allen—had demanded delay, it would have been necessary to pause; but none appear to have made open opposition; and all must share in the responsibility for subsequent events.

Phips says that the affair at Salem Village was represented to him as "much like that of Sweden,

"about thirty years ago." This Swedish case was Cotton Mather's special topic. In his *Wonders of the Invisible World*, he says that "other "good people have in this way been harassed, "but none in circumstances more like to ours, "than the people of God in Sweedland." He introduces, into the *Wonders*, a separate account of it; and reproduces it in his *Life of Phips*, incorporated subsequently into the *Magnalia*. The first point he makes, in presenting this case, is as follows: "The inhabitants had earnestly sought "God in prayer, and yet their affliction con-"tinued. Whereupon Judges had a Special "Commission to find, and root out the hellish "crew; and the rather, because another County "in the Kingdom, which had been so molested, "was delivered upon the execution of the Witch-"es."—*The Wonders of the Invisible World.* Edit. London, 1693, p. 48.

The importance attached by Cotton Mather to the affair in Sweden, especially viewed in connection with the foregoing extract, indicates that the change, I have conjectured, had come over him, as to the way to deal with Witches; and that he had reached the conclusion that prayer would not, and nothing but the gallows could, answer the emergency. In the Swedish case, was found the precedent for a "Special Commission "of Oyer and Terminer."

Well might the Governor have felt the importance of relieving himself, as far as possible, from the responsibility of having organized such a Court, and of throwing it upon his advisers. The tribunal consisted of the Deputy-governor, as Chief-justice, and eight other persons, all members of the Council, and each, as has been shown, owing his seat, at that Board, to the Mathers.

The recent publication of this letter of Governor Phips enables us now to explain certain circumstances, before hardly intelligible, and to appreciate the extent of the outrages committed by those who controlled the administration of the Province, during the Witchcraft trials.

In 1767, Andrew Oliver, then Secretary of the Province, was directed to search the Records of the Government to ascertain precedents, touching a point of much interest at that time. From his Report, part of which is given in Drake's invaluable *History of Boston*, [p. 728.] it appears that the Deputy-governor, Stoughton, by the appointment of the Governor, attended by the Secretary, administered the oaths to the members of the House of Representatives, convened on the eighth of June, 1692; that, as Deputy-governor, he sat in Council, generally, during that year, and was, besides, annually elected to the Council, until his death, in 1701. All that time, he was sitting, in the double capacity of an *ex-officio* and an elected member; and for much the greater part of it, in the absence of Phips, as acting Governor. The

Records show that he sat in Council when Sir William Phips was present, and presided over it, when he was not present, and ever after Phips's decease, until a new Governor came over in 1699. His annual election, by the House of Representatives, as one of the twenty-eight Councillors, while, as Deputy or acting Governor, he was entitled to a seat, is quite remarkable. It gave him a distinct legislative character, and a right, as an elected member of the body, to vote and act, directly, in all cases, without restraint or embarrassment, in debate and on Committees, in the making, as well as administering, the law.

In the letter now under consideration, Governor Phips says: "I was almost the whole time "of the proceeding abroad, in the Service of "their Majesties in the Eastern part of the coun-"try."

The whole tenor of the letter leaves an impression that, being so much away from the scene, in frequent and long absences, he was not cognizant of what was going on, He depended "upon "the judgment of the Court," as to its methods of proceeding; and was surprised when those methods were brought to his attention. Feeling his own incapacity to handle such a business, he was willing to leave it to those who ought to have been more competent. Indeed, he passed the whole matter over to the Deputy-governor. In a letter, for which I am indebted to Mr. Goodell, dated the twentieth of February, 1693, to the Earl of Nottingham, transmitting copies of laws passed by the General Court, Governor Phips says: "Not being versed in law, I have depended up-"on the Lieu' Gov', who is appointed Judge of "the Courts, to see that they be exactly agreea-"ble to the laws of England, and not repugnant "in any part. If there be any error, I know "it will not escape your observation, and de-"sire a check may be given for what may be "amiss."

The closing sentence looks somewhat like a want of confidence in the legal capacity and judgment of Stoughton, owing perhaps, to the bad work he had made at the Salem trials, the Summer before; but the whole passage shows that Phips, conscious of his own ignorance of such things, left them wholly to the Chief-justice.

The Records show that he sat in Council to the close of the Legislature, on the second of July. But the main business was, evidently, under the management of Stoughton, who was Chairman of a large Joint Committee, charged with adjusting the whole body of the laws to the transition of the Colony, from an independent Government, under the first Charter, to the condition of a subject Province.

One person had been tried and executed; and the Court was holding its second Session when the Legislature adjourned. Phips went to the eastward, immediately after the eighth of July. Again, on the first of August, he embarked from Boston with a force of four hundred and fifty men, for the mouth of the Kennebec. In the Archives of Massachusetts, Secretary's office, State House, Vol. LI, p. 9, is the original document, signed by Phips, dated on the first of August, 1692, turning over the Government to Stoughton, during his absence. It appears by Church's *Eastern Expeditions*, Part II. p. 82, edited by H. M. Dexter, and published by Wiggin & Lunt, Boston, 1867, that, during a considerable part of the month of August, the Governor must have been absent, engaged in important operations on the coast of Maine. About the middle of September, he went again to the Kennebec, not returning until a short time before the twelfth of October. In the course of the year, he also was absent for a while in Rhode Island. Although an energetic and active man, he had as much on his hands, arising out of questions as to the extent of his authority over Connecticut and Rhode Island and the management of affairs at the eastward, as he could well attend to. His Instructions, too, from the Crown, made it his chief duty to protect the eastern portions of his Government. The state of things there, in connection with Indian assaults and outrages upon the outskirt settlements, under French instigation, was represented as urgently demanding his attention. Besides all this, his utmost exertions were needed to protect the sea-coast against buccaneers. In addition to the public necessities, thus calling him to the eastward, it was, undoubtedly, more agreeable to his feelings, to revisit his native region and the home of his early years, where, starting from the humblest spheres of mechanical labor and maritime adventure, as a ship-carpenter and sailor, he had acquired the manly energy and enterprise that had conducted him to fortune, knightly honor, and the Commission of Governor of New England. All the reminiscences and best affections of his nature made him prompt to defend the region thus endeared to him. It was much more congenial to his feelings than to remain under the ceremonial and puritanic restraints of the seat of Government, and involved in perplexities with which he had no ability, and probably no taste, to grapple. He was glad to take himself out of the way; and as his impetuous and impulsive nature rendered those under him liable to find him troublesome, they were not sorry to have him called elsewhere.

I have mentioned these things as justifying the impression, conveyed by his letter, that he knew but little of what was going on until his return in the earlier half of October. Actual absence at a distance, the larger part of the time, and engrossing cares in getting up expeditions and supplies for them while he was at home—particularly as, from the beginning, he had passed over the business of the Court entirely to his Deputy, Stoughton—it is not difficult to suppose, had prevented his mind being much, if at all, turned towards it. We may, therefore, consider that the witchcraft prosecutions were wholly under the control of Stoughton and those who, having given him power, would naturally have influence over his exercise of it.

Calling in question the legality of the Court, Hutchinson expresses a deep sense of the irregularity of its proceedings; although, as he says, "the most important Court to the life of the subject which ever was held in the Province," it meets his unqualified censure, in many points. In reference to the instance of the Jury's bringing in a verdict of "Not guilty," in the case of Rebecca Nurse, and being induced, by the dissatisfaction of the Court, to go out again, and bring her in "Guilty," he condemns the procedure. Speaking of a wife or husband being allowed to accuse one the other, he breaks out: "I shudder "while I am relating it;" and giving the results at the last trial, he says: "This Court of Oyer and "Terminer, happy for the country, sat no more." Its proceedings were arbitrary, harsh, and rash. The ordinary forms of caution and fairness were disregarded. The Judges made no concealment of a foregone conclusion against the Prisoners at the Bar. No Counsel was allowed them. The proceedings were summary, and execution followed close upon conviction. While it was destroying the lives of men and women, of respectable position in the community, of unblemished and eminent Christian standing, heads of families, aged men and venerable matrons, all the ordinary securities of society, outside of the tribunal, were swept away. In the absence of Sir William Phips, the Chief-justice absolutely absorbed into his own person the whole Government. His rulings swayed the Court, in which he acted the part of prosecutor of the Prisoners, and overbore the Jury. He sat in judgment upon the sentences of his own Court; and heard and refused applications and supplications for pardon or reprieve. The three grand divisions of all constitutional or well-ordered Governments were, for the time, obliterated in Massachusetts. In the absence of Phips, the Executive functions were exercised by Stoughton. While presiding over the Council, he also held a seat as an elected ordinary member, thus participating in, as well as directing, its proceedings, sharing, as a leader, in legislation, acting on Committees, and framing laws. As Chief-justice, he was the head of the Judicial department. He was Commander-in-chief of the military and naval forces and forts within the Province proper. All administrative, legislative, judicial, and military powers were concentrated in his person and wielded by his hand. No more shameful tyranny or shocking despotism was ever endured in America, than, in "the dark and awful "day," as it was called, while the Special Commission of Oyer and Terminer was scattering destruction, ruin, terror, misery and death, over the country. It is a disgrace to that generation, that it was so long suffered; and, instead of trying to invent excuses, it becomes all subsequent generations to feel—as was deeply felt by enlightened and candid men, as soon as the storm had blown over and a prostrate people again stood erect, in possession of their senses—that all ought, by humble and heart-felt prayer, to implore the divine forgiveness, as one of the Judges, fully as misguided at the time as the rest, did, to the end of his days.

As all the official dignities of the Province were combined in Stoughton, he seems hardly to have known in what capacity he was acting, as different occasions arose. He signed the Death-warrant of Bridget Bishop, without giving himself any distinctive title, with his bare name and his private seal. It is easy to imagine how this lodging of the whole power of the State in one man, destroyed all safeguards and closed every door of refuge. When the express messenger of the poor young wife of John Willard, or the heroic daughter of Elizabeth How, or the agents of the people of the village, of all classes, combined in supplication in behalf of Rebecca Nurse, rushing to Boston to lay petitions for pardon before the Governor, upon being admitted to his presence, found themselves confronted by the stern countenance of the same person, who, as Chief-justice, had closed his ears to mercy and frowned the Jury into Conviction; their hearts sunk within them, and all realized that even hope had taken flight from the land.

Such was the political and public administration of the Province of Massachusetts, during the Summer of 1692, under which the Witchcraft prosecutions were carried on. It was conducted by men whom the Mathers had brought into office, and who were wholly in their counsels. If there is, I repeat, an instance in history where particular persons are responsible for the doings of a Government, this is one. I conclude these general views of the influence of Increase and Cotton Mather upon the ideas of the people and the operations of the Government, eventuating in the Witchcraft tragedy, by restating a proposition, which, under all the circumstances, cannot, I think, be disputed, that, if they had been really and earnestly opposed to the proceedings, at any stage, they could and would have stopped them.

I now turn to a more specific consideration of the subject of Cotton Mather's connection with the Witchcraft delusion of 1692.

VL

COTTON MATHER'S CONNECTION WITH THE COURT.
SPECTRAL EVIDENCE. LETTER TO JOHN RICH-
ARDS. ADVICE OF THE MINISTERS.

I am charged with having misrepresented the part Cotton Mather, in particular, bore in this passage of our history. As nearly the whole community had been deluded at the time, and there was a general concurrence in aiding oblivion to cover it, it is difficult to bring it back, in all its parts, within the realm of absolute knowledge. Records—municipal, ecclesiastical, judicial, and provincial—were willingly suffered to perish; and silence, by general consent, pervaded correspondence and conversation. Notices of it are brief, even in the most private Diaries. It would' have been well, perhaps, if the memory of that day could have been utterly extinguished; but it has not. On the contrary, as, in all manner of false and incorrect representations, it has gone into the literature of the country and the world and become mixed with the permanent ideas of mankind, it is right and necessary to present the whole transaction, so far as possible, in the light of truth. Every right-minded man must rejoice to have wrong, done to the reputation of the dead or living, repaired; and I can truly say that no one would rejoice more than I should, if the view presented of Cotton Mather. in the *North American Review*, of April, 1869, could be shown to be correct. In this spirit, I proceed to present the evidence that belongs to the question.

The belief of the existence of a personal Devil was then all but universally entertained. So was the belief of ghosts, apparitions, and spectres. There was no more reluctance to think or speak of them than of what we call natural objects and phenomena. Great power was ascribed to the Devil over terrestrial affairs; but it had been the prevalent opinion, that he could not operate upon human beings in any other way than through the instrumentality of other human beings, in voluntary confederacy with him; and that, by means of their spectres he could work any amount of mischief. While this opinion prevailed, the testimony of a witness, that he had seen the spectre of a particular person afflicting himself or any one else, was regarded as proof positive that the person, thus spectrally represented, was in league with the Devil, or, in other words, a Witch. This idea had been abandoned by some writers, who held that the Devil could make use of the spectre of an innocent person, to do mischief; and that, therefore, it was not positive or conclusive proof that any one was a Witch because his spectre had been seen tormenting others. The logical conclusion, from the views of these later writers, was that spectral

evidence, as it was called, bearing against an accused party, was wholly unreliable and must be thown out, entirely, in all cases.

The Reviewer says the "Clergy of New Eng"land" adopted the views of the writers just alluded to, and held that spectral evidence was unreliable and unsafe, and ought to be utterly rejected; and particularly maintain that such was the opinion of Cotton Mather. It is true that they professed to have great regard for those writers; but it is also true, that neither Mather nor the other Ministers in 1692, adopted the conclusion which the Reviewer allows to be inevitably demanded by sound reason and common sense namely, that "no spectral evidence must be ad"mitted." On the contrary, they did authorise the "admission" of spectral evidence. This I propose to prove; and if I succeed in doing it, the whole fabric of the article in the *North American Review*, falls to the ground.

It is necessary, at this point, to say a word as to the *Mather Papers*. They were published by a Committee of the Massachusetts Historical Society, in 1868. My work was published in 1867. The Reviewer, and certain journals that have committed themselves to his support, charge me with great negligence in not having consulted those papers, *not then in print*. Upon inquiry, while making my researches, I was informed, by those having them in hand preparatory to their going to press, that they contained nothing at all essential to my work; and the information was correct. Upon examining the printed volume, I cannot find a single item that would require an alteration, addition, or omission to be made in my work. But they are quite serviceable in the discussion to which the article in the *North American Review* compels me.

To return to the issue framed by the Reviewer. He makes a certain absolute assertion, repeats it in various forms, and confidently assumes it, all the way through, as in these passages: "Stough"ton admitted spectral evidence; Mather, in his "writings on the subject, denounced it, as ille"gal, uncharitable, and cruel." "He ever testi"fied against it, both publicly and privately; "and, particularly in his Letter to the Judges, "he besought them that they would by no means "admit it; and when a considerable assembly "of Ministers gave in their *Advice* about the mat"ter, he not only concurred with the advice, but "he drew it up." "The *Advice* was very spe"cific in excluding spectral testimony."

He relies, in the first place, and I may say chiefly, in maintaining this position—namely, that Mather denounced the *admission* of spectral testimony and demanded its *exclusion*—upon a sentence in a letter from Cotton Mather to John Richards, called by the Reviewer "his Letter to "the Judges," among the *Mather Papers*, p. 391.

Hutchinson informs us that Richards came into the country in low circumstances, but became an opulent merchant, in Boston. He was a member of Mather's Church, and one of the Special Court to try the witches. Its Session was to commence in the first week, probably on Thursday, the second day of June. The letter, dated on Tuesday, the thirty-first of May, is addressed to John Richards alone; and commences with a strong expression of regret that quite a severe indisposition will prevent his accompanying him to the trials. "Excuse me," he says, "from waiting upon you, "with the utmost of my little skill and care, to "assist the noble service, whereto you are called "of God this week, the service of encountering "the wicked spirits in the high places of our air, "and of detecting and confounding of their "confederates." He hopes, before the Court "gets far into the mysterious affair," to be able to "attend the desires" of Richards, which, to him, "always are commands." He writes the letter, "for the strengthening of your honorable "hands in that work of God whereto, (I thank "him) he hath so well fitted you." After some other complimentary language, and assurances that God's "people have been fasting and pray- "ing before him for your direction," he proceeds to urge upon him his favorite Swedish case, wherein the "endeavours of the Judges to dis- "cover and extirpate the authors of that execra- "ble witchcraft," were "immediately followed "with a remarkable smile of God." Then comes the paragraph, which the Reviewer defiantly cites, to prove that Cotton Mather agreed with him, in the opinion that spectre evidence ought not to be "admitted."

Before quoting the paragraph, I desire the reader to note the manner in which the affair in Sweden is brought to the attention of Richards, in the clauses just cited, in connection with what I have said in this article, page 16. Cotton Math- er was in possession of a book on this subject. "It comes to speak English," he says, "by the "acute pen of the excellent and renowned Dr. "Horneck." Who so likely as Mather to have brought the case to the notice of Phips, pp. 14. It was urged upon Richards at about the same time that it was upon Phips; and as an argument in favor of "*extirpating*" witches, by the *action of a Court of Oyer and Terminer.*

The paragraph is as follows: "And yet I must "most humbly beg you that in the management "of the affair in your most worthy hands, you "do not lay more stress upon pure Spectre testi- "mony than it will bear. When you are satis- "fied, and have good plain legal evidence, that "the Demons which molest our poor neighbors "do indeed represent such and such people to "the sufferers, though this be a presumption, yet "I suppose you will not reckon it a conviction

"that the people so represented are witches to "be immediately exterminated. It is very cer- "tain that the Devils have sometimes represented "the Shapes of persons not only innocent, but "also very virtuous. Though I believe that the "just God then ordinarily provides a way for the "speedy vindication of the persons thus abused. "Moreover, I do suspect that persons, who "have too much indulged themselves in malig- "nant, envious, malicious ebullitions of their "souls, may unhappily expose themselves to the "judgment of being represented by Devils, of "whom they never had any vision, and with "whom they have, much less, written any cove- "nant. I would say this; if upon the bare sup- "posal of a poor creature being represented by a "spectre, too great a progress be made by the "authority in ruining a poor neighbor so repre- "sented, it may be that a door may be thereby "opened for the Devils to obtain from the Courts "in the invisible world a license to proceed unto "most hideous desolations upon the repute and "repose of such as have yet been kept from the "great transgression. If mankind have thus far "once consented unto the credit of diabolical rep- "resentations, the door is opened! Perhaps there "are wise and good men, that may be ready to "style him that shall advance this caution, a "Witch-advocate, but in the winding up, this "caution will certainly be wished for."

This passage, strikingly illustrative, as it is, of Mather's characteristic style of appearing, to a cursory, careless reader, to say one thing, when he is really aiming to enforce another, while it has deceived the Reviewer, and led him to his quixotic attempt to revolutionize history, cannot be so misunderstood by a critical interpreter.

In its general drift, it appears, at first sight, to disparage spectral evidence. The question is: Does it forbid, denounce, or dissuade, its intro- duction? By no means. It supposes and allows its introduction, but says, *lay not more stress upon it than it will bear.* Further, it affirms that it may afford "presumption" of guilt, though not sufficient for conviction, and removes objec- tion to its introduction, by holding out the idea that, if admitted by the Court and it bears against innocent persons, "the just God, then, "ordinarily provides a way for their speedy vin- "dication." It is plain that the paragraph re- fers, not to the *admission* of "diabolical repre- "sentations," but to the *manner* in which they are to be received, in the "management" of the trials, as will more fully appear, as we proceed.

The suggestion, to reconcile Richards to the use of spectral evidence, that something would "or- "dinarily" providentially turn up to rescue in- nocent persons, against whom it was borne, was altogether delusive. It was an opinion of the day, that one of the most signal marks of the

Devil's descent with power, would be the seduction, to his service, of persons of the most eminent character, even, if possible, of the very elect; and, hence, no amount of virtue or holiness of life or conversation, could be urged in defence of any one. The records of the world present no more conspicuous instances of Christian and saint-like excellence than were exhibited by Rebecca Nurse and Elizabeth How; but spectral testimony was allowed to destroy them. Indeed, it was impossible for a Court to put any restrictions on this kind of evidence, if once received. (If the accusing girls exclaimed—all of them concurring, at the moment, in the declaration and in its details—that they saw, at that very instant, in the Court-room, before Judges and Jury, the spectre of the Prisoner assailing one of their number, and that one showing signs of suffering, what could be done to rebut their testimony? The character of the accused was of no avail. An *alibi* could not touch the case. (The distance from the Prisoner to the party professing to be tormented, was of no account. The whole proceeding was on the assumption that, however remote the body of the Prisoner, his or her spectre was committing the assault.) No limitation of space or time could be imposed on the spectral presence.) "Good, plain, legal evidence" was out of the question, where the Judges assumed, as Mather did, that "the molestations" then suffered by the people of the neighborhood, were the work of Demons, and fully believed that the tortures and convulsions of the accusers, before their eyes, were, as alleged, caused by the spectres of the accused.

To cut the matter short. The considerations Mather presents of the "inconvenience," as he calls it, of the spectral testimony, it might be supposed, would have led him to counsel—not as he did, against making "too great a progress" in its use—but its abandonment altogether. Why did he not, as the Reviewer says ought always have been done, protest utterly against its admission at all? The truth is, that neither in this letter, nor in any way, at any time, did he ever recommend caution *against* its use, but *in* its use.

It may be asked, what did he mean by "not "laying more stress upon spectre testimony than "it will bear," and the general strain of the paragraph? A solution of this last question may be reached as we continue the scrutiny of his language and actions.

In this same letter, Mather says: "I look upon "wounds that have been given unto spectres, "and received by witches, as intimations, broad "enough, in concurrence with other things, to "bring out the guilty. Though I am not fond "of assaying to give such wounds, yet, the proof "[*of*] such, when given, carries with it what is "very palpable."

This alludes to a particular form of spectral evidence. One of the "afflicted children" would testify that she saw and felt the spectre of the accused, tormenting her, and struck at it. A corresponding wound or bruise was found on the body, or a rent in the garments, of the accused. Mather commended this species of evidence, writing to one of the Judges, on the eve of the trials. He not only commends, but urges it as conclusive of guilt. Referring to what constituted the bulk of the evidence of the accusing girls, and which was wholly spectral in its nature—namely, that they were "hurt" by an "unseen hand"—he charges Richards, if he finds such "hurt" to be inflicted by the persons accused, "Hold them, for "you have catched a witch." He recommends putting the Prisoners upon repeating the "Lord's "prayer" or certain "other Systems of Chris-"tianity." He endorses the evidence derived from "poppits," "witch-marks," and even the "water ordeal." He advised a Judge, just proceeding to sit in cases of life and death, to make use of "cross and swift questions," as the means of bringing the accused "into confusion, likely "to lead them into confession."

Whoever examines, carefully, this letter to Richards, cannot, I think, but conclude that, instead of exonerating Mather, it fixes upon him the responsibility for the worst features of the Witchcraft Trials.

The next document on which the Reviewer relies is the *Return of the Ministers consulted by his Excellency and the honorable Council, upon the present Witchcraft in Salem Village.* It is necessary to give it entire, as follows:

["I. The afflicted state of our poor neighbours, "that are now suffering by molestations from "the invisible world, we apprehend so deplora-"ble, that we think their condition calls for the "utmost help of all persons in their several ca-"pacities.

"II. We cannot but, with all thankfulness, "acknowledge the success which the merciful "God has given to the sedulous and assiduous "endeavours of our honorable rulers, to defeat the "abominable witchcrafts which have been com-"mitted in the country, humbly praying, that "the discovery of those mysterious and mischiev-"ous wickednesses may be perfected.]

"III. We judge that, in the prosecution of "these and all such witchcrafts, there is need of "a very critical and exquisite caution, lest by "too much credulity for things received only "upon the Devil's authority, there be a door "opened for a long train of miserable conse-"quences, and Satan get an advantage over us; "for we should not be ignorant of his devices.

"IV. As in complaints upon witchcrafts "there may be matters of enquiry which do not "amount unto matters of presumption, and there

"may be matters of presumption which yet may
"not be reckoned matters of conviction, so it is
"necessary, that all proceedings thereabout be
"managed with an exceeding tenderness towards
"those that may be complained of, especially if
"they have been persons formerly of an unblem-
"ished reputation.

"V. When the first inquiry is made into the
"circumstances of such as may lie under any just
"suspicion of witchcrafts, we could wish that
"there may be admitted as little as possible of
"such noise, company, and openness, as may
"too hastily expose them that are examined; and
"that there may nothing be used as a test for
"the trial of the suspected, the lawfulness
"whereof may be doubted among the people of
"God; but that the directions given by such
"judicious writers as Perkins and Barnard may
"be consulted in such a case.

"VI. Presumptions whereupon persons may
"be committed, and, much more, convictions
"whereupon persons may be condemned as guil-
"ty of witchcrafts, ought certainly to be more
"considerable than barely the accused persons
"being represented by a spectre unto the afflict-
"ed; [inasmuch as it is an undoubted and a no-
"torious thing, that a Demon may, by God's per-
"mission, appear, even to ill purposes, in the
"shape of an innocent, yea, and a virtuous man.]
"Nor can we esteem alterations made in the suf-
"ferers, by a look or touch of the accused, to be
"an infallible evidence of guilt, but frequently
"liable to be abused by the Devil's legerdemain.

"VII. We know not whether some remarka-
"ble affront, given the Devil, by our disbelieving
"of those testimonies, whose whole force and
"strength is from him alone, may not put a pe-
"riod unto the progress of the dreadful calam-
"ity begun upon us, in the accusation of so
"many persons, whereof some, we hope, are yet
"clear from the great transgression laid to their
"charge.

["VIII. Nevertheless, we cannot but humbly
"recommend unto the Government, the speedy and
"vigorous prosecutions of such as have rendered
"themselves obnoxious, according to the direc-
"tions given in the laws of God, and the whole-
"some Statutes of the English nation, for the
"detection of Witchcrafts."]

I have enclosed the *first, second* and *eighth* Sections, and a part of the *Sixth*, in brackets, for purposes that will appear, in a subsequent part of this
discussion. The *Advice of the Ministers* was written by Cotton Mather. As in his letter to Richards, he does not caution *against* the use, but *in*
the use, of spectral evidence. Not a word is said
denouncing its introduction or advising its entire rejection. We look in vain for a line or a
syllable disapproving the trial and execution just
had, resting as they did, entirely upon spectral

evidence; on the contrary, the *second* Section
applauds what had been done; and prays that
the work entered upon may be perfected. The
first clauses in the *fourth* Section sanction its admission, as affording ground of "presumption,"
although "it may not be matter of conviction."
The *sixth* Section, while it appears to convey the
idea that spectral evidence alone ought not to be
regarded as sufficient, contains, at the same time,
a form of expression, that not only requires its
reception, but places its claims on the highest
possible grounds. '[*A Demon may, by* GOD's
"PERMISSION, *appear, even to ill purposes, in the
"shape of an innocent, yea, and a virtuous man.*"
It is sufficiently shocking to think that anything,
to ill purposes, can be done by Divine permission; but horrible, indeed, to intimate that the
Devil can have that permission to malign and
murder an innocent person. If the spectre appears by God's permission, the effect produced
has his sanction] The blasphemous supposition
that God permits the Devil thus to bear false
witness, to the destruction of the righteous, over-
turns all the sentiments and instincts of our moral
and religious nature.] In using this language,
the Ministers did not have a rational apprehension of what they were saying, which is the only
apology for much of the theological phraseology
of that day. This phrase, "God's permission,"
had quite a currency at the time; and if it did
not reconcile the mind, subdued it to wondering
and reverent silence. It will be seen that Mather,
on other occasions, repeated this idea, in various
and sometimes stronger terms. The *third, fifth,
seventh*, and last clauses of the *fourth* Sections,
contain phrases which will become intelligible,
as we advance in the examination of Mather's
writings, relating to the subject of witchcraft.

Here it may, again, be safely said, that if Increase and Cotton Mather had really, as the Reviewer affirms, been opposed to the *admission* of
spectral testimony, this was the time for them to
have said so. If, at this crisis, they had "de-
"nounced it, as illegal, uncharitable and cruel,"
no more blood would have been shed. If the
Advice had even recommended, in the most
moderate terms, its absolute exclusion from every
stage of the proceedings, they would have come
to an end. But it assumes its introduction, and
only suggests "disbelief" of it, in avoiding to
act upon it, in "some" instances.

Hutchinson states the conclusion of the matter,
after quoting the whole document. "The Judges
"seem to have paid more regard to the last ar-
"ticle of this *Return*, than to several which pre-
"cede it; for the prosecutions were carried on
"with all possible vigor, and without that ex-
"quisite caution which is proposed."—*History*,
ii. 54.

The *Advice* was skilfully—it is not uncharitable to say—artfully drawn up. It has deceived the Reviewer into his statement that it was "very specific in excluding spectral testimony." A careless reader, or one whose eyes are blinded by a partisan purpose, may not see its real import. The paper is so worded as to mislead persons not conversant with the ideas and phraseology of that period. But it was considered by all the Judges, and the people in general, fully to endorse the proceedings in the trial of Bridget Bishop, and to advise their speedy and vigorous continuance. It was spectral testimony that overwhelmed her. It was the fatal element that wrought the conviction of every person put on trial, from first to last : as was fully proved, five months afterwards, when Sir William Phips, under circumstances I shall describe, bravely and peremptorily forbid, as the Ministers failed to do, the "trying," or even "committing," of any one, on the evidence of "the afflicted per-"sons," which was wholly spectral. When thus, by his orders, it was utterly thrown out, the life of the prosecutions became, at once, extinct; and, as Mather says, the accused were cleared as fast as they were tried.—*Magnalia*, Book II, page 64.

The suggestion that caution was to be used in handling this species of evidence, and that it was to be received as affording grounds of "pre-"sumption," to be corroborated or re-inforced by other evidence, practically was of no avail. If received, at all, in any stage, or under any name, it necessarily controlled every case. No amount of evidence, of other kinds, could counterbalance or stand against it : nothing was needed to give it full and fatal effect. It struck Court, Jury, and people, nay, even the Prisoners themselves, in many instances, with awe. It dispensed, as has been mentioned, with the presence of the accused, on the spot, where and when the crime was alleged to have been committed, or within miles or hundreds of miles of it. No reputation for virtue or piety could be pleaded against it. The doctrine which Cotton Mather proclaimed, on another occasion, that the Devil might appear as an Angel of Light, completed the demolition of the securities of innocence. There was no difficulty in getting "other testimony" to give it effect. In the then state of the public mind, indiscriminately crediting every tale of slander and credulity, looking at every thing through the refracting and magnifying atmosphere of the blindest and wildest passions, it was easy to collect materials to add to the spectral evidence, thereby, according to the doctrine of the Ministers, to raise the "presumption," to the "conviction" of guilt. Even our Reviewer finds evidence to "substantiate" that, given against George Burroughs, resting on spectres, in his feats of strength, in some malignant neighborhood scandals, and in exaggerated forms of parish or personal animosities.

VII.

ADVICE OF THE MINISTERS, FURTHER CONSIDERED. COTTON MATHER'S PLAN FOR DEALING WITH SPECTRAL TESTIMONY.

The *Advice of the Ministers* is a document that holds a prominent place in our public history ; and its relation to events needs to be elucidated.

In his *Life of Sir William Phips*, Cotton Mather has this paragraph : "And Sir William Phips "arriving to his Government, after this ensnaring "horrible storm was begun, did consult the "neighboring Ministers of the Province, who "made unto his Excellency and the Council, a "Return (drawn up, at their desire, by Mr. Math-"er, the younger, as I have been informed) where-"in they declared."—*Magnalia*, Book II, page 62.

He then gives, without intimating that any essential or substantial part of the *declaration*, or *Advice*, was withheld, the Sections *not* included in brackets.—*Vide*, pages 21, 22, *ante*.

It is to be observed that Phips is represented as having asked the Ministers for their advice, and their answer as having been made to his "Excel-"lency and the Council." There is no mention of this transaction in the Records of the Council. Phips makes no reference to it in his letter of the fourteenth of October, which is remarkable, as it would have been to his purpose, in explaining the grounds of his procedure, in organizing, and putting into operation, the judicial tribunal at Salem. It may be concluded, from all that I shall present.—Sir William, having given over the whole business to his Deputy and Chief-justice, with an understanding that he was authorized to manage it, in all particulars,—that this transaction with the Ministers may never have been brought to the notice of the Governor at all : his official character and title were, perhaps, referred to, as a matter of form. The Council, as such, had nothing to do with it ; but the Deputy-governor and certain individual members of the Council, that is, those who, with him, as Chief-justice, constituted the Special Court, asked and received the *Advice*.

Again : the paragraph, as constructed by Mather, just quoted, certainly leaves the impression on a reader, that Phips applied for the *Advice of the Ministers*, at or soon after his arrival. The evidence, I think, is conclusive, that the *Advice* was not asked, until after the first Session of the Court had been held. This is inferrible from the answer of the Ministers, which is dated thirteen days after the first trial, and five days after the execution of a sentence then passed. It alludes

to the *success* which had been given to the prosecutions. If the Government had asked counsel
of the Ministers before the trials commenced, it
is inexplicable and incredible, besides being inexcusable, that the Ministers should have delayed
their reply until after the first act of the awful
tragedy had passed, and blood begun to be shed.
Hutchinson expressly says: "The further trials
"were put off to the adjournment, the thirtieth
"of June. The Governor and Council thought
"proper, *in the mean time*, to take the opinion
"of several of the principal Ministers, upon the
"state of things, as they then stood. This was
"an old Charter practice."—*History*, ii, 53.

It has been regarded as a singular circumstance, that after such pains had been taken,
and so great a stretch of power practised, to
put a Court so suddenly in operation to try persons accused of witchcraft, on the pretence,
too, recorded in the Journal of the Council, of
the "thronged" condition of the jails, at that
"hot season," and after trying one person only,
it should have adjourned for four weeks. Perhaps, by a collation of passages and dates, we
may reach a probable explanation. In his letter to "the Ministers in and near Boston,"
written in January, 1696, after considering
briefly, and in forcible language, the fearful errors from which the Delusion of 1692 had risen,
and solemnly reminding them of what they
ought to have done to lead their people out of
such errors, Calef brings their failure to do it
home to them, in these pungent words: "If,
"instead of this, you have, some by word and
"writing propagated, an I others recommended,
"such doctrines, and abetted the false notions
"which are so prevalent in this apostate age, it
"is high time to consider it. If, when author-
"ity found themselves almost nonplust in such
"prosecutions, and sent to you for your advice
"what they ought to do, and you have then
"thanked them for what they had already done
"(and thereby encouraged them to proceed in
"those very by-paths already fallen into) it so
"much the more nearly concerns you. *Ezek,*
"xxxiii, 2 to 8."—*Calef*, 92.

Looking at this passage, in connection with
that quoted just before from Hutchinson, we
gather that something had occurred that "non-
"plust" the Court—some serious embarrassment,
that led to its sudden adjournment—after the
condemnation of Bridget Bishop, while many
other cases had been fully prepared for trial by
the then Attorney-general, Newton, and the
parties to be tried had, the day before, been
brought to Salem from the jail in Boston, and
were ready to be put to the Bar. What was the
difficulty? The following may be the solution.

Brattle informs us, and he was able to speak
with confidence, that "Major N. Saltonstall,
"Esq., who was one of the Judges, has left the
"Court, and is very much dissatisfied with the
"proceedings of it."—*Massachusetts Historical
Collections*, I, v., 78.

The questions arise; When and why did he
leave the Court? The Records of the Council
show that he was constant in his attendance at
that Board, his name always appearing at the
head of the roll of those present, until the sixteenth of June, from which date it does not ap-
p ar again until the middle of February, 1693.
The Legislature, in the exercise of its powers,
under the Charter, had, near the close of 1692,
established a regular Superior Court, consisting
of Stoughton, Danforth—who had disapproved
of the proceedings of the Special Court—Richards, Wait Winthrop, and Sewall. It continued,
in January, 1693, witchcraft trials; but spectral
evidence being wholly rejected, the prosecutions
all broke down; and Stoughton, in consequence,
left the Court in disgust. After all had been
abandoned, and his own course, thereby, vindicated, Major Saltonstall re-appeared at the
Council Board; and was re-elected by the next
House of Representatives. His conduct, therefore, was very marked and significant. In the
only way in which he, a country member, could
express his convictions, as there were no such
facilities, in the press or otherwise, for public
discussions, as we now have, he made them emphatically known; and is worthy of the credit
of being the only public man of his day who
had the sense or courage to condemn the proceedings, at the start. He was a person of amia-
ble and genial deportment; and, from the County
Court files, in which his action, as a Magistrate,
is exhibited in several cases, it is evident that
he was methodical and careful in official business, but susceptible of strong impressions and
convictions, and had, on a previous occasion,
manifested an utter want of confidence in certain parties, who, it became apparent at the first
Session of the Court, were to figure largely in
bearing spectral testimony, in most of the cases.
He had no faith in those persons, and was thus,
we may suppose, led to discredit, wholly, that
species of testimony.

From his attendance at the Council Board,
up to the sixteenth of June, the day when the
Advice of the Ministers was probably received,
it may be assumed that he attended also, to that
time, the sittings of the Court; and that when
he withdrew from the former, he did also f om
the latter. Th date indicates that his action,
in withdrawing, was determined by the import
of the *Advice*.

If a gentleman of his position and family, a
grandson of an original Patentee, Sir Richard
Saltonstall, and sitting as a Judge at the first
trial, had the independence and manly spirit to

express, without reserve, his disapprobation of the proceedings, the expression of Calef is explained; and the Court felt the obstacle that was in their way. Hence the immediate adjournment, and the resort to some extraordinary expedient, to remove it.

This may account for the appeal to the Ministers. Great interest must have been felt in their reply, by all cognizant of the unexpected difficulty that had occurred. The document was admirably adapted to throw dust into the eyes of those who had expressed doubts and misgivings; but it did not deceive Saltonstall. He saw that it would be regarded by the other Judges, and the public in general, as an encouragement to continue the trials; and that, under the phraseology of what had the aspect of caution, justification would be found for the introduction. to an extent that would control the trials, of spectral evidence. The day after its date, he left his seat at the Council Board, withdrew from the Court, and washed his hands of the whole matter.

The course of events demonstrates that the *Advice* was interpreted, by all concerned, as applauding what had been done at the first trial, and earnestly urging that the work, thus begun, should be speedily and vigorously prosecuted. Upon the Ministers, therefore, rests the stigma for all that followed.

There may have been, at that time, as there was not long afterward, some difference of opinion among the Ministers; and the paper may have had the character of a compromise—always dangerous and vicious, bringing some or all parties into a false position. Samuel Willard may have held, then, the opinion expressed in a pamphlet ascribed to him, published, probably, towards the close of the trials, that spectral evidence ought only to be allowed where it bore upon persons of bad reputation. The *fourth* Section conciliated his assent to the document. This might have been the view of Increase Mather, who, after the trials by the Special Court were over, indicated an opinion, that time for further diligent " search " ought to have been allowed, before proceeding to " the " execution of the most capital offenders; " and declared the very excellent sentiment, that " it " becomes those of his profession to be very " tender in the shedding of blood." The expressions, " exceeding tenderness," in the *fourth* Section, and " the first inquiry," in the *fifth*—the latter conveying the idea of repeated investigations with intervals of time—were well adapted to gain his support of the whole instrument. If they were led to concur in the *Advice*, by such inducements, they were soon undeceived. " Unblemished reputation " was no protection;

and the proceedings at the trials were swift, summary, and conclusive.

It may be proper, at this point, to inquire what was meant by the peculiar phraseology of the *third*, *fifth*, *seventh*, and latter part of the *fourth*, Sections. It is difficult, writing as Cotton Mather often did, and had great skill in doing, in what Calef calls " the ambidexter" style, to ascertain his ideas. After the reaction had taken effect in the public mind, and be was put upon the defensive, he had much to say about some difference between him and the Judges. It clearly had nothing to do with the " admission " of spectral evidence; for that was the point on which the opinion of the Ministers was asked, and on which he voluntarily proffered remarks in his letter to one of the Judges, Richards. If he had been opposed to its " admission," nothing would have been easier, safer, or more demanded by the truth and his own honor, than for him to have said so. Indeed, his writings everywhere show that he was almost a *one idea* man, on the subject of spectres; and, in some way or form, deemed their evidence indispensible and reliable. He, evidently, had some favorite plan or scheme, as to the method in which that kind of evidence was to be handled; and it was because he could not get it carried into effect, and for this reason alone, so far as we can discover, that he disapproved of the methods actually pursued by the Court. He never disclosed his plan, but shrunk from explaining it at length, " as too Icarian and " presumptuous " a task for him to undertake. Let us see if we can glean his ideas from his writings.

I call attention, in the first place, to the following clause, in his letter to Richards: " If upon " the bare supposal of a poor creature's being " represented by a spectre, too great a progress " be made by the authority, in ruining a poor " neighbor so represented, it may be that a " door may be thereby opened for the Devil " to obtain from the Courts, in the invisible " world, a license to proceed unto most hideous " desolations upon the repute and repose of such " as have been kept from the great transgres- " sion."

" Too great a progress " conveys the suggestion that, upon the introduction of spectral evidence, there should be a delay in the proceedings of the Court, for some intermediate steps to be taken, before going on with the trial.

We gather other intimations, to this effect, from other passages, as follows: " Now, in my " visiting of the miserable, I was always of this " opinion, that we were ignorant of what power " the Devils might have, to do their mischiefs in " the shapes of some that had never been explicitly engaged in diabolical confederacies,

"and that therefore, though many witchcrafts
"had been fairly detected on enquiries provoked
"and begun by spectral exhibitions, yet we
"could not easily be too jealous of the snares
"laid for us in the devices of Satan. The world
"knows how many pages I have composed and
"published, and particular gentlemen in the Gov-
"ernment know how many letters I have written,
"to prevent the excessive credit of spectral accu-
"sations; wherefore I have still charged the af-
"flicted that they should cry out of nobody for
"afflicting them; but that, if this might be any
"advantage, they might privately tell their
"minds to some one person of discretion enough
"to make no ill use of their communications;
"accordingly there has been this effect of it, that
"the name of no one good person in the world
"ever came under any blemish by means of an
"afflicted person that fell under my particular
"cognizance; yea, no one man, woman, or child
"ever came into any trouble, for the sake of any
"that were afflicted, after I had once begun to
"look after them. How often have I had this
"thrown into my dish, 'that many years ago I
"'had an opportunity to have brought forth such
"'people as have, in the late storm of witchcraft,
"'been complained of, but that I smothered it
"'all'; and after that storm was raised at Salem,
"I did myself offer to provide meat, drink, and
"lodging for no less than six of the afflicted,
"that so an experiment might be made, wh ther
"prayer, with fasting, upon the removal of the
"distressed, might not put a period to the troub-
"le then rising, without giving the civil authori-
"ty the trouble of prosecuting those things,
"which nothing but a conscientious regard unto
"the cries of miserable families could have over-
"come the reluctancies of the honorable Judges
"to meddle with. In short, I do humbly but
"freely affirm it, there is not a man living in this
"world who has been more desirous, than the
"poor man I, to shelter my neighbors from the
"inconveniences of spectral outcries: yea, I am
"very jealous I have done so much that way, as
"to sin in what I have done; such have been the
"cowardice and fearfulness where unto my re-
"gard to the dissatisfaction of other people has
"precipitated me. I know a man in the world,
"who has thought he has been able to convict
"some such witches as ought to die; but his re-
"spect unto the public peace has caused him
"rather to try whether he could not renew them
"by repentance."—*Calef*, 11.

The careful reader will notice that "six of the
"afflicted," at Salem Village, would have included nearly the whole circle of the accusing girls
there. If he had been allowed to take them into
his exclusive keeping, he would have had the
whole thing in his own hands.

In his account of "the afflictions of Margaret

"Rule," printed by Calef, in his book, and from
which the foregoing extracts have been made
speaking of the "eight cursed spectres" with
which she was assaulted, in the fall of 1693,
Mather says: "She was very careful of my reiter-
"ated charges, *to forbear blazing their names*,
"lest any good person should come to suffer any
"blast of reputation, through the cunning mal-
"ice of the great accuser; nevertheless, having
"since privately named them to myself, I will
"venture to say this of them. that they are a sort
"of wretches who, for these many years, have
"gone under as violent presumptions of witch-
"craft as, perhaps, any creatures yet living upon
"earth; although I am far from thinking that
"the visions of this young woman were evidence
"enough to prove them so."—*Calef*, 4.

The following is from his *Wonders of the Invisible World*. 12.: "If once a witch do ingen-
"iously confess among us, no more spectres do,
"in their shapes, after this, trouble the vicinage;
"if any guilty creatures will accordingly, to so
"good purpose, confess their crime to any Min-
"ister of God, and get out of the snare of the
"Devil, as no Minister will discover such a con-
"scientious confession, so, I believe, none in the
"authority will press him to discover it, but re-
"joice in a soul saved from death."

In his *Life of Phips*, he says: "In fine, the
"country was in a dreadful ferment, and wise
"men foresaw a long train of dismal and bloody
"consequences. Hereupon they first advised,
"that the *afflicted* might be kept asunder, in the
"closest privacy; and one particular person
"(whom I have cause to know), in pursuance of
"this advice, offered himself singly to provide
"accommodations for any six of them, that so the
"success of more than ordinary prayer, with fast-
"ing, might, with patience, be experienced, be-
"fore any other courses were taken."—*Magnalia*.
Book II. p. 62.

Hutchinson gives an extract from a letter, written by John Allyn, Secretary of Connecticut, dated. "HARTFORD, March 18, 1693." to Increase
Mather, as follows: "As to what you men-
"tion. concerning that poor creature in your
"town that is afflicted, and mentioned my name
"to yourself and son, I return you hearty thanks
"for your intimation about it. and for your char-
"ity therein mentioned; and I have great cause
"to bless God, who, of his mercy hitherto, hath
"not left me to fall into such an horrid evil."
—*History*, ii. 61, note.

Further. it was on account of some particular
plan, in reference to the management of this description of evidence, I am inclined to think.
that he felt the importance of being present at
the trials. For this reason, he laments the illness
that prevented his accompanying Richards to the
Court, at its opening, on the second of June, to

"assist the noble service," as he says, "with the "utmost of my little skill and care."

This language shows conclusively, by the way, the great influence he had, at that time, in directing the Government, particularly the Court. He would not have addressed one of the Judges, in such terms, had he not felt that his "skill and "care" would be recognized and permitted to take effect. We may well lament, with him, that he could not have been present at the first trial. It would not, then, have been left to conjecture and scrutiny, to determine what his plan was; and an open attempt, to bring the Court to adopt it, might have given another turn to affairs.

In his Diary, on the twenty-ninth of April, is the following: "This day I obtained help of "God, that he would make use of me, as of a John, "to be a herald of the Lord's Kingdom, now ap- "proaching." "My prayers did especially in- "sist upon the horrible enchantments and posses "sions, broke forth in Salem Village, things of "a most prodigious aspect, a good issue to those "things, and my own direction and protection ' thereabouts, I did especially petition for."

The date of this entry is important. On the eleventh, nineteenth, and twenty second of April, impressive scenes had been exhibited at Salem Village. Some of the most conspicuous cases of the preliminary examinations of persons arrested, had occurred. The necessary steps were then being taken to follow up those examinations with a procedure that would excite the country to the highest pitch. The arrangements, kept concealed at Salem, and unsuspected by the public at large, were made and perfected in Boston. On the day after the date of the foregoing memorandum, a Magistrate in that place issued the proper order for the arrest of the Rev. George Burroughs; and officers were started express to Maine for that purpose. This was "the most prodigious aspect "of affairs" at the time. All the circumstances must have been known by Mather. Hence his earnest solicitude that proceedings should be conducted under his own "direction and protection." The use of these terms, looks as if Mather contemplated the preliminary examinations as to take place under his direction and management, and will be borne in mind, when we come to consider the question of his having been, more or less, present at them.

Disposed to take the most favorable and charitable view of such passages as have now been presented, I would gather from them that his mind may have recurred to his original and favorite idea, that prayer and fasting were the proper weapons to wield against witchcraft: but if they failed, then recourse was to be had to the terrors of the law. He desired to have the afflicted and the accused placed under the treat-

ment of some one person, of discretion enough to make no ill use of their communications, to whom "they might privately tell their minds," and who, without "noise, company and openness," could keep, under his own control, the dread secrets of the former and exorcise the latter. He was willing, and desirous, of occupying this position himself, and of taking its responsibility. To signify this, he offered to provide "meat, "drink and lodging" for six of the afflicted children; to keep them "asunder, in the closest "privacy;" to be the recipient of their visions; and then to look after the accused, for the purpose of inducing them to confess and break loose from their league with Satan; to be exempt, except when he thought proper to do it, from giving testimony in Court, against parties accused; and to communicate with persons, thus secretly complained of, as he and his father afterwards did with the Secretary of Connecticut, and taking, as in that case, if he saw fit, a bare denial as sufficient, for "sheltering" them, altogether, by keeping the accusation a profound secret in his own breast, as he acknowledges he had done to a considerable extent—at once claiming and confessing that he had "done so much "that way, as to sin in what he had done."

In language that indicates a correspondence and familiarity of intercourse with persons, acting on the spot, at Salem Village, such as authorized him to speak for them, he gives us to understand that they concurred with him in his proposed method of treating the cases: "There are "very worthy men, who, having been called by "God, when and where this witchcraft first ap- "peared upon the stage, to encounter it, are ear- "nestly desirous to have it sifted unto the bot- "tom of it." "Persons, thus disposed, have "been men eminent for wisdom and virtue." "They would gladly contrive and receive as ex- "pedient, how the shedding of blood might be "spared, by the recovery of witches not beyond "the reach of pardon. And, after all, they in- "vite all good men, in terms to this purpose." "Being amazed at the number and quality of "those accused, of late, we do not know but Sa- "tan by his wiles may have enwrapt some inno- "cent persons; and therefore should earnestly "and humbly desire the most critical inquiry, "upon the place, to find out the fallacy."—*Wonders*, 11.

Indeed, Parris and his coadjutors, at Salem Village, to whom these passages refer, had, without authority, been, all along, exercising the functions Mather desired to have bestowed upon him, by authority. They had kept a controlling communication with the "afflicted children;" determined who were to be cried out publicly against, and when; rebuked and repressed the calling out, by name, of the Rev. Samuel Willard

and many other persons, of both sexes, of "quality," in Boston; and arranged and managed
matters, generally.

The conjecture I have ventured to make, as to
Mather's plan of procedure, explains, as the reader
will perceive, by turning back to the Minister's *Advice*, [*Pages* 21, 22. *ante*] much of the phraseology
of that curious document. "Very critical and ex-
"quisite caution," in the *third* Section; "that all
"proceedings thereabout be managed with an ex-
"ceeding tenderness towards those that may be
"complained of," in the *fourth*; "we could wish
"that there may be admitted as little as possi-
"ble of such noise, company and openness, as
"may too hastily expose them that are examin-
"ed," in the *fifth*; and the entire *seventh* Section, expressly authorize the suppression, disregard, and *disbelief*, of *some* of the Devil's
accusations, on the grounds of expediency and
public policy.

Mather's necessary absence from the Court, at
its first Session, prevented his "skill and care"
being availed of, or any attempt being made to
bring forward his plan. The proceedings, having thus commenced in an ordinary way, were
continued at the several adjournments of the
Court; and his experiment was never made.

The fallacy of his ideas and the impracticability of his scheme must, indeed, have become
evident, at the first moment it was brought under consideration. Inexperienced and blinded,
as they were, by the delusions of the time and the
excitements of the scene, and disposed, as they
must have been, by all considerations, to comply
with his wishes, the Judges had sense enough
left to see that it would never do to take the
course he desired. The trials could not, in that
event, have gone on at all. The very first step
would have been to abrogate their own functions
as a Court; pass the accusers and accused over to
his hands; and adjourn to wait his call. If the
spectre evidence had been excluded from the
"noise, confusion and openness" of the public
Court-room, there would have been nothing left
to go upon. If it had been admitted, under any
conditions or limitations, merely to disclose matter of "presumption," a fatal difficulty would
meet the first step of the enquiry. To the question, "Who hurts you?" no answer could be allowed to be given; and the "*Minister*," to whom
the witness had confidentially given the names
of persons whose spectres had tormented her, sitting, perhaps, in the Court-room at the time, would
have to countenance the suppression of the evidence, and not be liable to be called to the stand
to divulge his knowledge.

The attempt to leave the accusers and the accused to be treated by the Minister selected for
the purpose, in secure privacy, would have dissolved the Court before it had begun; and if this

was what Mather meant when, afterwards, at any
time, he endeavored to throw off the responsibility of the proceedings, by intimating that his
proffered suggestions and services were disregarded, his complaint was not unreasonable.
The truth is, the proposal was wholly inadmissi-
ble, and could not have been carried into effect.

Besides, it would have overthrown the whole
system of organized society, and given to whom-
soever the management of the cases had thus, for
the time, been relinquished, a power too fearful
to be thought of, as lodged in one man, or in any
private person. If he, or any other person, had
been allowed by the Court to assume such an office, and had been known to hold, in secret custody, the accusing parties, receiving their confidential communications, to act upon them as he saw
fit—sheltering some from prosecution and returning others to be proceeded against by the Court,
which would be equivalent to a conviction and
execution—it would have inaugurated a reign of
terror, such as had not even then been approached, and which no community could bear. Every
man and woman would have felt in the extremest peril, hanging upon the will of an irrespon-
sible arbiter of life and death.

Parris and his associates, acting without authority and in a limited sphere, had tried this
experiment; had spread abroad, terror, havoc, and
ruin; and incensed the surrounding region
with a madness it took generations to allay.

To have thought, for a moment, that it was
desirable to be invested with such a power, "by
"the authority," shows how ignorant Cotton
Mather was of human nature. However innocent, upright, or benevolent might be its exercise,
he would have been assailed by animosities of
the deepest, and approaches of the basest, kind.
A hatred and a sycophancy, such as no Priest,
Pope, or despot before, had encountered, would
have been brought against him. He would have
been assailed by the temptation, and aspersed by
the imputation, of "Hush money," from all
quarters; and, ultimately, the whole country would
have risen against what would have been regarded as a universal levy of "Black Mail." Whoever, at any time, in any country, should undertake such an office as this, would be, in the end,
the victim of the outraged sensibilities and passions of humanity. How long could it be endured, any where, if all men were liable to receive, from one authorized and enabled to determine their fate, such a missive as the Mathers
addressed to the Secretary of Connecticut, and,
at the best, to be beholden, as he felt himself to
be, to the "charity" that might prevent their
being exposed and prosecuted to the ruin of their
reputation, if not to an ignominious death?

Calef, alluding to Mather's pretensions to having been actuated by "exceeding tenderness to-

"wards persons complained of," expresses the
sentiments all would feel, in such a condition of
dependence upon the "charity" of one, armed
with such fatal power over them: "These are
"some of the destructive notions of this age;
"and however the asserters of them seem some-
"times to value themselves much upon shelter-
"ing their neighbors from spectral accusations,
"they may deserve as much thanks as that Tyrant,
"that having industriously obtained an unintel-
"ligible charge against his subjects, in matters
"wherein it was impossible they should be guil-
"ty, having thereby their lives in his power, yet
"suffers them of his mere grace to live, and
"will be called gracious Lord!"—*Preface.*

The mere suspicion that some persons were
behind the scene, exercising this power of pointing out some for prosecution and sheltering some
from trial or arrest, produced, as Phips says, "a
"strange ferment of dissatisfaction," threatening
ing to kindle "an inextinguishable flame." Brattle complained of it bitterly: "This occasions
"much discourse and many hot words, and is a
"very great scandal and stumbling block to many
"good people; certainly distributive justice should
"have its course, without respect to persons;
"and, although the said Mrs. Thatcher be moth-
"er-in-law to Mr. Curwin, who is one of the Jus-
"tices and Judges, yet, if justice and conscience
"do oblige them to apprehend others on account
"of the afflicted their complaints, I cannot see
"how, without injustice and violence to con-
"science, Mrs. Thatcher can escape, when it is
"well known how much she is, and has been,
"complained of."—Letter dated October 8th,
1692, in the *Massachusetts Historical Society's
Collections,* I., v., 69.

Hezekiah Usher, an eminent citizen of Boston,
was arrested by Joseph Lynde, one of the Council, but suffered to remain, "for above a fort-
"night," in a private house, and afterwards to
leave the Province. Brattle "cannot but admire"
at this, and says: "Methinks that same justice,
"that actually imprisoned others, and refused
"bail for them, on any terms, should not be sat-
"isfied without actually imprisoning Mr. U.,
"and refusing bail for him, when his case is
"known to be the very same with the case of
"those others."

Brattle was a friend of Usher, and believed
him innocent, yet was indignant that such bare-
faced partiality should be shown in judicial proceedings. The establishment of a regular sys-
tematized plan, committed to any individual, for
sheltering some, while others would be handed
back for punishment, would have been unendur-
able.

As it was, Mather exposed himself to much
odium, because it was understood that he was
practising, on his own responsibility and privately, upon the plan he wished the Judges to
adopt, as a principle and method of proceedure,
in all the trials. He says: "It may be, no man
"living ever had more people, under preternatu-
"ral and astonishing circumstances, cast by the
"providence of God into his more particular
"care than I have had."

Of course, those persons would be most obnoxious to ill-feeling in the community, who were
known, as he says of himself, in the foregoing
sentence, to have most intimacy with, and influence over, the accusers. For this reason, Cotton
Mather was the special object of resentment. No
wonder that he sometimes bewails, and sometimes
berates, the storm of angry passions raging
around. A very bitter feeling pervaded the
country, grounded on the conviction that there
was "a respect to persons," and a connivance, in
behalf of some, by those managing the affair.
The public was shocked by having such persons
as the Rev. Samuel Willard, Mrs. Hale of Beverly, and the Lady of the Governor, cried out
upon by the "afflicted children;" and the com-
motion was heightened by a cross-current of indignant enquiries: "Why, as these persons are
"accused, are they not arrested and imprisoned?"

Mather alludes, in frequent passages, to this
angry state of feeling, as the following: "It is
"by our quarrels that we spoil our prayers; and
"if our humble, zealous, and united prayers are
"once hindered! Alas, the Philistines of Hell
"have cut our locks for us; they will then blind
"us, mock us, ruin us. In truth, I cannot alto-
"gether blame it, if people are a little trans-
"ported, when they conceive all the secular in-
"terests of themselves and their families at stake,
"and yet, at the sight of these heart-burnings,
"I cannot forbear the exclamation of the sweet-
"spirited Austin, in his pacificatory epistle to
"Jerom, on the contest with Ruffin, '*O misera et
"'miseranda conditio!'*"—*Wonders,* 11.

There was another evil to which he exposed
himself by seeking to have such frequent, private, and confidential intercourse with the afflicted
accusers and confessing witches, who professed
to have so often seen, associated with, and suffered from, spectral images of the Devil's confederates; which spectral shapes, as was believed,
were, after all, the Devil himself. He came
under the imputation of what, in Scripture, is
pronounced one of the darkest of crimes. The
same charge was made to tell against Mr. Parris,
helping effectually to remove him from the ministry at Salem Village. *Leviticus* xx., 6. "And
"the soul that turneth after such as have familiar
"spirits, and after wizards, to go a whoring
"after them, I will set my face against that soul,
"and will cut him off from among his people."
1 Chronicles, x., 13. "So Saul died for his
"transgression, which he committed against the

"Lord, even against the word of the Lord,
"which he kept not; and also, for asking counsel
"of one that had a familiar spirit, to inquire of
"it, and inquired not of the Lord, therefore he
"slew him."

For having so much to do with persons professing to suffer from, and from others confessing to have committed, the sin of witchcraft, Mather became the object of a scathing rebuke in the letter of Brattle, in a passage I shall quote, in another connection.

Such, then, so far as I can gather, was Cotton Mather's plan for the management of witchcraft investigations; such its impracticability; and such the dangerous and injurious consequences to himself, of attempting to put it into practice. He never fully divulged it; but, in the *Advice* of the Ministers and various other writings, endeavored to pave the way for it. All the expressions, in that document and elsewhere, which have deceived the Reviewer and others into the notion that he was opposed to the admission of spectre evidence, at the trials, were used as arguments to persuade "authority" not to receive that species of evidence, in open Court, but to refer it to him, in the first instance, to be managed by him with exquisite caution and discretion, and, thereby avoid inconveniences and promote good results; and when he could not subdue the difficulties of the case, to deliver back the obdurate and unrepentant, to the Court, to be proceeded against in the ordinary course of law. With this view, he has much to say that indicates a tender regard to the prisoners. It is true that the scheme, if adopted, would have given him absolute power over the community, and, for this reason, may have had attraction. But, I doubt not, that he cherished it from benevolent feelings also. He thought that he might, in that way, do great good. But it could not be carried into effect. It was seen, at once, by all men, who had any sense left, to be utterly impracticable, and had to be abandoned. That being settled and disposed of, he went into the prosecutions without misgivings, earnestly and vehemently sustaining the Court, in all things, spectre evidence included, as remains to be shown.

VIII.

COTTON MATHER AND SPECTRAL EVIDENCE.

I shall continue to draw, at some length, upon Mather's writings, to which I ask the careful attention of the reader. The subject to which they mostly relate, is of much interest, presenting views of a class of topics, holding, for a long period, a mighty sway over the human mind.

In his *Life of Phips*, written in 1697, and constituting the concluding part of the Second Book of the *Magnalia*, he gives a general account of what had transpired, in the preliminary examinations at Salem, before the arrival of Sir William, at Boston. In it, he spreads out, with considerable fullness, what had been brought before the Magistrates, consisting mainly of spectral testimony; and narrates the appearances and doings of spectres assaulting the "afflicted "children," not as mere matters alleged, but as facts. It is true that he appears as a narrator; yet, in the manner and tenor of his statement, he cannot but be considered as endorsing the spectral evidence. Speaking of the examining Magistrates, and saying that it is "now," that is, in 1697, "generally thought they went out of "the way," he expresses himself as follows:
"The afflicted people vehemently accused sev-
"eral persons, in several places, that the *spectres*
"which afflicted them, did exactly resemble
"*them;* until the importunity of the accusations
"did provoke the Magistrates to examine them.
"When many of the accused came upon their
"examination, it was found, that the demons,
"then a thousand ways abusing of the poor af-
"flicted people, had with a marvellous exact-
"ness represented them; yea, it was found
"that many of the accused, but casting their
"eye upon the afflicted, the afflicted, though
"their faces were never so much another way,
"would fall down and lie in a sort of a swoon,
"wherein they would continue, whatever hands
"were laid upon them, until the hands of the
"accused came to touch them, and then they
"would revive immediately: and it was found,
"that various kinds of natural actions, done by
"many of the accused in or to their own bodies,
"as leaning, bending, turning awry, or squeez-
"ing their hands, or the like, were presently
"attended with the like things preternaturally
"done upon the bodies of the afflicted, though
"they were so far asunder, that the afflicted
"could not at all observe the accused."—*Magnalia*, Book II., p. 61.

Indeed, throughout his account of the appearances and occurrences, at the examinations before the committing Magistrates, it must be allowed that he exposed a decided bias, in his own mind, to the belief and reception of the spectral evidence. He commences that account in these words: "Some scores of people, first about Sa-
"lem, the centre and first-born of all the towns
"in the Colony, and afterwards in several other
"places, were arrested with many preternatural
"vexations upon their bodies, and a variety of
"cruel torments, which were evidently inflicted
"from the demons of the invisible world. The
"people that were infected and infested with
"such Demons, in a few days time, arrived at
"such a refining alteration upon their eyes, that
"they could see their tormentors; they saw a
"Devil of a little stature and of a tawny color,
"attended still with spectres that appeared in

"more human circumstances."—*Page 60.*

And he concludes it as follows: ("Flashy peo-
"ple may burlesque these things, but when hun-
"dreds of the most sober people in a country,
"where they have as much mother-wit certainly
"as the rest of mankind, know them to be *true,*
"nothing but the absurd and froward spirit of
"Sadduceeism can question them.) I have not yet
"mentioned so much as one thing, that will not
"be justified, if it be required, by the oaths of
"more considerate persons, than any that can
"ridicule these odd phenomena."—*Page 61.*

When he comes to the conclusion of the affair,
and mentions the general pardon of the convicted
and accused, he says: "there fell out several
"strange things that caused the spirit of the
"country to run as vehemently upon the acquit-
"ting of all the accused, as it had, by mistake,
"ran at first upon the condemning of them."
"In fine, the last Courts that sate upon this
"thorny business, finding that it was impossible
"to penetrate into the whole meaning of the
"things that had happened, and that so many
"unsearchable cheats were interwoven into the
"conclusion of a mysterious business, which
"perhaps had not crept thereinto at the begin-
"ning of it, they cleared the accused as fast as
"they tried them." But, even then, Mather
could not wholly disengage his mind from the
"mistake." "More than twice twenty," he says,
in connection with the fact that the confessions
had been receded from, "had made such volun-
"tary, and harmonious, and uncontrollable con-
"fessions, that if they were all sham, there was
"therein the greatest violation, made by the effi-
"cacy of the invisible world, upon the rules of
"understanding human affairs, that was ever
"seen since God made man upon the earth."

In this same work he presents, in condensed
shape, the views of the advocates and of the opponents of spectral testimony, without striking
the balance between them or avowedly taking
sides with either, although it may fairly be observed that the weight he puts into the scale of
the former is quite preponderating. From incidental expressions, too, it might be inferred that
he was to be classed with the former, as he
ascribes to them some "philosophical schemes,"
in explanation of the phenomena of witchcraft,
that look like his notion of the " Plastic spirit of
" the world." Another incidental remark seems to
point to Increase Mather, as to be classed with
the latter, as follows: "Though against some
"of them that were tried, there came in so much
"other evidence of their diabolical compacts,
"that some of the most judicious, and yet vehe-
"ment, opposers of the notions then in vogue,
"publicly declared, *Had they themselves been on*
"*the Bench, they could not have acquitted them;*
"nevertheless, divers were condemned, against

"whom the chief evidence was founded in the
"spectral exhibitions."

Increase Mather, in the Postscript to his *Cases
of Conscience,* says: "I am glad that there is
"published to the World (by my Son) a *Breviate*
"*of the Tryals* of some who were lately executed,
"whereby I hope the thinking part of Mankind
"will be satisfied, that there was more than that
"which is called *Spectre Evidence* for the Con-
"viction of the Persons condemned. I was not
"my self present at any of the Tryals, excepting
"one, *viz.* that of *George Burroughs;* had I
"been one of his Judges, I could not have ac-
"quitted him: For several Persons did upon Oath
"testifie, that they saw him do such things as no
"Man that has not a Devil to be his Familiar
"could perform."

It is observable that Increase Mather does not
express or intimate, in this passage, any objection to the introduction of spectre evidence.
When we come to consider Cotton Mather's *Breviate* of the trial of George Burroughs, we shall
see how slight and inadequate was what Increase
Mather could have heard, *at the Trial,* to prove
that Burroughs had exhibited strength which the
Devil only could have supplied. The most trivial
and impertinent matter was all that was needed,
to be added to spectral testimony, to give it fatal
effect. The value, by the way, of Increase
Mather's averment, that "more than that which is
"called Spectre Evidence" was adduced against
the persons convicted, is somewhat impaired by
the admission of Cotton Mather, just before
quoted, that "divers were condemned," against
whom it was the "chief evidence."

In stating the objection, by some, to the admission of spectral evidence, on the ground that the
Devil might assume the shape of an innocent person, and if that person was held answerable for
the actions of that spectral appearance, it would
be in the power of the Devil to convict and destroy any number of innocent and righteous people, and thereby "subvert Government and dis-
"band and ruin human society," Cotton Mather
gets over the difficulty thus: "And yet God may
"sometimes suffer such things to evene, that we
"may know, thereby, how much we are beholden
"to him, for that restraint which he lays upon
"the infernal spirits, who would else reduce a
"world into a chaos."

This is a striking instance of the way in which
words may be made, not only to cover, but to
transform, ideas. A reverent form of language
conceals an irreverent conception. The thought
is too shocking for plain utterance; but, dressed
in the garb of ingenious phraseology, it assumes
an aspect that enables it to pass as a devout acknowledgment of a divine mystery. The real
meaning, absurd as it is dreadful, to state or
think, is that the Heavenly Father sometimes

may, not merely permit, but will, the lies of the
Devil to mislead tribunals of justice to the shedding of the blood of the righteous, that he may,
thereby show how we are beholden to Him, that
a like outrage and destruction does not happen
to us all.   He allows the Devil, by false testimony, to bring about the perpetration of the most
horrible wrong.   It is a part of the "Rectoral
"Righteousness of God," that it should be so.
What if the Courts do admit the testimony of
the Devil in the appearance of a spectre, and, on
its strength, consign to death the innocent ?   It
is th will of God, that it should be so.   Let that
will be done.

But however the sentiment deserves to be char-
acterised, it removes the only ground upon which,
in that day, spectral evidence was objected to—
namely, that it might endanger the innocent.   If
such was the will of God, the objectors were silenced.

In concluding the examination of the question
whether Cotton Mather denounced, or countenanced, the admission of spectral testimony—for
that is the issue before us—I feel confident that
it has been made apparent, that it was not in reference to the *admission* of such testimony, that
he objected to the "principles that some of the
"Judges had espoused," but to the method in
which it should be *handled* and *managed*.   I de-
ny, utterly, that it can be shown that he opposed
its *admission*.   In none of his public writings
did he ever pretend to this.   The utmost upon
which he ventured, driven to the defensive on
this very point, as he was during all the rest of
his days, was to say that he was opposed to its
"excessive use."   Once, indeed, in his private
Diary, under that self-delusion which often led
him to be blind to the import of his language,
contradicting, in one part, what he had said in
another part of the same sentence, evidently, as
I believe, without any conscious and intentional
violation of truth, he makes this statement : "For
"my own part, I was always afraid of proceed-
"ing to convict and condemn any person, as a
"confederate with afflicting Demons, upon so
"feeble an evidence as a spectral representation.
"Accordingly, I ever protested against it, both
"publicly and privately; and, in my letter to
"the Judges, I particularly besought them that
"they would, by no means, admit it; and
"when a considerable assembly of Ministers
"gave in their advice about that matter, I not
"only concurred with them, but it was I who
"drew it up."

This shows how he indulged himself in forms
of expression that misled nim.   His letter to
"the Judges" means, I suppose, that written to
Richards; and he had so accustomed his mind
to the attempt to make the *Advice* of the Ministers bear this construction, as to deceive him-

self.   That document does not say a word, much
less, protest, against the "admission" of that
evidence: it was not designed, and was not understood by any, at the time, to have that bearing,
but only to urge suggestions of caution, in its
use and management.   Charity to him requires us
to receive his declaration in the Diary as subject
to the modifications he himself connects with it,
and to mean no more than we find expressed in
the letter to Richards and in the *Advice*.   But,
if he really had deluded himself into the idea
that he had protested against the *admission* of
spectral evidence, he has not succeeded, probably, in deluding any other persons than his son
Samuel, who repeated the language of the Diary,
and our Reviewer.

The question, I finally repeat, is as to the admission of that species of evidence, *at all*, in any
stage, in any form, to any extent.   Cotton Mather never, in any public writing, "denounced the
"admission" of it, never advised its absolute
exclusion; but, on the contrary recognised it as
a ground of "presumption."   Increase Mather
stated that the "Devil's accusations," which
he considered spectral evidence really to be,
"may be so far regarded as to cause an enquiry
"into the truth of things."   These are the facts
of history, and not to be moved from their
foundation in the public record of that day.
There is no reason to doubt that all the Ministers, in the early stages of the delusion, concurred in these views.   All partook of the "awe,"
mentioned by Mather, which filled the minds
of Juries, Judges, and the people, whenever
this kind of testimony was introduced.   No
matter how nor when, whether as "presumption"
to build other evidence upon or as a cause for
further "enquiry," nothing could stand against
it.   Character, reason, common sense, were swept
away.   So long as it was suffered to come in,
any how, or to be credited at all, the horrid
fanaticism and its horrible consequences continued.   When it was wholly excluded, the reign of
terror and of death ceased.

IX.

COTTON MATHER AND THE PRELIMINARY EXAMINA-
TIONS.   JOHN PROCTOR.   GEORGE BURROUGHS.

The spectral evidence was admitted; and the
examinations and trials went on.   The question
now arises, what was Cotton Mather's attitude
towards them ?   The scrutiny as to the meaning
of his words is exhausted; and now we are to in-
terpret his actions.   They speak louder and clear-
er than words.   Let us, in the first place, make
the proper distinction between the Examinations,
on the arrest of the prisoners and leading to
their commitment, and the Trials.   The first
Warrants were issued on the twenty-ninth of

February, 1692; and the parties arrested were brought before the Magistrates the next day. Arrests and Examinations occurred, at short intervals, during three months, when the first trial was had; and they were continued, from time to time, long after, while the Special Court was in operation. They were, in some respects, more important than the Trials. Almost all the evidence, finally adduced before the Jury, was taken by the examining Magistrates; and being mostly in the form of carefully-written depositions, it was simply reproduced, and sworn to, before the Court. Further, as no Counsel was allowed the Prisoners, the Trials were quite summary affairs. Hutchinson says, no difficulty was experienced; and the results were quickly reached, in every case but that of Rebecca Nurse.

These two stages in the proceedings became confounded in the public apprehension, and have been borne down by tradition, indiscriminately, under the name of Trials. It was the succession, at brief intervals, through a long period, of these Examinations, that wrought the great excitement through the country; which met Phips on his arrival; and which is so graphically described by Cotton Mather, as a "dreadful ferment." He says he was not present at any of the Trials. Was he present at any of the Examinations? The considerations that belong to the solution of this question are the following:

When the special interest he must have taken in them is brought to mind, from the turn of his prevalent thoughts and speculations, exhibited in all his writings, and from the propensity he ever manifested to put himself in a position to observe and study such things, it may be supposed he would not have foregone opportunities like those presented in the scenes before the Magistrates. While all other people, Ministers especially, were flocking to them, it is difficult to conclude that he held back. That he attended some of them is, perhaps, to be inferred from the distinctive character of his language that he never attended a *Trial*. The description given, in his *Life of Phips*, of what was exhibited and declared by the "afflicted children," at the Examinations, exhibits a minuteness and vividness, seeming to have come from an eye-witness; but there is not a particular word or syllable, I think, in the account, from which an inference, either way, can be drawn whether, or not, he was present at them, personally. This is observable, I repeat, inasmuch as he was careful to say that he was *not* present at the *Trials*.

The Examinations, being of a character to arrest universal attention, and from the extraordinary nature of their incidents, as viewed by that generation, having attractions, all but irresistible, it is not surprising that, as incidentally appears, Magistrates and Ministers came to them, from all quarters. No local occurrences, in the history of this country, ever awakened such a deep, awe-inspiring, and amazed interest. It can hardly be doubted that he was attracted to them. Can any other inference be drawn from the passage already quoted, from his Diary, that he felt called, "as a herald of the Lord's Kingdom, now approaching," to give personal attendance, in "the horrible enchantments and possessions broke "forth at Salem Village?" There was a large concourse of Magistrates and Ministers, particularly, on the twenty-fourth of March, when Deodat Lawson preached his famous Sermon, after the Examination of Rebecca Nurse; on the eleventh of April, when the Governor and Council themselves conducted the Examination of John Proctor and others; and, on the ninth of May, when Stoughton, from Dorchester, and Sewall, from Boston, sat with the local Magistrates, and the Rev. George Burroughs was brought before them. It is strange, indeed, if Mather was not present, especially on the last occasion; and it may appear, as we advance, that it is almost due to his reputation to suppose that he was there, and thus became qualified and authorized to pass the judgment he afterwards did.

Local tradition, of less value, in some respects, for reasons given in my book, in reference to this affair than most others, but still of much weight, has identified Cotton Mather with these scenes. The family, of which John Proctor was the head, has continued to this day in the occupancy of his lands. Always respectable in their social position, they have perpetuated his marked traits of intellect and character. They have been strong men, as the phrase is, in their day, of each generation; and have constantly cherished in honor the memory of their noble progenitor, who bravely breasted, in defence of his wife, the fierce fanaticism of his age, and fell a victim to its fury and his own manly fidelity and integrity. They have preserved, as much as any family, a knowledge of the great tragedy; and it has been a tradition among them that Cotton Mather took an active part in the prosecution of Proctor. The representative of the family, in our day, a man of vigorous faculties, of liberal education, academical and legal, and much interested in antiquarian and genealogical enquiries, John W. Proctor, presided at the Centennial Celebration, in Danvers, on the fifteenth of June, 1852; and in his Address, expressed, no doubt, a transmitted sentiment—although, as has generally been done, confounding the Examinations with the Trials—in stating that Cotton Mather rendered himself conspicuous in the proceedings against his ancestor.

Cotton Mather was the leading champion of the Judges. In his Diary, he says: "I saw, in "most of the Judges, a most charming instance of "prudence and patience; and I know the exam-

"plary prayer and anguish of soul, wherewith
"they had sought the direction of heaven, above
"most other people; whom I generally saw en-
"chanted into a raging, railing, scandalous and
"unreasonable disposition, as the distress in-
"creased upon us. For this cause, *though I*
"*could not allow the principles that some of the*
"*Judges had espoused,* yet I could not but speak
"honorably of their persons, on all occasions; and
"my compassion upon the sight of their difficult-
"ies, raised by *my journeys to Salem,* the chief
"seat of those diabolical vexations, caused me
"yet more to do so."

How, as he had not been present at any of the
Trials, could he have given this commendation of
the bearing of the Judges, based, as he says, upon
what he had witnessed in visits to Salem? I can
think of but one way in which his statements can
be reconciled. Five of the eight Judges (Saltonstall's seat being vacant) Stoughton, Sewall, Gedney, Corwin and Hathorne, severally, at
different times, sat as Magistrates, at the Examinations, which occasions were accompanied with
vexations and perplexities, calling for prudence
and patience, much more than the Trials. It is
due, therefore, to Mather to suppose that he had
frequented the Examinations, and, thus acquired
a right to speak of the deportment of the Judges,
"upon the *sight* of their difficulties."

Much of the evidence given by the "afflicted
"children," at the Examinations, can hardly be
accounted for except as drawn from ideas suggested by Mather, on the spot, so as to reach
their ears. [In the testimony of Susannah Shel-
don, against John Willard, on the ninth of May,
is the following singular statement: "There ap-
"peared to me a Shining White man." She represents it as a good and friendly angel, or spirit,
accompanied by another "angel from Heaven,"
protecting her against the spectre of John Willard.

Prefixed to the London Edition of the *Cases
of Conscience,* printed in 1862, is a narrative,
by Deodat Lawson, of some remarkable things he
saw and heard, connected with the witchcraft
transactions at Salem Village. In it, is the following statement: "The first of April, Mercy
"Lewis saw in her fit, a white man, and was
"with him in a glorious place, which had no
"candles nor sun, yet was full of light and
"brightness; where was a great multitude in
"white glittering robes; and they sung the Song
"in *Revelation,* v. 9, and the one hundred and
"tenth Psalm, and the one hundred and forty-
"ninth Psalm; and said with herself, ' How long
"'shall I stay here?' 'Let me be along with you!'
"She was loth to leave the place; and grieved
"that she could tarry no longer. This White man
"hath appeared several times to some of them,
"and given them notice how long it should be

"before they had another fit, which was, some-
"times, a day, or day and half, or more or less.
"It hath fallen out accordingly."

In the case of Margaret Rule, in Boston, the
year after the Salem Delusion, of which it is not to
be questioned that Mather had the management,
this same "*White*" Spirit is made to figure; and
also, in another instance. Mather alludes to the
"glorious and signal deliverance of that poor
"damsel," Mercy Short, six months before. In-
"deed," says he, "Margaret's case was, in sev-
"eral points, less remarkable than Mercy's; and
"in some other things the entertainment did
"a little vary." Margaret, Mercy, and the "af-
"flicted children" at Salem Village, all had
their "White angel," as thus stated by Mather:
"Not only in the Swedish, but also in the
"Salem Witchcraft, the enchanted people have
"talked much of a White Spirit, from whence
"they received marvellous assistances in their
"miseries. What lately befell Mercy Short,
"from the communications of such a Spirit,
"hath been the just wonder of us all; but
"by such a Spirit was Margaret Rule now
"also visited. She says that she could never
"see his face; but that she had a frequent view
"of his bright, shining and glorious garments;
"he stood by her bed-side, continually, hearten-
"ing and comforting her, and counselling her
"to maintain her faith and hope in God, and
"never comply with the temptations of her ad-
"versari a."—*Calef,* 3, 8.

This appearance of the "White and Shining,"
Spirit, or "White Angel," exercising a good and
friendly influence, was entirey out of the line
of ordinary spectral manifestations; constituted
a speciality in the cases mentioned; and seems
to have originated in the same source. Let it,
then, be considered that Cotton Mather's favorite precedent, which was urged upon Sir William Phips, and which Mather brought to the
notice of Richards, and was so fond of citing in
his writings, had a "White Angel." In his account of the "most horrid outrage, committed
"in Sweedland by Devils, by the help of witch-
"es," we find the following: "Some of the chil-
"dren talked much of a White Angel, which
"did use to forbid them, what the Devil had
"bid them to do, and assure them that these
"things would not last long; but that what
"had been done was permitted for the wicked-
"ness of the people. This White Angel would
"sometimes rescue the children, from going in
"with the witches."— *Wonders,* 50.

Mr. Hale also notices this feature of the Salem Trials—that the witnesses swore to "repre-
"sentations of heavenly beauty, white men."

Mather brought the story of this witchcraft "in
"Sweedland," before the public, in America; he
had the book that contained it; and was active

in giving it circulation. There can be little doubt that he was the channel through which it found its way to the girls in the hamlet of Salem Village. He was, it is evident, intimate with Parris. How far the latter received his ideas from him, is, *as yet*, unknown. That they were involved in the same responsibility is clear from the fact that Parris fell back upon him for protection, and relied upon him, as his champion, throughout his controversy with his people, occasioned by the witchcraft transactions.

When these considerations are duly weighed, in connection with his language in the passage of his Diary, just quoted—"I saw a most charm-"ing instance of prudence and patience" in the Judges: "My compassion upon the sight of "their difficulties," "raised by my journeys to "Salem, the chief seat of those diabolical vexa-"tions"—it seems necessary to infer, that his opportunities of *seeing* all this, on the occasions of his "journeys to Salem," must have been afforded by attending the Examinations, held by the Magistrates who were also Judges; as it is established, by his own averment, that he never saw them on the Bench of the Court, at the Jury-trials. It is, therefore, rendered certain, by his own language and by all the facts belonging to the subject, that the purpose of his "journeys to Salem" was to attend the Examinations. We are, indeed, shut up to this conclusion.

The Examinations were going on from the first of March, far into the Summer of 1692. There is no intimation that either of the Mathers uttered a syllable against the course pursued in them, before or after the middle of May, when the Government passed into their almost exclusive possession. All the way through, spectral evidence was admitted, without restraint or a symptom of misgiving, on their part; and, whether present or absent, they could not but have known all that was going on.

Cotton Mather's "*journeys to Salem*," must have been frequent. If only made two or three times, he would have said so, as he speaks of them in an apologetic passage and when trying to represent his agency to have been as little as the truth would allow.

The Reviewer states that the journeys were made for another purpose. He states it positively and absolutely. "He made visits to Sa-"lem, as we shall presently see, for quite anoth-"er purpose than that which has been alleged." This language surprised me, as it had wholly escaped my researches; and the surprise was accompanied with pleasure, for I supposed there must be some foundation for the declaration. I looked eagerly for the disclosure about to be made, in some document, now, for the first time, to be brought to light, from "original sources,"

such as he, in a subsequent passage, informs us, Mr. Longfellow has had access to. Great was my disappointment, to find that the Reviewer, notwithstanding his promise to let us know the "other purpose" of Mather's visits to Salem, has not given us a single syllable of *information* to that effect, but has endeavored to palm off, upon the readers of the *North American Review*, a pure fiction of his own brain, a mere conjecture, as baseless as it is absurd. He says that Mather made his visits to Salem, as the "spiritual comforter" of John Proctor and John Willard!

He further says, in support of this statement, "that Proctor and Willard had been confined "several months in the Boston Jail, and there, "doubtless, made Mr. Mather's acquaintance, as "he was an habitual visitor of the prison." This hardly accounts for "journeys to Salem," during *those* months. Salem was not exactly in Mr. Mather's way from his house in Boston to the Jail in Boston.

As only a few days over four months elapsed between Proctor's being put into the Boston Jail and his execution, deducting the "several "months" he spent there, but little time remained, after his transfer to the Salem Jail, for Mather's "journeys to Salem," for the purpose of administering spiritual consolation to him. So far as making his "acquaintance," while in Boston Jail is regarded, upon the same ground it might be affirmed that he was the spiritual adviser of the Prisoners generally; for most of those, who suffered, were in Boston Jail as long as Proctor; and he visited them all alike,

The Reviewer adduces not a particle of evidence to prove his absolute statement, nor even to countenance the idea; but, as is his custom, he transforms a conjecture into an established fact. On a bare surmise, he builds an argument, and treats the whole, basis and superstructure, as History. To show, more particularly, how he thus *makes History*, I must follow this matter up a little further. Brattle, in his *Account of the Witchcraft in the County of Essex, 1692*, has this paragraph, after stating that the persons executed "went out of the world, not only "with as great protestations, but also with "as great shows, of innocency, as men could "do:" "They protested their innocency as in "the presence of the great God, whom forth-"with they were to appear before: they wish-"ed, and declared their wish, that their blood "might be the last innocent blood shed "upon that account. With great affection, "they entreated Mr. C. M. to pray with "them: they prayed that God would dis-"cover what witchcrafts were among us: they "forgave their accusers: they spake without "reflection on Jury and Judges, for bringing

"them in guilty and condemning them: [they
"prayed earnestly for pardon for all *other sins,*
"and for an interest in the precious blood of
"our dear Redeemer:] and seemed to be very
"sincere, upright, and sensible of their circum-
"stances on all accounts; especially Proctor
"and Willard, whose whole management of
"themselves, from the Jail to the Gallows, [and
"whilst at the Gallows,] was very affecting
"and melting to the hearts of some considera-
"ble spectators, whom I could mention to you:
"—[but they are executed and so I leave
"them.]"—*Massachusetts Historical Collections,*
I. v. 68.

The Reviewer cites this paragraph, omitting
the clauses I have placed within brackets, *without any indication of the omissions.* The first
of the omitted clauses is a dying declaration of
the innocence of the sufferers, as to the crime
alleged. The second proves that they "man-
"aged themselves" after, as well as before,
reaching the Gallows, and to their dying moment—seeming to preclude the idea that their
exercises of prayer and preparation were directed or guided by any spiritual adviser. The
last is an emphatic and natural expression of
Brattle's feelings and judgment on the occasion.

The Reviewer follows his citation, thus:
"Mr. Brattle mentions no other person than Mr.
"C. M. as the comforter and friend of the suf-
"ferers, especially Proctor and Willard." "In
"the above statement we trace the character of
"their spiritual counsellor." "We now see the
"object of Mr. Mather's visits to Salem."
"Would these persons have asked Mr. Mather
"to be be their spiritual comforter, if he had
"been the agent, as has been alleged, of bring-
"ing them into their sad condition?"

In other forms of language and other connections, he speaks of Mr. Mather's presence,
at these executions, as "the performance of a
"sad duty to Proctor and Willard," and represents Brattle as calling him "the spiritual
"adviser of the persons condemned." All this
he asserts as proved and admitted fact; and
the whole rests upon the foregoing *mutilated*
paragraph of Brattle.

Let the reader thoroughly examine and consider that paragraph, and then judge of this
Reviewer's claim to establish History. The
word "affection," was used much at that time
to signify *earnest desire.* "They"—that is, the
persons then about to die, namely, the Rev.
George Burroughs, an humble, laborious, devoted Minister of the Gospel; John Proctor, the
owner of valuable farms and head of a large
family; John Willard, a young married man of
most respectable connections; George Jacobs,
an early settler, land-holder, and a grandfather,
of great age, with flowing white locks, sus-

tained, as he walked, by two staffs or crutches;
and Martha Carrier, the wife of a farmer in Andover, with a family of children, some of them
quite young—"entreated Mr. C. M. to pray with
"them." Why did they have to "entreat"
him, if he had come all the way from Boston
for that purpose? They all had Ministers near
at hand—Carrier had two Ministers, either or
both of whom would have been prompt to come,
if persons suffering for the imputed crime of
witchcraft had been allowed to have the attendance of "spiritual comforters," at their executions. If Mather had prayed with them,
Brattle would have said so. His language is
equivalent to a statement, that "Mr. C. M." was
reluctant, if he did not absolutely refuse to do
it; and the only legitimate inferences from the
whole passage are, that the sufferers did their own
praying,—from Brattle's account of their dying prayers, they did it well—and that without
"spiritual comforter," "adviser," or "friend,"
in the last dread hour, they were left to the
"management of themselves."

When the paragraph is taken in connection
with the relations of Brattle to Mather, not
approving of his course in public affairs, but,
at the same time, delicately situated, being associated with him in important public interests
and leading circles, the conclusion seems probable that he meant, in an indirect mode of expression, to notice the fact that Mather refused
to pray with the sufferers on the occasion. In
fact, we know that Nicholas Noyes, who was
Proctor's Minister, refused to pray with him,
unless he would confess. Mather and Noyes
were intimately united by personal and professional ties of friendship and communion, and
probably would not run counter to each other,
at such a time, and in the presence of such a
multitude of Ministers and people.

It is to be regarded exclusively as illustrating
the shocking character of the whole procedure
of the witchcraft prosecutions, and not as a
personally harsh or cruel thing, that Noyes or
Mather was unwilling to pray with persons, at
their public executions, who stood convicted of
being confederates of the Devil, and who, refusing to confess, retained that character to the
last. Ministers, like them, believing that the
convicts were malefactors of a far different and
deeper dye than ordinary human crime could
impart, rebels against God, apostates from
Christ, sons of Belial, recruits of the Devil's
army, sworn in allegiance to his Kingdom, baptized into his church, beyond the reach of hope
and prayer, could hardly be expected to pray
with them. To *join* them in prayer was impossible. To go through the forms of united prayer
would have been incongruous with the occasion,
and not more inconsistent with the convictions

of the Ministers, than repugnant to the conscious innocence and natural sensibilities of the sufferers. Condemned, unconfessing, unrepentant witches might be prayed *for*, or *at*, but not *with*.

The superior greatness of mind of Burroughs and his fellow sufferers, the true spirit of Christian forgiveness elevating them above a sense of the errors and wrongs of which they were the victims, are beautifully and gloriously shown in their earnestly wishing and entreating Noyes and Mather to pray with them. They pitied their delusion, and were desirous, in that last hour, to regard them and all others as their brethren, and bow with them before the Father of all. The request they made of Christian Ministers, who, at the moment, regarded them as in league with the Devil, might not be exactly logical; a failure to comply with it is not a just matter of reproach; but the fact that it was repeated with earnestness, "entreated with affec-"tion," shows that the last pulsations of their hearts were quickened by a holy and heavenly Love.

The Reviewer asks: "Were those five per-"sons executed that day without any spiritual "adviser?" There is no evidence, I think, to show that a Minister ever accompanied, in that character, persons convicted of witchcraft, at the place of execution. All that can be gathered from Brattle's account is, that, on the occasion to which he is referring, the sufferers *themselves* offered public prayers. We know that Martha Corey, at a subsequent execution, pronounced a prayer that made a deep impression on the assembled multitude. Mr. Burroughs's prayer is particularly spoken of. So, also, in England, when the Reverend Mr. Lewis, an Episcopal clergyman, eighty years of age, and who, for fifty years, had been Vicar of Brandeston, in the County of Suffolk, was executed for alleged witchcraft, the venerable man read his own funeral service, according to the forms of his Church, "committing his own body to "the ground, in sure and certain hope of the "resurrection to eternal life."

This whole story of the spiritual relation between Mather and Proctor is a bare fiction, entirely in conflict with all tradition and all probability, without a shadow of support in any document adduced by the Reviewer; and yet he would have it received as an established fact, and incorporated, as such, in history. Liberties, like this, cannot be allowed.

Sewall's Diary, at the date of the nineteenth of August, 1692, has this entry: "This day "George Burrough, John Willard, John Proc-"tor, Marther Carrier, and George Jacobs were "executed at Salem, a very great number of "spectators being present. Mr. Cotton Mather

"was there, Mr. Sims, Hale, Noyes, Cheever, etc. "All of them said they were innocent, Carrier "and all. Mr. Mather says they all died by a "righteous sentence. Mr. Burrough, by his "Speech, Prayer, protestation of his innocence, "did much move unthinking persons, which "occasioned the speaking hardly concerning his "being executed."

It is quite remarkable that Cotton Mather should have gone directly home to Boston, after the execution, and made himself noticeable by proclaiming such a harsh sentiment against *all* the sufferers, if he had just been performing friendly offices to them, as "spiritual adviser, "counsellor, and comforter." Clergymen, called to such melancholy and affecting functions, do not usually emerge from them in the frame of mind exhibited in the language ascribed to Mather, by Sewall. It shows, at any rate, that Mather felt sure that Proctor went out of the world, an unrepenting, unconfessing wizard, and, therefore, not a fit subject for a Christian Minister to unite with in prayer.

One other remark, by the way. The account Sewall gives of the impression made by Burroughs, on the spectators, now first brought to light, in print, is singularly confirmatory of what Calef says on the subject.

My chief purpose, however, in citing this passage from Sewall's Diary, is this. Mather was not present at the Trial of Burroughs. If he was not present at his Examination before the Magistrates, how could he have spoken, as he did, of the righteousness of his sentence? There had been no Report or publication, in any way, of the evidence; and he could only have received a competent knowledge of it from personal presence, on one or the other of those occasions. He could not have been justified in so confident and absolute a judgment, by mere hearsay. If that had been the source of his information, he would have modified his language accordingly.

There is one other item to be considered, in treating the question of Mather's connection with the Examinations of the Prisoners, before the Magistrates.

When Proctor was awaiting his trial, during the short period, previous to that event, that he was in the Salem Jail, he had addressed a letter to "Mr. Mather, Mr. Allen, Mr. Moody, Mr. "Willard and Mr. Baily," all Ministers, begging them to intercede, in behalf of himself and fellow-prisoners, to secure to them better treatment, especially a fairer trial than they could have in Salem, where such a violent excitement had been wrought up against them. From the character of the letter, it is evident that it was addressed to them in the hope and belief that they were accessible to such an appeal. But one of the Mathers is named. They were associate Ministers of the same Church. Although the father was President of the College at Cambridge, he resided in Boston, and was in the active exercise of his ministry there. The question is, Which of them is meant? In my book, I expressed the opinion that it was Increase, the father. The Reviewer says it was Cotton, the son. It is a fair question; and every person can form a judgment upon it. The other persons named, comprising the rest of the Ministers then connected with the Boston Churches, are severally, more or less, indicated by what has come to us, as not having gone to extremes, in support of the witchcraft prosecutions.

Increase Mather was commonly regarded, upon whatever grounds, as not going so far as his son, in that direction. The name, " Mr. Math- " er," heads the list. From his standing, as presiding over the College and the Clergy, it was proper to give him this position. His age and seniority of settlement, also entitled him to it. Usage, and all general considerations of propriety, require us to assume that by " Mr. Mather," the *elder* is meant. Cotton Mather, being the youngest of the Boston Ministers, would not be likely to be the first named, in such a list. Besides, he was considered, as he himself complains, as the " doer of all the hard things, " that were done, in the prosecution of the " witchcraft." Whoever concludes that Increase Mather was the person, in Proctor's mind, will appreciate the fact that Cotton Mather is omitted in the list. It proves that Proctor considered him beyond the reach of all appeals, in behalf of accused persons; and tends to confirm the tradition, in the family, that his course towards Proctor, when under examination, either before the Magistrates or in Court, had indicated a fixed and absolute prejudice or conviction against him. This Letter of Proctor's, printed in my book, [*ii. 310.*] utterly disperses the visionary fabric of the Reviewer's fancy, that Cotton Mather was his " spiritual adviser," counselling him in frequent visits to the Salem Jail. It denounces, in unreserved language, " the " Magistrates, Ministers, Juries," as under the " delusion of the Devil, which we can term no " other, by reason we know, in our own con- " sciences, we are all innocent persons;" and is couched in a bold, outspoken and trenchant style, that would have shocked and incensed Cotton Mather to the highest possible degree. It is absolutely certain, that if Cotton Mather had been Proctor's " friend and counsellor," a more prudent and cautious tone and style would have been given to the whole document.

In concluding the considerations that render it probable that Cotton Mather had much to do with the Examinations, it may be said, in general, that he vindicates the course taken at them, in language that seems to identify himself with them, and to prove that he could not have been opposed to the methods used in them.

X

COTTON MATHER AND THE WITCHCRAFT TRIALS. THE EXECUTIONS.

I now proceed to examine Cotton Mather's connection with the Trials at Salem. It is fully admitted that he did not personally attend any of them. His averment to this effect does not allow the supposition that he could have deceived himself, on such a point. In his letter to Richards, as has been seen, he expressed his great disappointment in not being well enough to accompany him to the first Session of the Special Court; and the tenor of the passage proves that he had fully expected and designed to be present, at the trials, generally. Whether the same bodily indisposition continued to forbid his attendance at its successive adjournments, we cannot obtain information.

The first point of connection I can find between him and the trials, is brought to view in a meeting of certain Ministers, after executions had taken place, and while trials were pending.

Increase Mather, in his *Cases of Conscience*, has the following: " As for the judgment of the " Elders in New Engl nd, so far as I can learn, " they do generally concur with Mr. Perkins and " Mr. Bernard. This I know, that, at a meet- " ing of Ministers at Cambridge, August 1, " 1692, where were present seven Elders, besides " the President of the College, the question " then discoursed on, was, whether the Devil " may not sometimes have a permission to rep- " resent an innocent person, as tormenting such " as are under diabolical molestations? The " answer, which they all concurred in, was in " these words, viz. 'That the Devil may some- " 'times have a permission to represent an inno- " 'cent person as tormenting such as are under " 'diabolical molestations; but that such things " 'are rare and extraordinary, especially when " 'such matters come before civil judicatures'; " and that some of the most eminent Ministers of " the land, who were not at that meeting, are of " the same judgment, I am assured. And I am " also sure that, in cases of this nature, the Priest's " lips should keep knowledge, and they should " seek the law at his mouth. *Mal. 2. 7.*"

What was meant by the quotation from Malachi is left to conjecture. It looks like the notion I have supposed Cotton Mather to have, more or less, cherished, at different times—to have such cases committed to the confidential custody and management of one or more Ministers. Whether Cotton Mather, as well as his father, was at this meeting, is not stated. The

expressions "rare and extraordinary" and "sometimes have a permission," and the general style of the language, are like his. At any rate, in referring to the meeting, in his *Wonders of the Invisible World*, he speaks of the Ministers present "as very pious and learned;" says that they uttered the prevailing sense of others "eminently cautious and judicious;" and declares that they "have both argument and his-"tory to countenance them in it."

It is to be noticed, that this opinion of the Ministers, given on the first of August, if it did not authorize the admission, without reserve or limitation, of spectral evidence, in judicial proceedings, reduces the objection to it to an almost inappreciable point.

Observe the date. Already six women, heads of families, many of them of respectable positions in society, all in advanced life, one or two quite aged, and two, at least, of the most eminent Christian character, had suffered death, wholly from spectral evidence, that is, no other testimony was brought against them, as all admit, that could, even then, have convicted them. Twelve days had elapsed since five of them had been executed; in four more days, six others were to be brought to trial, among them the Rev. George Burroughs; and the Ministers pass a vote, under the lead of Increase Mather, and with the express approval of Cotton Mather, that there is very little danger of innocent people suffering, in judicial proceedings, from spectral evidence.

Let us hear no more that the Clergy of New England accepted the doctrines of those writers who had "declared against the admission of "spectral testimony;" that "the Magistrates re-"jected those doctrines;" that "all the evils "at Salem, grew out of the position taken by "the Magistrates;" and that "it had been well "with the twenty victims at Salem, if the Min-"isters of the Colony, instead of the Lawyers, "had determined their fate."

The Clergy of New England did, indeed, entertain great regard for the authority of certain writers, who were considered as, more or less, discrediting spectral evidence. The Mathers professed to concur with them in that judgment; but the ground taken at the meeting on the first of August, as above stated, was, it must be allowed, inconsistent with it. The passages I have given, and shall give, from the writings of Cotton Mather, will illustrate the elaborate ingenuity he displayed in trying to reconcile a respect for the said writers with the admission of that species of evidence, to an extent they were considered as disallowing.

I am indebted to George H. Moore, LL.D., of New York city, for the following important document. John Foster was, at its date, a member of the Council. Hutchinson, who was his grandson, speaks of him [*History, ii. 21*] as a "merchant "of Boston of the first rank," "who had a great "share in the management of affairs from 1689 "to 1692." In the latter year, he was raised to the Council Board, being named as such in the new Charter; and held his seat, by annual elections, to the close of his life, in 1710. He seems to have belonged to the Church of the Mathers, as the father and son each preached and printed a Sermon on the occasion of his death.

Autograph Letter of COTTON MATHER, *on Witchcraft, presented to the Literary and Historical Society, by the Honorable Chief-justice Sewell.*[*]

"17th 8ber, 1692.

"Sr:

"You would know whether I still retain my "opinion about ye horrible Witchcrafts among "us, and I acknowledge that I do.

"I do still Think That when there is no fur-"ther Evidence against a person but only This, "That a Spectre in their shape does afflict a "neighbour, that Evidence is not enough to con-"vict ye * * of Witchcraft.

"That the Divels have a natural power wch "makes them capable of exhibiting what shape "they please I suppose nobody doubts, and I "have no absolute promise of God that they shall "not exhibit mine.

"It is the opinion generally of all protestant "writers that ye Divel may thus abuse ye innocent, "yea, tis ye confession of some popish ones. "And or Honorable Judges are so eminent for "their Justice, Wisdom. & Goodness that what-"ever their own particular sense may bee, yett "they will not proceed capitally against any, "upon a principle contested with great odds on "ye other side in ye Learned and Godly world.

"*Nevertheless, a very great use is to bee made* "*of ye Spectral impressions upon ye sufferers.* "*They Justly Introduce, and Determine, an En-*"*quiry into ye circumstances of ye person ac-*"*cused; and they strengthen other presumptions.* "*When so much use is made of those Things,* "*I believe ye use for such ye Great God intends* "*ym is made.* And accordingly you see that ye "Excellent Judges have had such an Encourag-"ing presence of God with them, as that scarce "any, if at all any, have been Tried before them, "against whom God has not strangely sent in "other, & more Humane & most convincing Tes-"timonies.

"If any persons have been condemned, about "whom any of ye Judges, are not easy in their "minds, that ye Evidence against them, has been "satisfactory, it would certainly bee for ye glory

* *Transactions of the Literary and Historical Society of Quebec*—Octavo, Quebec, 1861—2, 212—214.

"of the whole Transaction to give that person a
"Reprieve.

"It would make all matters easier if at least
"Bail were taken for people Accused only by y^e
"invisible tormentors of ye poor sufferers and not
"Blemished by any further Grounds of suspi-
"cion against them.

"The odd Effects produced upon the sufferers
"by ye look or touch of the accused are things
"wherein ye Divels may as much Impose upon
"some Harmless people as by the Representacõn
"of their shapes.

"My notion of these matters is this. A Sus-
"pected and unlawful com'union with a Famil-
"iar Spirit, is the Thing enquired after. The
"communion on the *Divel's* part may bee prov-
"ed, while, for ought I can say, The man may
"bee Innocent; the Divel may impudently Im-
"pose his com'union upon some that care not for
"his company. But if the com'union on ye man's
"part bee proved, then the Business is done.

"I am suspicious Lest ye Divel may at some
"time or other, serve us a trick by his constancy
"for a long while in one way of Dealing. Wee
"may find the Divel using one constant course in
"Nineteen several Actions, and yett bee bee too
"hard for us at last, if wee thence make a Rule
"to form an Infallible Judgement of a Twentieth.
"It is o^r singular Happiness That wee are blessed
"with Judges who are Aware of this Danger.

"For my own part if the Holy God should
"permitt such a Terrible calamity to befal my-
"self as that a Spectre in my Shape should so
"molest my neighbourhood, as that they can have
"no quiet, altho' there should be no other Evi-
"dence against me, I should very patiently sub-
"mit unto a Judgement of *Transportation*, and
"all reasonable men would count o^r Judges to
"Act, as they are like ye Fathers of ye public,
"in such a Judgment. What if such a Thing
"should be ordered for those whose Guilt is
"more Dubious, and uncertain, whose presence
"ye perpetuates ye miseries of o^r sufferers?
"They would cleanse ye Land of Witchcrafts,
"and yett also prevent ye shedding of Innocent
"Blood, whereof some are so apprehensive of
"Hazard. If o^r Judges want any Good Bottom,
"to act thus upon, You know, that besides y^e
"usual power of Govern^t, to Relax many Judg-
"ments of Death, o^r General Court can soon
"provide a law.

"S^r,
"You see ye Incoherency of my Thoughts
"but I hope, you will also some Reasonableness
"in those Thoughts.

"In the year 1645, a Vast Number of persons
"in ye county of *Suffolk* were apprehended, as
"Guilty of Witchcraft; whereof, some con-
"fessed. The parlament granted a special com-
"ission of *Oyer & Terminer* for ye Trial of those
"Witches; in wch com'ission, there were a fa-
"mous Divine or two, Mr *Fairclough* particu-
"larly inserted. That Eccellent man did preach
"two sermons to ye Court, before his first sitting
"on ye Bench : Wherein having first proved the
"Existence of Witches, bee afterwards showed
"ye Evil of Endeavouring ye Conviction of any
"upon Defective Evidence. The Sermon had
"the Effect that none were Condemned, who
"could bee saved w^thout an Express Breach of
"ye Law; & then tho' 'twas possible some Guilty
"did Escape, yett the troubles of those places,
"were, I think Extinguished.

"O^r case is Extraordinary. And so, you and
"others will pardon ye Extraordinary Liberty I
"take to address You on this occasion. But af-
"ter all, I Entreat you, that whatever you do,
"you Strengthen ye Hands of o^r Honourable
"Judges in ye Great work before y^m. They are
"persons, for whom no man living has a greater
"veneration, than
"S^r,
"Your Servant
"C. MATHER.
"For the Honourable JOHN FOSTER, Esq."

This letter must be considered, I think, as set-
tling the question. It was written two days before the execution of Burroughs, Proctor, and
others. It entirely disposes of the assertions of
the Reviewer, that Mather "denounced" the
"admission" of spectral testimony, and demonstrates the truth of the positions, taken in this
article, that he authorized fully its admission, as
affording occasion of enquiry and matter of presumption, sufficient, if reinforced by other evidence, to justify conviction. The sentences I
have italicised leave no further room for discussion. The language in which the Judges and
their conduct of the Trials are spoken of, could
not have been stronger. The reference to the
course taken in England, in 1645, sheds light
upon the suggestions I have made, as to Mather's notion, that one or more Ministers—"a fa-
"mous Divine or two,"—ought to have been connected, "by authority," with the Court of Oyer
and Terminer, in the management of the cases.
The idea thrown out, as to Transportation, could
hardly, it would seem, but have been apparent to
a reflecting person, as utterly impracticable. No
convicts or parties under indictment or arrest
for the crime of witchcraft, could have been
shipped off to any other part of the British do-
minions. A vessel, with persons on board, with
such a stamp upon them, would have been everywhere repelled with as much vehemence and
panic, as if freighted with the yellow fever, small-
pox, or plague. If the unhappy creatures she
bore beneath her hatches, should have been landed
in any other part of the then called Christian or
civilized world, stigmatized with the charge of

witchcraft, they would have met with the halter or the fagot; and scarcely have fared better, if cast upon any savage shore.

We have seen how our Reviewer *makes*, let us now see how he *unmakes*, history.

Robert Calef, in his book entitled *More Wonders of the Invisible World*, Part V., under the head of "An impartial account of the most "memorable matters of fact, touching the sup- "posed Witchcraft in New England," [*p. 103*,] says:/"Mr. Burroughs was carried in a cart, "with the others, through the streets of Salem "to execution. When he was upon the ladder, "he made a speech for the clearing of his inno- "cency, with such solemn and serious expres- "sions, as were to the admiration of all present; "his prayer (which he concluded by repeating "the Lord's prayer) was so well worded, and "uttered with such composedness, and such (at "least seeming) fervency of spirit, as was very "affecting, and drew tears from many, so that "it seemed to some that the spectators would "hinder the execution. The accusers said the "black man stood and dictated to him. As "soon as he was turned off, Mr. Cotton Mather, "being mounted upon a horse, addressed himself "to the people, partly to declare that he (Bur- "roughs) was no ordained Minister, and partly "to possess the people of his guilt, saying that "the Devil has often been transformed into an "Angel of Light; and this somewhat appeased "the people; and the executions went on. "When he was cut down, he was dragged by "the halter to a hole, or grave, between the "rocks, about two feet deep, his shirt and "breeches being pulled off, and an old pair of "trowsers of one executed, put on his lower "parts; he was so put in, together with Will- "ard and Carrier, that one of his hands and his "chin, and a foot of one of them, were left un- "covered."

The Reviewer undertakes to set aside this statement; to erase it altogether from the record; and to throw it from the belief and memory of mankind. But this cannot be done, but by an arbitrary process, that would wipe out all the facts of all history, and leave the whole Past an utter blank. If any record has passed the final ordeal, this has. It is beyond the reach of de- nial; and no power on earth can start the solid foundation on which it stands. It consists of distinct, plainly stated, averments, which, as a whole, or severally, if not true, and known to be true, might have been denied, or questioned, at the time. Not disputed, nor controverted, then, it never can be. If not true to the letter, so far as Cotton Mather is concerned, hundreds, nay thousands, were at hand, who would have con- tradicted it. Certificates without number, like that of John Goodwin, would have been pro-

cured to invalidate it. Consisting of specifica- tions, in detail, if there had been in it the mi- nutest item that could have admitted contra- di tion, it would have been seized upon, and used with the utmost eagerness to break the force of the statement. It was printed at Lon- don, in 1700, in a volume accredited there, and immediately put into circulation here, twenty- eight years before the death of Mather. He had a copy of it. now in possession of the Massa- chusetts Historical Society, and wrote on the inside of the front cover, "My desire is, that "mine adversary had written a book," etc. His father, the President of Harvard University, had a copy; for the book was burned in the College- square. Everything contributed to call univer- sal attention to it. Its author was known, avowed, and his name printed on the title page; he lived in the same town with Mather; and was in all respects a responsible man.

No attempt was made, at the time, nor at any time, until now, to overthrow the statement or disprove any of its specifications.

Let us see how the Reviewer undertakes to controvert it. As to Mather's being on horse- back, the argument seems to be, that it was customary, then, for people to travel in that way !

The harangue to the people to prevail upon them to pay no heed to the composed, de- vout, and forgiving deportment of the suffer- ers, because the Devil often appeared as an Angel of Light, sounded strangely from one who had attended the prisoners as their "spirit- "ual comforter and friend." It was a queer conclusion of his services of consolation and pastoral offices, to proclaim to the crowd, that the truly Christian expressions of the persons in his charge were all a diabolical sham. One would have thought, if he accompanied them in the capacity alleged, he would have dis- mounted before ascending the hill, and tenderly waited upon them, side by side, holding them by the hand and sustaining them by his arm, as they approached the fatal ladder; and that his last benedictions, upon their departing souls, would have been in somewhat different lan- guage. That language was entirely natural, however, believing, as he did, that they were all guilty of the unpardonable sin, in its black- est dye; that, obstinately refusing to confess, they were reprobates, sunk far below the ordi- nary level of human crime, beyond the pale of sympathy or prayer, enemies of God, in covenant with the Devil, and firebrands of Hell. All this he believed. Of course, he could not pray *with*, and could hardly be expected to pray *for*, them. The language ascribed to him by Calef, expressed his honest convictions; bears the stamp of credi- bility; was not denied or disavowed, then; and cannot be discredited, now.

If those sufferers, wearing the resplendent aspect of faith, forgiveness, and piety, in their dying hour, were, in reality, "the Devil appear-"ing as the Angel of Light," nobody but the Reviewer is to blame for charging Mather with being his "spiritual adviser and counsellor."

The Reviewer says that the horse Mather rode on that occasion, "has been tramping through "history, for nearly two centuries. It is time "that he be reined up." Not having been reined up by Mather, it is in vain for the Reviewer to attempt it. Mazeppa, on his wild steed, was not more powerless. The "man on horse-"back," described by Calef, will go tramping on through all the centuries to come, as through the "nearly two centuries" that have passed.

To discredit another part of the statement of Calef, the Reviewer cites the *Description and History of Salem*, by the Rev. William Bentley, in the Sixth Volume of the First Series of the *Massachusetts Historical Collections*, printed in 1800, quoting the following passage: "It was "said that the bodies were not properly buried; "but, upon an examination of the ground, the "graves were found of the usual depth, and re-"mains of the bodies, and of the wood in "which they were interred."

At the time when this was written, there was a tradition to that effect. But it is understood that, early in this century, an examination was made of the spot, pointed out by the tradition upon which Bentley had relied, and nothing was found to sustain it. It is apparent that this tradition was, to some extent, incorrect, because it is quite certain that three, and probably most, of the bodies were recovered by their friends, at the time; but chiefly because it is believed, on sufficient grounds, that the locality, indicated in the tradition that had reached Doctor Bentley, was, in 1692, covered by the original forest. Of course, a passage through woods, to a spot, even now, after the trees have been wholly removed from the hill and all its sides, so very difficult of access, would not have been encountered; neither can it be supposed that an open area would have been elaborately prepared for the place of execution, in the midst of a forest, entirely shut in from observation, by surrounding trees, with their thick foliage, in that season of the year. If seclusion had been the object, a wooded spot might have been found, near at hand, on level areas, anywhere in the neighborhood of the town. But it was not a secluded, but a conspicuous, place that was sought; not only an elevated, but an open, theatre for the awe-inspiring spectacle, displaying to the whole people and world—to use the language employed by Mather, in the *Advice of the Ministers* and in one of his letters to Richards—the "Success" of the Court, in "extin-"guishing that horrible witchcraft."

Another tradition, brought down through a family, ever since residing on the same spot, in the neighborhood, and from the longevity of its successive heads, passing through but few memories, and for that reason highly deserving of credit, is, that its representative, at that time, lent his aid in the removal of the bodies of the victims, in the night, and secretly, across the river, in a boat. The recollections of the transaction are preserved in considerable detail. From the locality, it is quite certain that the bodies were brought to it from the southern end of Witch-hill. From a recently-discovered letter of Dr. Holyoke, mentioned in my book [ii, 377], it appears that the executions must have taken place there. The earth is so thin, scattered between projecting ledges of rock, which, indeed, cover much of the surface, that few trees probably ever grew there; and a bare, elevated platform afforded a conspicuous site, and room for the purpose. These conclusions, to which recent discoveries and explorations have led, remarkably confirm Calef's statements. From Sheriff Corwin's *Return*, we know that the first victim was buried "in the place" where she was executed; and it may be supposed all the rest were. The soil is shallow, near the brow of the precipice and between the clefts of the rock.

The Reviewer desires to know my authority for saying that the ground, where Burroughs was buried, "was trampled down by the mob." I presume that when, less than five weeks afterwards, eight more persons were hanged there, belonging to respectable families in what are now Peabody, Marblehead, Topsfield, Rowley and Andover, as well as Salem, and a spectacle again presented to which crowds flocked from all quarters, and to which many particularly interested must have been drawn, besides those from the populous neighborhood, especially if men "on "horseback" mingled in the throng, the ground must have been considerably trampled upon. Poor Burroughs had been suddenly torn from his family and home, more than a hundred miles away; there were no immediate connections, here, who would have been likely to recover his remains; and, it is therefore probable, they had been left where they were thrown, near the foot of the gallows.

There is one point upon which the Reviewer is certain he has "demolished" Calef. The latter speaks of the victims, as having been hanged, one after another. The Reviewer says, the mode of execution was to have them "swung off at "once;" and further uses this argument: "Calef "himself furnishes us with evidence that such "was the practice in Salem, where eight persons "were hanged thirty-six days later. He says, "'After the execution, Mr. Noyes, turning him "'to the bodies, said—What a sad thing it is to

" ' see eight firebrands of Hell hanging there.' ".

The argument is, eight were hanging there together, after the execution ; therefore, they must have been swung off at the same moment !

This is a kind of reasoning with which—to adopt Mather's expression in describing diabolical horrors, capital trials, and condemnations to death—we are " entertained " throughout by the Reviewer. The truth is, we have no particular knowledge of the machinery, or its operations, at these executions. A " halter," a " ladder," a " gallows," a " hangman," are spoken of. The expression used for the final act is, " turned off." There is no shadow of evidence to contradict Calef. The probabilities seem to be against the supposition of a structure, on a scale so large, as to allow room for eight persons to be turned off at once. The outstretching branches from large trees, on the borders of the clearing, would have served the purpose, and a ladder, connected with a simple frame, might have been passed from tree to tree.

The Regicides, thirty years before, had been executed in England, in the method Calef understood to have been used here. Hugh Peters was carried to execution with Judge Cook. The latter suffered first ; and when Peters ascended the ladder, turning to the officer of the law, he uttered these memorable words, exhibiting a state of the faculties, a grandeur of bearing, and a force and felicity of language and illustration, all the circumstances considered, not surpassed in the records of Christian heroism or true eloquence : " Sir, you have slain one of the servants " of God, before mine eyes, and have made me " to behold it, on purpose to terrify and dis- " courage me ; but God hath made it an ordi- " nance unto me, for my strengthening and en- " couragement."

While the trials were going on, Mather made use of his pulpit to influence the public mind, already wrought up to frenzy, to greater heights of fanaticism, by portraying, in his own peculiar style, the out-breaking battle between the Church and the Devil. On the day before Burroughs, who was regarded as the head of the Church, and General of the forces, of Satan, was brought to the Bar, Mather preached a Sermon from the text, *Rev. xii., 12.* " Wo to the inhabiters of the earth, " and of the Sea! for the Devil is come down " unto you, having great wrath, because he " knoweth he hath but a short time." It is thickly interspersed with such passages as these: " Now, at last, the Devils are, (if I may so " speak), *in Person* come down upon us, with " such a wrath, as is most justly *much*, and will " quickly be *more*, the astonishment of the world." " There is little room for hope, that the great " wrath of the Devil will not prove the ruin of " our poor New England, in particular. I be-

" lieve there never was a poor plantation more " pursued by the wrath of the Devil than our " poor New England." " We may truly say, 'Tis " *the hour and power of darkness.* But, though " the wrath be so great, the time is but short: " when we are pursued with the wrath of the " Devil, the word of our God, at the same time, " unto us, is that in *Rom. xvi. 20.* ' *The God of* " ' *Peace shall bruise Satan under your feet short-* " ' *ly.*' Shortly, didst thou say, dearest Lord ! O " gladsome word ! Amen, even so, come Lord ! " Lord Jesus, come quickly ! We shall never be " rid of this troublesome Devil, till thou do come " to chain him up."—*Wonders, etc.*

There is much in the Sermon that relates to the sins of the people, generally, and some allusions to the difficulties that encompass the subject of diabolical appearances ; but the witchcraft in Salem is portrayed in colors, which none but a thorough believer in all that was there brought forward, could apply ; the whole train of ideas and exhortations is calculated to inflame the imaginations and passions of the people ; and it is closed by " An hortatory and necessary Address to a " country now extraordinarily alarum'd by the " Wrath of the Devil." In this Address, he goes, at length, into the horrible witchcraft at Salem Village. " Such," says he, " is the descent of " the Devil, at this day, upon ourselves, that I " may truly tell you, the walls of the whole world " are broken down. He enumerates, as undoubtedly true, in detail, all that was said by the " af- " flicted children" and " confessing witches." He says of the reputed witches : " They each of " them have their spectres or devils, commissioned " by them, and representing of them, to be the " engines of their malice." Such expressions as these are scattered over the pages, " wicked spec- " tres," " diabolical spectres," " owners of spec- " tres," " spectre's hands," " spectral book," etc.

And yet it is stated, by the Reviewer, that Mather was opposed to spectral evidence, and denounced it ! He gave currency to it, in the popular faith, during the whole period, while the trials and executions were going on, more than any other man.

He preached another Sermon, of the same kind, entitled, *The Devil Discovered.*

After the trials by the Special Court were over, and that body had been forbidden to meet on the day to which it had adjourned, he addressed another letter to John Richards, one of its members, dated " Dec. 14th, 1692," to be found in the *Mather Papers, p. 397.* It is a characteristic document, and, in some points of view, commendable. Its purpose was to induce Richards to consent to a measure he was desirous of introducing into his pastoral administration, to which Richards and one other member of his Church had manifested repugnance. Cotton Mather was in advance of his times, in liberality of views, relating to denominational matters. He desired to open the door to the Ordinances, particularly Baptism, wider than was the prevalent practice. He urges his sentiments upon Richards in earnest and fitting tones; but resorts, also, to flattering, and what may be called coaxing, tones. He calls him. "My ever-honored Richards," "Dearest Sir," "my dear Major," and reminds him of the public and constant support he had given to his official conduct: "I have signalized my perpetual re- "spects before the whole world." In this letter, he refers to the Salem witchcraft prosecutions, and pronounces unqualified approval and high encomiums upon Richards's share in the proceedings, as one of the Judges. "God has made "more than an ordinary use of your honorable "hand," in "the extinguishing" of "that horri- "ble witchcraft," into which "the Devils have "been baptizing so many of our miserable neigh- "bors." This language is hardly consistent with a serious, substantial, considerable, or indeed with any, disapprobation of the proceedings of the Court.

XI.

LETTER TO STEPHEN SEWALL.   "WONDERS OF THE "INVISIBLE WORLD." ITS ORIGIN AND DESIGN. COTTON MATHER'S ACCOUNT OF THE TRIALS.

I com · now to the examination of matters of interest and importance, not only as illustrating the part acted by Mather in the witchcraft affair, but as bearing upon the public history of the Province of Massachusetts Bay, at that time.

The reader is requested carefully to examine the following letter, addressed by Cotton Mather to Stephen Sewall, Clerk of the Court at Salem.

"BOSTON, Sept. 20. 1692.

"MY DEAR AND MY VERY OBLIGING STEPHEN,

"It is my hap, to bee continually * * * with all "sorts of objections, and objectors against the * * "work now doing at Salem, and it is my further "good hap, to do some little Service for God and "you, in my encounters.

"But, that I may be the more capable to assist, "in lifting up a standard against the infernal en- "emy, I must renew my most IMPORTUNATE RE- "QUEST, that would please quickly to perform, "what you kindly promised, of giving me a nar- "rative of the evidence given in at the trials of "half a dozen, or if you please, a dozen, of the "principal witches, that have been condemned. "I know 'twill cost you some time; but when "you are sensible of the benefit that will follow, "I know you will not think much of that "cost, and my own willingness to expose myself "unto the utmost for the defence of my friends "with you, makes me presume to plead some- "thing of merit, to be considered.

"I shall be content, if you draw up the desir-

"ed narrative by way of letter to me, or at least, "let it not come without a letter, wherein you "shall, if you can, intimate over again, what you "have sometimes told me, of the awe, which is "upon the hearts of your Juries, with * * * unto "the validity of the spectral evidences.

"Please also to * * * some of your observations "about the confessors, and the credibility of "what they assert; or about things evidently pre- "ternatural in the witchcrafts, and whatever else "you may account an entertainment, for an in- "quisitive person, that entirely loves you, and "Salem. Nay, though I will never lay aside the "character which I mentioned in my last words, "yet, I am willing that, when you write, you "should imagine me as obstinate a Sadducee "and witch-advocate, as any among us: address "me as one that believed nothing reasonable; "and when you have so knocked me down, in a "spectre so unlike me, you will enable me to "box it about, among my neighbors, till it come, "I know not where at last.

"But, assure yourself, as I shall not wittingly "make what you write prejudicial to any worthy "design, which those two excellent persons, Mr. "Hale and Mr. Noyes, may have in hand, so "you shall find that I shall be,

"Sir, your grateful friend,

C. MATHER."

"P. S.   That which very much strengthens the "charms of the request, which this letter makes "you, is that his Excellency, the Governor, laid "his positive commands upon me to desire this "favor of you ; and the truth is, there are some "of his circumstances with reference to this af- "fair, which I need not mention, that call for "the expediting of your kindness, *kindness*, I "say, for such it will be esteemed, as well by "him, as by your servant, C. MATHER."

The point, on which the Reviewer raises an objection to the statement in my book, in reference to this letter, is, as to the antecedent of "it," in the expression, "box it about." The opinion I gave was that it referred to the document requested to be sent by Sewall. The Reviewer says it refers to "a Spectre," in the preceding line, or as he expresses it, "the fallen Spectre of Saddu- "ceeism." Every one can judge for himself on inspection of the passage. After all, it is a mere quibbling about words, for the meaning remains substantially the same. Indeed, that which he gives is more to my purpose. Let it go, that Mather desired the document, and intended to use it, to break down all objectors to the work then doing in Salem. Whoever disapproved of such proceedings, or intimated any doubt concerning the popular notions about witchcraft, were called "Sadducees and witch-advocates." These terms were used by Mather, on all occasions, as marks of opprobium, to stigmatize and make odious such persons. If they could once be silenced, witchcraft demonstrations and prosecutions might be continued, without impediment or restraint, until they should "come," no one could tell "where, at last." "The fallen Spectre of, "Sadducceism" was to be the trophy of Mather's victory; and Sewall's letter was to be the weapon to lay it low.

Each of the paragraphs of this letter demonstrates the position Mather occupied, and the part he had taken, in the transactions at Salem. Mr. Hale had acted, up to this time, earnestly with Noyes and Parris; and the letter shows that Mather had the sympathies and the interests of a co-operator with them, and in their "designs." Every person of honorable feelings can judge for himself of the suggestion to Sewall, to be a partner in a false representation to the public, by addressing Mather "in a spectre so unlike" him—that is, in a character which he, Sewall, knew, as well as Mather, to be wholly contrary to the truth. Blinded, active, and vehement, as the Clerk of the Court had been, in carrying on the prosecutions, it is gratifying to find reason to conclude that he was not so utterly lost to self-respect as to comply with the jesuitical request, or lend himself to any such false connivance.

The letter was written at the height of the fury of the delusion, immediately upon a Session of the Court, at which all tried had been condemned, eight of whom suffered two days after its date. Any number of others were under sentence of death. The letter was a renewal of "a most "importunate request."

I cite it, here, at this stage of the examination of the subject, particularly on account of the postscript. Every one has been led to suppose that "His Excellency, the Governor," who had laid such "positive commands" upon Mather to obtain the desired document from Sewall, was Sir William Phips. The avowed purpose of Mather, in seeking it, was to put it into circulation—to "box it "about"—thereby to produce an effect, to the putting down of Sadducceism, or all further opposition to witchcraft prosecutions. He, undoubtedly, contemplated making it a part of his book, the *Wonders of the Invisible World*, printed, the next year, in London. The statement made by him always was, that he wrote that book in compliance with orders laid upon him to that effect by "His Excellency, the Governor." The imprimatur, in conspicuous type, in front of one of the editions of the book, is "Published by the "special command of his Excellency, the Gov- "ernor of the Province of the Massachusetts Bay "in New England."

On the sixteenth of September, Sir William Phips had notified the Council of his going to the eastward; and that body was adjourned to the fourteenth of October. From his habitual promptness, and the pressing exigency of affairs in the neighborhood of the Kennebec, it is to be presumed that he left immediately; and, as it was expected to be a longer absence than usual, it can hardly be doubted that, as on the first of August, he formally, by a written instrument, passed the Government over to Stoughton. At any rate, while he was away from his Province proper, the Deputy necessarily acceded to the Executive functions.

In the Sewall Diary we find the following: "SEPT. 21. A petition is sent to Town, in behalf "of Dorcas Hoar, who now confesses. Accord- "ingly, an order is sent to the Sheriff to forbear "her execution, notwithstanding her being in the "Warrant to die to-morrow. This is the first con- "demned person who has confessed."

The granting of this reprieve was an executive act, that would seem to have belonged to the functions of the person filling the office of Governor; and Phips being absent, it could only have been performed by Stoughton, and shows, therefore, that he, at that time, acted as Governor. As such, he was, by custom and etiquette, addressed—"His Excellency." The next day, eight were executed, four of them having been sentenced on the ninth of September, and four on the seventeenth, which was on Saturday. The whole eight were included, as is to be inferred from the foregoing entry, and is otherwise known, in the same Warrant, which could not, therefore, have been made out before the nineteenth. The next day, Mather wrote the letter to Sewall; and the language, in its Postscript, may have referred to Stoughton; particularly this clause: "There "are some of his circumstances, with reference "to this affair." As Phips had, from the first, left all the proceedings with the Chief-Justice, who had presided at all the trials, and was, by universal acknowledgment, especially responsible for all the proceedings and results, the words of Mather are much more applicable to Stoughton than to Phips.

Upon receiving these "importunate requests" from Mather, proposing such a form of reply, to be used in such a way, Sewall thought it best to adopt the course indicated in the following entry, in the Diary of his brother, the Judge: "THURS- "DAY, SEPT. 22, 1692. William Stoughton, Esq., "John Hathorne, Esq., Mr. Cotton Mather, and "Capt. John Higginson, with my brother St. "were at our house, speaking about publishing "some trials of the witches."

It appears that Stephen Sewall, instead of answering Mather's letter in writing, went directly to Boston, accompanied by Hathorne and Higginson, and met Mather and Stoughton at the house of the Judge. No other Minister was present; and Judge Sewall was not Mather's parishioner. The whole matter was there talked over. The project Mather had been contemplating was matured; and arrangements made with Stephen Sewall, who had them in his custody, to send to Mather the Records of the trials; and, thus provided, he proceeded, without further delay, in obedience to the commands laid upon him by "his Excellency," to prepare for the press, *The Wonders of the Invisible World*, which was designed to send to the shades, "Sad- "ucceism," to extirpate "witch-advocates," and to leave the course clear for the indefinite continuance of the prosecutions, until, as Stoughton expressed it, "the land was cleared" of all witches.

The presence of the Deputy-governor, at this private conference, shows the prominent part he bore in the movement, and corroborates, what is inferrible from the dates, that he was " His Ex- " cellency, the Governor," referred to in the documents connected with this transaction. It is observable, by the way, that the references are always to the official character and title, and not to the name of the person, whether Phips or Stoughton.

I now proceed to examine the book, written and brought forward, under these circumstances and for this purpose. It contains much of which I shall avail myself, to illustrate the position and the views of Mather, at the time. The length to which this article is extended, by the method I have adopted of quoting documents so fully, is regretted; but it seems necessary, in order to meet the interest that has been awakened in the subject, by the article in the *North American Review*, to make the enquiry as thorough as possible.

Only a part of the work is devoted to the main purpose for which it was ostensibly and avowedly designed. That I shall first notice. It is introduced as follows: " I shall no longer detain my "reader from his expected entertainment, in a "brief account of the Trials which have passed "upon some of the Malefactors lately executed "at Salem, for the witchcrafts whereof they stood "convicted. For my own part, I was not pres- "ent at any of them; nor ever had I any per- "sonal prejudice at the persons thus brought "upon the Stage; much less, at the surviving re- "lations of those persons, with and for whom I "would be as hearty a mourner, as any man liv- "ing in the world: *The Lord comfort them!* "But having received a command so to do, I can "do no other than shortly relate the chief *Mat- "ters of Fact*, which occurred in the trials of "some that were executed; in an abridgement "collected out of the *Court Papers*, on this oc- "casion put into my hands. You are to take the "*Truth*, just as it was."— *Wonders of the Invisible World, p. 54.*

He singles out five cases and declares: " I report "matters, not as an *Advocate*, but as an *Historian*."

After further prefacing his account, by relating, *A modern instance of Witches, discovered and condemned, in a trial before that celebrated Judge, Sir Matthew Hale,* he comes to the trial of George Burroughs. He spreads out, without reserve, the spectral evidence, given in this as in all the cases, and without the least intimation of objection from himself, or any one else, to its being *admitted*, as, " with other things to render it " credible " enough for the purpose of conviction. Any one reading his account, and at the same time examining the documents on file, will be able to appreciate how far he was justified in saying, that he reported it in the spirit of an historian rather than an advocate.

Let us first, see what the " Court papers, put " into his hands," amounted to; as we find them in the files.

" The Deposition of Simon Willard, aged about " 42 years, saith: I being at Saco, in the year 1689, " some in Capt. Ed. Sargent's garrison were speak- " ing of Mr. George Burroughs his great strength, " saying he could take a barrel of molasses out of " a canoe or boat, alone; and that he could take it " in his hands, or arms, out of the canoe or boat, " and carry it, and set it on the shore; and Mr. " Burroughs being there, said that he had carried " one barrel of molasses or cider out of a canoe, " that had like to have done him a displeasure; " said Mr. Burroughs intimated, as if he did not " want strength to do it, but the disadvantage of " the shore was such, that, his foot slipping " in the sand, he had liked to have strained his " leg."

Willard was uncertain whether Burroughs had stated it to be molasses or cider. John Brown testified about a " barrel of cider." Burroughs denied the statement, as to the molasses, thereby impliedly admitting that he had so carried a barrel of cider.

Samuel Webber testified that, seven or eight years before, Burroughs told him that, by putting his fingers into the bung of a barrel of molasses, he had lifted it up, and " carried it " round him, and set it down again."

Parris, in his notes of this trial, not in the files, says that " *Capt. Wormwood* testified about the " gun and the molasses." But the papers on file give the name as " *Capt. Wm Wormall*," and represents that he, referring to the gun, " swore " that he, " saw George Burroughs raise it from " the ground." His testimony, with this exception, was merely confirmatory, in general terms, of another deposition of Simon Willard, to the effect, that Burroughs, in explanation of one of the stories about his great strength, showed him how he held a gun of " about seven foot barrel," by taking it " in his hand behind the lock," and holding it out; Willard further stating that he did not see him " hold it out then, " and that he, Willard, so taking the gun with both hands, could not hold it out long enough to take sight. The testimony, throughout, was thus loose and conflicting, almost wholly mere hearsay, of no value, logically or legally. All that was really proved being what Burroughs admitted, that is, as to the cider.

But, in the statement made by him to Willard, at Saco, as deposed by the latter, he mentioned a circumstance, namely, the straining of his leg, which, if not true, could easily have been disproved, that demonstrated the effort to have been made, and the feat accomplished, by the natural exercise of muscular power. If preternatural force had aided him, it would have been supplied in sufficient quantity to have prevented such a mishap. To convey the impression that the exhibitions of strength ascribed to Burroughs were proofs of diabolical assistance, and demonstrations that he was guilty of the crime of witchcraft, Mather says "he was a very puny "man, yet he had often done things beyond the "strength of a giant." There is nothing to justify the application of the word "puny" to him, except that he was of small stature. Such persons are often very strong. Burroughs had, from his college days, been noted for gymnastic exercises. There is nothing, I repeat, to justify the use of the word, by Mather, in the sense he designed to convey, of bodily weakness.

The truth is, that his extraordinary muscular power, as exhibited in such feats as lifting the barrel of cider, was the topic of neighborhood talk; and there was much variation, as is usual in such cases, some having it a barrel of cider, and some, of molasses. There is, among the Court papers, a *Memorandum, in Mr. George Burroughs trial, besides the written evidences*. One item is the testimony of Thomas Evans, "that he carried out barrels of "molasses, meat, &c., out of a canoe, whilst his "mate went to the fort for hands to help out "with." Here we see another variation of the story. The amount of it is, that, while the mate thought assistance needed, and went to get it, Burroughs concluded to do the work himself. If the Prisoner had been allowed Counsel; or any discernment been left in the Judges, the whole of this evidence would have been thrown out of account, as without foundation and frivolous in its character; yet Increase Mather, who was present, was entirely carried away with it, and declared that, upon it alone, if on the Bench or in the jury-box, he would have convicted the Prisoner.

It is quite doubtful, however, whether the above testimony of Evans was given in, at the trial; for the next clause, in the same paragraph, is Sarah Wilson's confession, that: "The night before Mr. Burroughs was executed, there was

"a great meeting of the witches, nigh Sargeant "Chandler's, that Mr. Burroughs was there, and "they had the sacrament, and after they had "done, he took leave, and bid them stand to "their faith, and not own any thing. Martha "Tyler saith the same with Sarah Wilson, and "several others."

The testimony of these two confessing witches, "and several others," relating, as it did, to what was alleged to have happened "the night before "Mr. Burroughs was executed," could not have been given at his trial, nor until after his death. Yet, as but three other confessing witches are mentioned in the files of this case, Mather must have relied upon this Memorandum to make up the "eight" said, by him, to have testified, "in the "prosecution of the charge" against Burroughs. Hale, misled, perhaps, by the Memorandum, uses the indefinite expression "seven or eight." We know that one of the confessing witches, who had given evidence against Burroughs, retracted it before the Court, previous to his execution; but Mather makes no mention of that fact.

To go back to the barrel Mr. Burroughs lifted. I have stated the substance of the whole testimony relating to the point. Mather characterizes it, thus, in his report of the trial: "There was "evidence likewise brought in, that he made "nothing of taking up whole barrels, filled with "molasses or cider, in very disadvantageous po-"sitions, and carrying them off, through the most "difficult places, out of a canoe to the shore."

He made up this statement, as its substance and phraseology show, from Willard's deposition, then lying before him. In his use of that part of the evidence, in particular, as of the whole evidence, generally, the reader can judge whether he exhibited the spirit of an historian or of an advocate; and whether there was any thing to justify his expression, "made nothing of."

Any one scrutinizing the evidence, which, strange to say, was allowed to come in on a trial for witchcraft, relating to alleged misunderstandings between Burroughs and his two wives, involved in an alienation between him and some of the relations of the last, will see that it amounts to nothing more than the scandals incident to imbittered parish quarrels, and inevitably engendered in such a state of credulity and malevolence, as the witchcraft prosecutions produced. Yet our "historian," in his report of the case, says: "Now G. B. had been infamous, for the bar-"barous usage of his two successive wives, all "the country over."

In my book, in connection with another piece of evidence in the papers, given, like that of the confessing witches just referred to, long after Burroughs's execution, I expressed surprise that the irregularity of putting such testimony among the documents belonging to the trial, escaped the notice of Hutchinson, eminent jurist as he was, and also of Calef. The Reviewer represents this remark as one of my " very grave and unsupported " charges against the honesty of Cotton Mather." I said nothing about Mather in connection with that point, but expressed strong disapprobation of the conduct of the official persons who procured the deposition to be made, and of those having the custody of the papers. The Reviewer, imagining that my censure was levelled at Mather, and resolved to defend him, through thick and thin, denies that the document in question was " surreptitiously foisted in." But there it was, when Mather had the papers, and there it now is,—its date a month after Burroughs was in his rocky grave. The Reviewer says that if I had looked to the end of Mather's notice of the document, or observed the brackets in which it was enclosed, I would have seen that Mather says that the paper was not used at the trial. I stated the fact, expressly, and gave Mather's explanation " that the man was overpersuaded by others to be " out of the way upon George Burroughs's trial " [ii. 300, 303.] I found no fault with Mather, in connection with the paper; and am not answerable, at all, for the snarl in which the Reviewer's mind has become entangled, in his eagerness to assail my book.

I ask a little further attention to this matter, because it affords an illustration of Mather's singular but characteristic, method of putting things, often deceiving others, and sometimes, perhaps, himself. I quote the paragraph from his report of the trial of Burroughs, in the *Wonders of the Invisible World.* p. 64: " There " were two testimonies, that G. B. with only " putting the fore-finger of his right hand into " the muzzle of an heavy gun, a fowling-piece of " about six or seven foot barrel, did lift up the " gun, and hold it out at arms end; a gun which " the deponents, though strong men, could not, " with both hands, lift up, and hold out, at the " butt end, as is usual. Indeed, one of these witnesses was overpersuaded by some persons to " be out of the way, upon G. B's. trial; but he " came afterwards, with sorrow for his withdraw; " and gave in his testimony; nor were either of " these witnesses made use of as evidences in the " trial."

The Reviewer says that Mather included the above paragarph in " brackets," to apprise the reader that the evidence, to which it relates, was not given at the trial. It is true that the brackets are found in the Boston edition; but they are omitted, in the London edition, of the same year, 1693. If it was thought expedient to prevent misunderstanding, or preserve the appearance of fairness, *here,* the precaution was not provided for the English reader, He was left to re-

ceive the impression from the opening words, " there were two testimonies," that they were given at the trial, and to run the luck of having it removed by the latter part of the paragraph. The whole thing is so stated as to mystify and obscure. There were " *two* " testimonies; " *one* " is said not to have been presented; and then, that neither was presented. The reader, not knowing what to make of it, is liable to carry off nothing distinctly, except that, somehow, " there were testimonies " brought to bear against Burroughs; whereas not a syllable of it came before the Court.

Never going out of my way to criticise Cotton Mather, nor breaking the thread of my story for that purpose, I did not, in my book, call attention to this paragraph, as to its bearing upon him, but the strange use the Reviewer has made of it against me, compels its examination, in detail.

What right had Mather to insert this paragraph, at all, in his report of the *trial* of George Burroughs? It refers to extra-judicial and gratuitous statements that had nothing to do with the trial, made a month after Burroughs had passed out of Court and out of the world, beyond the reach of all tribunals and all Magistrates. It was not true that " there were two testimonies" to the facts alleged, *at the trial,* which, and which alone, Mather was professing to report. It is not a sufficient justification, that he contradicted, in the last clause, what he said in the first. This was one of Mather's artifices, as a writer, protecting himself from responsibility, while leaving an impression.

Mather says there were " *two* " witnesses of the facts alleged in the paragraph. Upon a careful re-examination of the papers on file, there appears to have been only *one,* in support of it. It stands solely on the single deposition of Thomas Greenslitt, of the fifteenth of September, 1692. The deponent mentions two other persons, by name, " and some others that are dead," who witnessed the exploit. But no evidence was given by them; and the muzzle story, according to the papers on file, stands upon the deposition of Greenslitt alone. The paragraph gives the idea that Greenslitt put himself out of the way, at the time of the trial of Burroughs; but there is reason to believe that he lived far down in the eastern country, and subsequently came voluntarily to Salem, from his distant home, to be present at the trial of his mother. The deposition was obtained from him in the period between her condemnation and execution. The motives that may have led the prosecutors to think it important to procure, and the probable inducement that led him to give, the deposition are explained in my book [*ii. 298*]. Greenslitt states that " the gun was of " six-foot barrel or thereabouts." Mather reports him as saying " about six or seven foot barrel." The account of the trial of Burroughs, throughout, is charged with extreme prejudice against the Prisoner; and the character of the evidence is exaggerated.

One of the witnesses, in the trial of Bridget Bishop, related a variety of mishaps, such as the stumping of the off-wheel of his cart, the breaking of the gears, and a general coming to pieces of the harness and vehicle, on one occasion; and his not being able, on another, to lift a bag of corn as easily as usual; and he ascribed it all to the witchery of the Prisoner. Mather gives his statement, concluding thus: "Many other pranks "of this Bishop this deponent was ready to tes-"tify." He endorses every thing, however absurd, especially if resting on spectral evidence, as absolute, unquestionable, and demonstrated facts.

Nothing was proved against the moral character of Susannah Martin; and nothing was brought to bear upon her, but the most ridiculous and shameful tales of blind superstition and malignant credulity. The extraordinary acumen and force of mind, however, exhibited in her defence, to the discomfiture of the examining Magistrates and Judges, excited their wrath and that of all concerned in the prosecution. Mather finishes the account of her trial in these words: "NOTE. "This woman was one of the most impudent, "scurrilous, wicked creatures in the world; and "she did now, throughout her whole trial, dis-"cover herself to be such an one. Yet when she "was asked what she had to say for herself, her "chief plea was, 'that she had led a most virtu-"'ous and holy life.'"— Wonders, ect. 126.

Well might he, and all who acted in bringing this remarkable woman to her death, have been exasperated against her. She will be remembered, in perpetual history, as having risen superior to them all, in intellectual capacity, and as having utterly refuted the whole system of spectral doctrine, upon which her life and the lives of all the others were sacrificed. Looking towards "the "afflicted children," who had sworn that her spectre tortured them, the Magistrate asked, "How comes your appearance to hurt these?" Her answer was, "How do I know? He that appeared "in the shape of Samuel, a glorified Saint, may "appear in any one's shape."

It is truly astonishing that Mather should have selected the name of Elizabeth How, to be held up to abhorrence and classed amon the "Male-"factors." It shows how utterly blinded and perverted he was by the horrible delusion that "possessed" him. If her piety and virtue were of no avail in leading him to pause in aspersing her memory, by selecting her case to be included in the "black list" of those reported by him in his Wonders, one would have thought he would have paid some regard to the testimony of his clerical brethren and to the feelings of her relatives, embracing many most estim-

able families. She was nearly connected with the venerable Minister of Andover, Francis Dane, and belonged to the family of Jackson.

There was, and is, among the papers, a large body of evidence in her favor, most weighty and decisive, yet Mather makes no allusion to it whatever; although he must have known of it, from outside information as well as the documents before him. Two of the most respectable Ministers in the country, Phillips and Payson of Rowley, many of her neighbors, men and women, and the father of her husband, ninety-four years of age, testified to her eminent Christian graces, and portrayed a picture of female gentleness, loveliness, and purity, not surpassed in the annals of her sex. The two Clergymen exposed and denounced the wickedness of the means that had been employed to bring the stigma of witchcraft upon her good name. Mather not only withholds all this evidence, but speaks with special bitterness of this excellent woman, calling her, over and over again, throughout his whole account, "This "How."

There is reason to apprehend that much cruelty was practised upon the Prisoners, especially to force them to confess. The statements made by John Proctor, in his letter to the Ministers, are fully entitled to credit, from his unimpeached honesty of character, as well as from the position of the persons addressed. It is not to be imagined, that, at its date, on the twenty-third of July, twelve days before his trial, he would have made, in writing, such declarations to them, had they not been true. He says that brutal violence was used upon his son to induce him to confess. He also states that two of the children of Martha Carrier were "tied neck and heels, till the blood "was ready to come out of their noses." The outrages, thus perpetrated, with all the affrighting influences brought to bear, prevailed over Carrier's children. Some of them were used as witnesses against her. A little girl, not eight years old, was made to swear that she was a witch; that her mother, when she was six years old, made her so, baptizing her, and compelling her "to set her hand to a book," and carried her, "in her spirit," to afflict people; that her mother, after she was in prison, came to her in the shape of "a black cat;" and that the cat told her it was her mother. Another of her children testified that he, and still another, a brother, were witches, and had been present, in spectra, at Witch-sacraments, telling who were there, and where they procured their wine. All this the mother had to hear.

Thomas Carrier, her husband, had, a year or two before, been involved in a controversy about the boundaries of his lands, in which hard words had passed. The energy of character, so strikingly displayed by his wife, at her Examination, rendered her liable to incur animosities, in the course of a neighborhood feud. The whole force of angry superstition had been arrayed against her; and she became the object of scandal, in the form it then was made to assume, the imputation of being a witch. Her Minister, Mr. Dane, in a strong and bold letter, in defence of his parishioners, many of whom had been accused, says: "There was a suspicion of Goodwife Carrier "among some of us, before she was apprehend- "ed, I know." He avers that he had lived above forty years in Andover, and had been much conversant with the people, "at their habitations;" that, hearing that some of his people were inclined to indulge in superstitious stories, and give heed to tales of the kind, he preached a Sermon against all such things; and that, since that time, he knew of no person that countenanced practices of the kind; concluding his statement in these words: "So far as I had the understanding of "any thing amongst us, do declare, that I be- "lieve the reports have been scandalous and un- "just, neither will bear the light."

Atrocious as were the outrages connected with the prosecutions, in 1692, none, it appears to me, equalled those committed in the case of Martha Carrier. The Magistrates who sat and listened, with wondering awe, to such evidence from a little child against her mother, in the presence of that mother, must have been bereft, by the baleful superstitions of the hour, of all natural sensibility. They countenanced a violation of reason, common sense, and the instincts of humanity, too horrible to be thought of.

The unhappy mother felt it in the deep recesses of her strong nature. That trait, in the female and maternal heart, which, when developed, assumes a heroic aspect, was brought out in terrific power. She looked to the Magistrates, after the accusing girls had charged her with having "killed thirteen at Andover," with a stern bravery to which those dignitaries had not been accustomed, and rebuked them: "It is a shameful "thing, that you should mind those folks that "are out of their wits;" and then, turning to the accusers, said, "You lie, and I am wronged." This woman, like all the rest, met her fate with a demeanor that left no room for malice to utter a word of disparagement, protesting her innocence. Mather witnessed her execution; and in a memorandum to the report, written in the professed character of an historian, having great compassion for "surviving relatives," calls her a "rampant hag."

Bringing young children to swear away the life of their mother, was probably felt by the Judges to be too great a shock upon natural sensibilities to be risked again, and they were not produced at the trial; but Mather, notwithstanding, had no reluctance to publish the substance of their

testimony, as what they would have sworn to if called upon; and says they were not put upon the stand, because there was evidence "enough" without them.

Such were the reports of those of the trials, which had then taken place, selected by Mather to be put into the *Wonders of the Invisible World*, and thus to be "boxed about,"—to adopt the Reviewer's interpretation—to strike down the "Spectre of Sadducceism," that is, to extirpate and bring to an end all doubts about witchcraft and all attempts to stop the prosecutions.

This book was written while the proceedings at Salem were at their height, during the very month in which sixteen persons had been sentenced to death and eight executed, evidently, from its whole tenor, and as the Reviewer admits, for the purpose of silencing objectors and doubters, Sadducees and Witch-advocates, before the meeting of the Court, by adjournment, in the first week of November, to continue—as the Ministers, in their *Advice*, expressed it—their "sedulous and "assiduous endeavours to defeat the abominable "witchcrafts which have been committed in the "country."

Little did those concerned, in keeping up the delusion and prolonging the scenes in the Salem Court-house and on Witch-hill, dream that the curtain was so soon to fall upon the horrid tragedy and confound him who combined, in his own person, the functions of Governor, Commander-in chief, President of the Council, Legislative leader of the General Court, and Chief-justice of the Special Court, and all his aiders and abettors, lay and clerical.

XII.

"WONDERS OF THE INVISIBLE WORLD"—CONTIN-
UED. PASSAGES FROM THE "CASES OF CON-
"SCIENCE." INCREASE MATHER.

In addition to the reports of the trials of the five "Malefactors," as Mather calls them, the *Wonders of the Invisible World* contains much matter that helps us to ascertain the real opinions, at the time, of its author, to which justice to him, and to all, requires me to ask attention. The passages, to be quoted, will occupy some room; but they will repay the reading, in the light they shed upon the manner in which such subjects were treated in the most accredited literature, and infused into the public mind, at that day. The style of Cotton Mather, while open to the criticisms generally made, is lively and attractive; and, for its ingenuity of expression and frequent felicity of illustration, often quite refreshing.

The work was written under a sense of the necessity of maintaining the position into which the Government of the Province had been led, by so suddenly and rashly organizing the Special Court and putting it upon its bloody work, at Salem ; and this could only be done by renewing and fortifying the popular conviction, that such proceedings were necessary, and ought to be vigorously prosecuted, and all Sadduceeism, or opposition to them, put down. It was especially necessary to reconcile, or obscure into indistinctness, certain conflicting theories that had more or less currency. "I do not believe," says Mather, "that the progress of Witchcraft among us, "is all the plot which the Devil is managing in "the Witchcraft now upon us. It is judged that "the Devil raised the storm, whereof we read in "the eighth Chapter of Matthew, on purpose to "overset the little vessel wherein the disciples of "our Lord were embarked with him. And it "may be feared that, in the Horrible Tempest "which is now upon ourselves, the design of the "Devil is to sink that happy Settlement of Gov- "ernment, wherewith Almighty God has gracious- "ly inclined their Majesties to favor us."— *Wonders, p. 10.*

He then proceeds to compliment Sir William Phips, alluding to his "continually venturing "his all," that is, in looking after affairs and fighting Indians in the eastern parts; to applaud Stoughton as "admirably accomplished" for his place; and continues as follows: "Our Councel- "lours are some of our most eminent persons, and "as loyal to the Crown, as hearty lovers of their "country. Our Constitution also is attended "with singular privileges. All which things are "by the Devil exceedingly envied unto us. And "the Devil will doubtless take this occasion for "the raising of such complaints and clamors, as "may be of pernicious consequence unto some "part of our present Settlement, if he can so far "impose. But that, which most of all threat- "ens us, in our present circumstances, is the mis- "understandings, and so, the animosities, where- "into the Witchcraft, now raging, has enchant- "ed us. The embroiling, first, of our Spirits, "and then, of our affairs." "I am sure, we "shall be worse than brutes, if we fly upon one "another, at a time when the floods of Belial "are upon us." "The Devil has made us like "a troubled sea, and the mire and mud begins "now also to heave up apace. Even good and "wise men suffer themselves to fall into their "paroxysms, and the shake which the Devil is "now giving us, fetches up the dirt which be- "fore lay still at the bottom of our sinful hearts. "If we allow the mad dogs of Hell to poison "us by biting us, we shall imagine that we see "nothing but such things about us, and like such "things, fly upon all that we see."

After deprecating the animosities and clamors that were threatening to drive himself and his friends from power, he makes a strenuous appeal

to persevere in the witchcraft prosecutions.

"We are to unite in our endeavours to deliver "our distressed neighbors from the horrible an- "noyances and molestations wherewith a dread- "ful witchcraft is now persecuting of them. "To have an hand in any thing that may stifle "or obstruct a regular detection of that witch- "craft, is what we may well with an holy fear "avoid. Their Majesties good subjects must not "every day be torn to pieces by horrid witches, "and those bloody felons be left wholly unpros- "ecuted. The witchcraft is a business that will "not be shammed, without plunging us into sore "plagues, and of long continuance. But then "we are to unite in such methods for this deliv- "erance, as may be unquestionably safe, lest the "latter end be worse than the beginning. And "here, what shall I say ? I will venture to say "thus much. That we are safe, when we make "just as much use of all advice from the invisi- "ble world, as God sends it for. It is a safe "principle, that when God Almighty permits "any spirits, from the unseen regions, to visit us "with surprising informations, there is then some- "thing to be enquired after; we are then to en- "quire of one another, what came there is for "such things ? The peculiar government of God, "over the unbodied Intelligences, is a sufficient "foundation for this principle. When there has "been a murder committed, an apparition of the "slain party accusing of any man, although "such apparitions have oftener spoke true than "false, is not enough to convict the man as guil- "ty of that murder; but yet it is a sufficient oc- "casion for Magistrates to make a particular en- "quiry whether such a man have afforded any "ground for such an accusation."—*Page 13.*

He goes on to apply this principle to the spectres of accused persons, seen by the "afflicted," as constituting sufficient ground to institute proceedings against the persons thus accused. After modifying, apparently, this position, although in language so obscure as to leave his meaning quite uncertain, he says: "I was going to make "one venture more ; that is, to offer some safe "rules, for the finding out of the witches, which "are to this day our accursed troublers : but this "were a venture too presumptuous and Icarian "for me to make. I leave that unto those Ex- "cellent and Judicious persons with whom I "am not worthy to be numbered : All that I shall "do, shall be to lay before my readers, a brief "synopsis of what has been written on that sub- "ject, by a Triumvirate of as eminent persons as "have ever handled it."—*Page 14.*

From neither of them, Perkins, Gaule and Bernard, as he cites them, can specific authority be obtained for the admission of spectral testi- mony, as offered by accusing witnesses, not them- selves confessing witches. The third Rule, attributed to Perkins, and the fifth of Bernard, apply to persons confessing the crime of witchcraft, and, after confession, giving evidence affecting another person—the former considering such evidence "not sufficient for condemnation, but a "fit presumption to cause a strait examination;" the latter treating it as sufficient to convict a fellow-witch, that is, another person also accused of being in "league with the Devil." Bernard specifies, as the kind of evidence, sufficient for conviction, such witnesses might give: "If they "can make good the truth of their witness and "give sufficient proof of it; as that they have "seen them with their Spirits, or that they have "received Spirits from them, or that they can tell "when they used witchery-tricks to do harm, or "that they told them what harm they had done, "or that they can show the mark upon them, or "that they have been together in their meetings, or "such like."

Mather remarks, in connection with his synopsis of these Rules: "They are considerable things, "which I have thus related." Those I have particularly noticed were enough to let in a large part of the evidence given at the Salem trials—in many respects, the most effective and formidable part—striking the Jury and Court, as well as the people, with an "awe," which rendered no other evidence necessary to overwhelm the mind and secure conviction. The Prisoners themselves were amazed and astounded by it. Mr. Hale, in his account of the proceedings, says: "When "George Burroughs was tried, seven or eight of "the confessors, severally called, said, they knew "the said Burroughs; and saw him at a Witch-"meeting at the Village; and heard him exhort "the company to pull down the Kingdom of "God and set up the Kingdom of the Devil. "He denied all, yet said he justified the Judges "and Jury in condemning him; because there "were so many positive witnesses against him; "but said he died by false witnesses." Mr. Hale proceeds to mention this fact: "I seriously spake "to one that witnessed (of his exhorting at the "Witch-meeting at the Village) saying to her; "'You are one that bring this man to death: if "'you have charged any thing upon him that is "'not true, recall it before it be too late, while he "'is alive.' She answered me, she had nothing to "charge herself with, upon that account."

Mather omits this circumstance in copying Mr. Hale's narrative. It has always been a mystery, what led the "accusing girls" to cry out, as they afterwards did, against Mr. Hale's wife. Perhaps this expostulation with one of their witnesses, awakened their suspicions. They always struck at every one who appeared to be wavering, or in the least disposed to question the correctness of what was going on. The statement of Mr. Hale shows how effectual and destructive

the evidence, authorized by Bernard's book, was; and it also proves how unjust, to the Judges and Magistrates, is the charge made upon them by the Reviewer, that they disregarded and violated the advice of the Ministers. In admitting a species of evidence, wholly spectral, which was fatal, more than any other, to the Prisoners, they followed a rule laid down by the very authors whose "directions" the Ministers, in their *Advice*, written by "Mr. Mather the younger," enjoined upon them to follow. It is noticable, by the way, that, in that document, they left Gaule out of the "triumvirate;" Mather finding nothing in his book to justify the admission of spectral testimony.

He urges the force of the evidence, from confessions, with all possible earnestness.

"One would think all the rules of under-"standing human affairs are at an end, if after "so many most voluntary harmonious confes-"sions, made by intelligent persons, of all ages, "in sundry towns, at several times, we must not "believe the main strokes, wherein those confes-"sions all agree."—*Page 8*.

He continues to press the point thus: "If "the Devils now can strike the minds of men "with any poisons of so fine a composition and "operation, that scores of innocent people shall "unite, in confessions of a crime, which we see "actually committed, it is a thing prodigious, "beyond the wonders of the former ages; and it "threatens no less than a sort of a dissolution "upon the world. Now, by these confessions, "it is agreed, that the Devil has made a dreadful "knot of witches in the country, and by the "help of witches has dreadfully increased that "knot; that these witches have driven a trade of "commissioning their confederate spirits, to do "all sorts of mischiefs to the neighbors, where-"upon there have ensued such mischievous con-"sequences upon the bodies and estates of the "neighborhood, as could not otherwise be ac-"counted for; yea, that at prodigious Witch-"meetings the wretches have proceeded so far "as to concert and consult the methods of root-"ing out the Christian religion from this coun-"try, and setting up, instead of it, perhaps a more "gross Diabolism, than ever the world saw be-"fore. And yet it will be a thing little short of "miracle, if, in so spread a business as this, the "Devil should not get in some of his juggles, to "confound the discovery of all the rest."

In the last sentence of the foregoing passage, we see an idea, which Mather expressed in several instances. It amounts to this. Suppose the Devil does "sometimes" make use of the spectre of an innocent person—he does it for the purpose of destroying our faith in that kind of evidence, and leading us to throw it all out, thereby "con-"founding the discovery" of those cases in which, as ordinarily, he makes use of the spectres of his guilty confederates, and, in effect, sheltering "all the rest," that is, the whole body of those who are the willing and covenanted subjects of his diabolical kingdom, from detection. He says: "The witches have not only intimated, "but some of them acknowledged, that they have "plotted the representations of innocent persons "to cover and shelter themselves in their witch"crafts."

He further suggests—for no other purpose, it would seem, than to reconcile us to the use of such evidence, even though it may, in "rare and "extraordinary" instances, bear against innocent persons, scarcely, however, to be apprehended, "when matters come before civil judicature"— that it may be the divine will, that, occasionally, an innocent person *may be cut off:* "Who of us "can exactly state how far our God may, for our "chastisement, permit the Devil to proceed in "such an abuse?" He then alludes to the meeting of Ministers, under his father's auspices, at Cambridge, on the first of August; quotes with approval, the result of the "Discourse," then held; and immediately proceeds: "It is rare and "extraordinary, for an honest Naboth to have "his life itself sworn away by two children of "Belial, and yet no infringement hereby made "on the Rectoral Righteousness of our eternal "Sovereign, whose judgments are a great deep, "and who gives none account of his matters." —*Page 9.*

The amount of all this is, that it is so rare and extraordinary for the Devil to assume the spectral shape of an innocent person, that it is best, "when," as his expression is, in another place, "the public safety makes an exigency," to receive and act upon such evidence, even if it should lead to the conviction of an innocent person—a thing so seldom liable to occur, and, indeed, barely possible. The procedure would be but carrying out the divine "permission," and a fulfilment of "the Rectoral Righteousness" of Him, whose councils are a great deep, not to be accounted for to, or by, us.

In summing up what the witches had been doing at Salem Village, during the preceding Summer, Mather says: "The Devil, exhibiting him"self ordinarily as a small black man, has decoy"ed a fearful knot of proud, froward, ignorant, "envious and malicious creatures to list them"selves in his horrid service, by entering their "names in a book, by him tendered unto them." "That they, each of them, have their spectres "or Devils, commissioned by them, and repre"senting them, to be the engines of their mal"ice." He enumerates, as facts, all the statements of the "afflicted" witnesses and confessing witches, as to the horrible and monstrous things perpetrated by the spectres of the accused

parties; and he applauds the Court,—testifying to the successful and beneficial issue of its proceedings. "Our honorable Judges have used, as "Judges have heretofore done, the spectral evi"dence, to introduce their further enquiries into "the lives of the persons accused; and they "have, thereupon, by the wonderful Providence "of God, been so strengthened with other evi"dences, that some of the Witch-gang have been "fairly executed."—*Pages 41, 43.*

The language of Cotton Mather, as applied to those who had suffered, as witches, "a fearful "knot of proud, froward, ignorant, envious and "malicious creatures—a Witch-gang,"—is rather hard, as coming from a Minister who, as the Reviewer asserts, had officiated in their death scenes, witnessed their devout and Christian expressions and deportment, and been their comforter, consoler, counsellor and friend.

The dissatisfaction that pervaded the public mind, about the time of the last executions at Salem, which Phips describes, was so serious, that both the Mathers were called in to allay it. The father also, at the request of the Ministers, wrote a book, entitled, *Cases of Conscience, concerning Evil Spirits, personating men, Witchcrafts,* &c., the general drift of which is against spectral evidence. He says: "Spectres are Devils, in the "shape of persons, either living or dead." Speaking of bewitched persons, he says: "What "they affirm, concerning others, is not to be ta"ken for evidence. Whence had they this su"pernatural sight? It must needs be either from "Heaven or from Hell. If from Heaven (as "Elisha's servant and Balaam's ass could discern "Angels) let their testimony be received. But "if they had this knowledge from Hell, though "there may possibly be truth in what they af"firm, they are not legal witnesses: for the "Law of God allows of no revelation from any "other Spirit but himself. *Isa. viii. 19.* It is a "sin against God, to make use of the Devil's "help to know that which cannot be otherwise "known; and I testify against it, as a great "transgression, which may justly provoke the "Holy One of Israel, to let loose Devils on the "whole land. *Luke, ii. 38.*"

After referring to a couple of writers on the subject, the very next sentence is this: "Al"though the Devil's accusations may be so far "regarded as to cause an enquiry into the truth "of things, *Job, i. 11, 12,* and *ii. 5, 6;* yet not "so as to be an evidence or ground of convic"tion."

It appears, therefore, that Increase Mather, while writing with much force and apparent vehemence against spectral evidence, still in reality countenanced its introduction, as a basis of "en"quiry into the truth of things," preliminary to other evidence. This was, after all, to use the form of thought of these writers, letting the Devil into the case; and that was enough, from the nature of things, in the then state of wild superstition and the blind delusions of the popular mind, to give to spectral evidence the controlling sway it had in the Salem trials, and would necessarily have, every where, when introduced at all.

In a Postscript to *Cases of Conscience*, Increase Mather says that he hears that "some have taken "up a notion," that there was something contradictory between his views and those of his son, set forth in the *Wonders of the Invisible World*. "'Tis strange that such imaginations "should enter into the minds of men." He goes on to say he had read and approved of his son's book, before it was printed; and falls back, as both of them always did, when pressed, upon the *Advice* of the Ministers, of the fifteenth of June, in which, he says, they concurred.

There can be no manner of doubt that the "strange" opinion did prevail, at the time, and has ever since, that the father and son did entertain very different sentiments about the Salem proceedings. The precise form of that difference is not easily ascertained. The feelings, so natural and proper, on both sides, belonging to the relation they sustained to each other, led them to preserve an appearance of harmony, especially in whatever was committed to the press. Then, again, the views they each entertained were in themselves so inconsistent, that it was not difficult to persuade themselves that they were substantially similar. There was much in the father, for the son to revere : there was much in the son, for the father to admire. Besides, the habitual style in which they and the Ministers of that day indulged, of saying and unsaying, on the same page—putting a proposition and then linking to it a countervailing one—covered their tracks to each other and to themselves. This is their apology; and none of them needs it more than Cotton Mather. He was singularly blind to logical sequence. With wonderful power over language, he often seems not to appreciate the import of what he is saying; and to this defect, it is agreeable to think, much, if not all, that has the aspect of a want of fairness and even truthfulness, in his writings, may be attributed.

As associate Ministers of the same congregation, it was desirable for the Mathers to avoid being drawn into a conflicting attitude, on any matter of importance. Drake, however, in his *History of Boston*, (p. 545.) says that there was supposed, at the formation of the New North Church, in that place, in 1712, to have been a jealousy between them. There were, indeed, many points of dissimilarity, as well as of similarity, in their culture, experience, manners, and ways; and men conversant with them, at the time, may have noticed a difference in their judgments and expressions, relating to the witchcraft affair, of which no knowledge has come to us, except the fact, that it was so understood at the time.

Cotton Mather brought all his ability to bear in preparing the *Wonders of the Invisible World*. It is marked throughout by his peculiar genius, and constructed with great ingenuity and elaboration; but it was " water spilt on the ground." So far as the end, for which it was designed, is regarded, it died before it saw the light.

<h2 style="text-align:center">XIII.</h2>

THE COURT OF OYER AND TERMINER BROUGHT TO A SUDDEN END. SIR WILLIAM PHIPS.

When Sir William Phips went to the eastward, it was expected that his absence would be prolonged to the twelfth of October. We cannot tell exactly when he returned; probably some days before the twelfth. Writing on the fourteenth, he says, that before any application was made to him for the purpose, he had put a stop to the proceedings of the Court. He probably signified, informally, to the Judges, that they must not meet on the day to which they had adjourned. Brattle, writing on the eighth, had not heard any thing of the kind. But the Rev. Samuel Torrey of Weymouth, who was in full sympathy with the prosecutors, had heard of it on the seventh, as appears by this entry in Sewall's Diary : " Oct. 7th, 1692. Mr. Torrey seems to be " of opinion, that the Court of Oyer and Termin- " er should go on, regulating any thing that may " have been amiss, when certainly found to be so."

Sewall and Stoughton were among the principal friends of Torrey ; and he, probably, had learned from them, Phips's avowed purpose to stop the proceedings of the Court, in the witchcraft matter. The Court, however, was allowed to sit, in other cases, as it held a trial in Boston, on the tenth, in a capital case of the ordinary kind. The purpose of the Governor gradually became known. Danforth, in a conversation with Sewall, at Cambridge, on the fifteenth, expressed the opinion that the witchcraft trials ought not to proceed any further.

It is not unlikely that Phips, while at the eastward, had received some communication that hastened his return. He describes the condition of things, as he found it. We know that the lives of twenty people had been taken away, one of them a Minister of the Gospel. Two Ministers had been accused, one of them the Pastor of the Old South Church; the name of the other is not known. A hundred were in prison ; about two hundred more were under accusation, including some men of great estates in Boston, the mother-in-law of one of the Judges, Corwin, and a member of the family of Increase Mather, although, as he says, in no way related to him. A Magistrate, who was a member of the House of Assembly, had fled for his life; and Phips's trusted naval commander, a man of high standing in the Church and in society, as well as in the service, after having been committed to Jail, had escaped to parts unknown. More than all, the Governor's wife had been cried out upon. We can easily imagine his state of mind. Sir William Phips was noted for the sudden violence of his temper. Mather says that he sometimes "showed choler "enough." Hutchinson says that "he was of a "benevolent, friendly disposition; at the same "time quick and passionate;" and, in illustration of the latter qualities, he relates that he got into a fisticuff fight with the Collector of the Port, on the wharf, handling him severely; and that, having high words, in the street, with a Captain of the Royal Navy, "the Governor made use of his "cane and broke Short's head." When his Lady told her story to him, and pictured the whole scene of the "strange ferment" in the domestic and social circles of Boston and throughout the country, it was well for the Chief-justice, the Judges, and perhaps his own Ministers, that they were not within the reach of those "blows," with which, as Mather informs us, in the *Life of Phips*, the rough sailor was wont, when the gusts of passion were prevailing, to "chastise incivili-"ties," without reference to time or place, rank or station.

But, as was his wont, the storm of wrath soon subsided; his purpose, however, under the circumstances, as brave as it was wise and just, was, as the result showed, unalterable. He communicated to the Judges, personally, that they must sit no more, at Salem or elsewhere, to try cases of witchcraft; and that no more arrests must be made, on that charge.

Mather's book, all ready as it was for the press, thus became labor thrown away. It was not only rendered useless for the purpose designed, but a most serious difficulty obstructed its publication. Phips forbade the "printing of "any discourses, one way or another;" and the *Wonders* had incorporated in it some Sermons, impregnated, through and through, with combustible matter, in Phips's view, likely to kindle an inextinguishable flame.

All that could be done was to keep still, in the hope that he would become more malleable. In the meanwhile, public business called him away, perhaps to Rhode Island or Connecticut, from the eighteenth to the twenty-seventh of October. In his absence, whether in consequence of movements he had put in train, or solely from what had become known of his views, the circumstance occurred which is thus related in Sewall's Diary— the Legislature was then in Session: "Oct. 26, "1692. A Bill is sent in about calling a Fast and

"Convocation of Ministers, that may be led in the "right way, as to the Witchcrafts. The season, "and manner of doing it, is such, that the Court "of Oyer and Terminer count themselves thereby "dismissed. 29 nos & 33 yeas to the Bill. "Capt. Bradstreet, and Lieut. True, Wm. Hutch-"ins, and several other interested persons, in the "affirmative."

The course of Nathaniel Saltonstall, of Haverhill, and the action in the Legislature of the persons here named, entitle the Merrimac towns of Essex-county to the credit of having made the first public and effectual resistance to the fanaticism and persecutions of 1692.

The passage of this Bill, in the House of Representatives, shows how the public mind had been changed, since the June Session. Dudley Bradstreet was a Magistrate and member from Andover, son of the old Governor, and, with his wife, had found safety from prosecution by flight; Henry True, a member from Salisbury, was son-in-law of Mary Bradbury, who had been condemned to death; Samuel Hutchins, (inadvertently called "Wm.," by Sewall) was a member from Haverhill, and connected by marriage with a family, three of whom were tried for their lives. Sewall says there were "several other" members of the House, interested in like manner. This shows into what high circles the accusers had struck.

It appears, by the same Diary, that on the twenty-seventh, Cotton Mather preached the Thursday Lecture, from *James i. 4.* The day of trial was then upon him and his fellow-actors; and patience was inculcated as the duty of the hour.

The Diary relates that at a meeting of the Council, on the twenty-eighth, in the afternoon, Sewall, "desired to have the advice of the Gov-"ernor and Council, as to the sitting of the Court "of Oyer and Terminer, next week; said, should "move it no more; great silence prevailed, as if "should say, Do not go."

The entry does not state whether Phips was present; as, however, the time fixed for his recent brief absence had expired, probably he was in his seat. The following mishap, described by Sewall, as occurring that day, perhaps detained the Deputy-governor: "Oct. 28. Lt. Gov", com-"ing over the causey, is, by reason of the high "tide, so wet, that is fain to go to bed, till sends "for dry clothes to Dorchester."

The "great silence" was significant of the embarrassment in which they were placed, and their awe of the "choler" of the Governor.

The Diary gives the following account of the Session the next day, at which, (as Sewall informs us,) the Lieutenant-governor was not present: "Oct. 29. Mr. Russel asked, whether the Court "of Oyer and Terminer should sit, expressing "some fear of inconvenience by its fall. Gover-"nor said, it must fall."

Thus died the Court of Oyer and Terminer. Its friends cherished, to the last, the hope that Sir William might be placated, and possibly again brought under control; but it vanished, when the emphatic and resolute words, reported by Sewall, were uttered.

The firmness and force of character of the Governor are worthy of all praise. Indeed, the illiterate and impulsive sailor has placed himself, in history, far in front of all the honored Judges and learned Divines, of his day. Not one of them penetrated the whole matter as he did, when his attention was fully turned to it, and his feelings enlisted, to decide, courageously and righteously, the question before him. He saw that no life was safe while the evidence of the "afflicted persons" was received, "either to the "committing or trying" of any persons. He thus broke through the meshes which had bound Judges and Ministers, the writers of books and the makers of laws; and swept the whole fabric of "spectral testimony" away, whether as matter of "enquiry" and "presumption," or of "conviction." The ship-carpenter of the Kennebec laid the axe to the root of the tree.

The following extract from a letter of Sir William Phips, just put into my hands, and for which I am indebted to Mr. Goodell, substantiates the conclusions to which I have been led.

"*Governor Phips to the Lords of the Commit-*
"*tee of Trade and Plantations, 3 April, 1693.*

"MAY IT PLEASE YOUR LORDSHIPS:

"I have intreated M'Blathwayte to lay "before your Lordships several letters, wherein "I have given a particular account of my stop-"ping a supposed witchcraft, which had proved "fatall to many of their Maj'ties good subjects, "had there not been a speedy end putt thereto; "for a stop putt to the proceedings against such "as were accused, hath caused the thing itself "to cease."

This shows that, addressing officially his Home Government, he assumed the responsibility of having "stopped and put a speedy end to the "proceedings;" that he had no great faith in the doctrines then received touching the reality of witchcraft; and that he was fully convinced that, if he had allowed the trials to go on, and the inflammation of the public mind to be kept up by "discourses," the bloody tragedy would have been prolonged, and "proved fatal to many "good" people.

There are two men—neither of them belonging to the class of scholars or Divines; both of them guided by common sense, good feeling, and a courageous and resolute spirit—who stand alone, in the scenes of the witchcraft delusions. NATHANIEL SALTONSTALL, who left the Council and the Court, the day the Ministers' *Advice*, to go on

with the prosecutions, was received, and never appeared again until that *Advice* was abandoned and repudiated: and Sir WILLIAM PHIPS, who stamped it out beneath his feet.

But how with Cotton Mather's Book, the *Wonders of the Invisible World?* On the eleventh of October, Stoughton and Sewall signed a paper, printed in the book, [*p. 88.*] endorsing its contents, especially as to "matters of fact and evidence" and the "methods of conviction used in the pro-"ceedings of the Court at Salem." The certificate repeats the form of words, so often used in connection with the book, that it was written "at "the direction of His Excellency the Governor," without, as in all cases, specifying who, whether Phips or Stoughton, was the Governor referred to. As all the Judges were near at hand, and as the certificate related to the proceedings before them, is is quite observable that only the two mentioned signed it. As they were present, in the private conference, with Cotton Mather, at the house of one of them, on the twenty-second of September, when its preparation for publication was finally arranged, they could not well avoid signing it. The times were critical; and the rest of the Judges, knowing the Governor's feelings, thought best not to appear. Of the three other persons, at that conference, Hathorne, it is true, was a Judge of that Court, but it is doubtful whether he often, or ever, took his seat as such; besides, he was too experienced and cautious a public man, unnecessarily to put his hand to such a paper, when it was known, as it was probably to him, that Sir William Phips had forbidden publications of the kind.

There is another curious document in the *Wonders*—a letter from Stoughton to Mather, highly applauding the book, in which he acknowledges his particular obligations to him for writing it, as "more nearly and highly concerned" than others, considering his place in the Court, expressing in detail his sense of the great value of the work, "at this juncture of time," and concluding thus: "I do therefore make it my par-"ticular and earnest Request unto you, that, as "soon as may be, you will commit the same un-"to the press, accordingly." It is signed, without any official title of distinction, simply "WILL-"IAM STOUGHTON," and is *without date.*

It is singular, if Phips was the person who requested it to be written and was the "Ex-"cellency" who authorized its publication, that it was left to William Stoughton to "request" its being put to press.

The foregoing examination of dates and facts seems, almost, to compel the conclusion, to be drawn also from his letter, that Sir William Phips really had nothing whatever to do with procuring the preparation or sanctioning the publication of the *Wonders of the Invisible World.*

The same is true as to the request to the Ministers, for their *Advice*, dated the fifteenth of June. It was " laid before the Judges;" and was, undoubtedly, a response to an application from them. Having, very improperly, it must be confessed, given the whole matter of the trials over to Stoughton, and being engrossed in other affairs, it is quite likely that he knew but little of what had been going on, until his return from the eastward, in October. And his frequent and long absences, leaving Stoughton, so much of the time, with all the functions and titles of Governor devolved upon him, led to speaking of the latter as " His Excellency." When bearing this title and acting as Governor, for the time being, the Chief-justice, with the side Judges—all of them members of the Council, and in number meeting the requirement in the Charter for a quorum, seven—may have been considered, as substantially, " The Governor and Council."

Thinking it more than probable that, in this way, great wrong has been done to the memory of an honest and noble-hearted man, I have endeavored to set things in their true light. The perplexities, party entanglements, personal collisions, and engrossing cares that absorbed the attention of Sir William Phips, during the brief remainder of his life, and the little interest he felt in such things, prevented his noticing the false position in which he had been placed by the undistinguishing use of titular phrases.

Judge Sewall's Diary contains an entry that, also, sheds light upon the position of the Mathers. It will be borne in mind, that Elisha Cook was the colleague of Increase Mather, as Colonial Agents in London. Cook refused assent to the new Charter, and became the leader of the anti-Mather party. He was considered an opponent of the witchcraft prosecutions, although out of the country at the time. " TUESDAY, NOV. 15. "1692. M' Cook keeps a Day of Thanksgiv- "ing for his safe arrival." * * * [*Many mentioned as there, among them Mr. Willard.*] " Mr. Allen preached from Jacob's going to Beth- "el, * * * Mr. Mather not there, nor Mr. "Cotton Mather. The good Lord unite us in "his fear, and remove our animosities."

The manner in which Sewall distinguished the two Mathers confirms the views presented on pages 37, 38.

It may be remarked, that, up to this time, Sewall seems to have been in full sympathy with Stoughton and Mather. He was, however, beginning to indulge in conversations that indicate a desire to feel the ground he was treading. After a while, he became thoroughly convinced of his error; and there are scattered, in the margins of his Diary, expressions of much sensibility at the extent to which he had been misled. Over against an entry, giving an account of his presence at an Examination before Magistrates, of whom he was one, on the eleventh of April, 1692, at Salem, is the interjection, thrice repeated, " *Vae, Vae, Vae.*" At the opening of the year 1692, he inserted, at a subsequent period, this passage: " *Attonitus tamen est, ingens discrim-* " *ine parvo committi potuisse Nefas.*"[*]

XIV.

COTTON MATHER'S WRITINGS SUBSEQUENT TO THE WITCHCRAFT PROSECUTIONS.

I propose, now, to enquire into the position Cotton Mather occupied, and the views he expressed, touching the matter, after the witchcraft prosecutions had ceased and the delusion been dispelled from the minds of other men.

During the Winter of 1692 and 1693, between one and two hundred prisoners, including confessing witches, remained in Jail, at Salem, Ipswich, and other places. A considerable number were in the Boston Jail. It seems, from the letter to Secretary Allyn of Connecticut, that, during that time, the Mathers were in communication with them, and receiving from them the names of persons whose spectres, they declared, they had seen and suffered from, as employed in the Devil's work. After all that had happened, and the order of Sir William Phips, forbidding attempts to renew the excitement, it is wonderful that the Mathers should continue such practices. In the latter part of the Summer of 1693, they were both concerned in the affair of Margaret Rule; and Cotton Mather prepared, and put into circulation, an elaborate account of it, some extracts from which have been presented, and which will be further noticed, in another connection.

His next work, in the order of time, which I shall consider, is his *Life of Sir William Phips*, printed in London, in 1697, and afterwards included in the *Magnalia*, also published in London, a few years afterwards, constituting the last part of the Second Book. *The Life of Phips* is, perhaps, the most elaborate and finished of all Mather's productions; and " adorned," as his uncle Nathaniel Mather says, in a commendatory note, " with a very grateful variety of learning." In it, Sir William , who had died, at London, three years before, is painted in glowing colors, as one of the greatest of conquerors and rulers, " drop- "ped, as it were, from the Machine of Heaven;" "for his exterior, he was one tall, beyond the "common lot of men ; and thick, as well as tall,

---

* For the privilege of inspecting and seeing Judge Sewall's Diary I am indebted to the kindness of the Massachusetts Historical Society; and I would also express my thanks, for similar favors and civilities, to the officers in charge of the Records and Archives in the Massachusetts State House, the Librarian of Harvard University the Essex Institute, and many individuals, not mentioned in the text, especially those devoted collectors and lovers of our old New England literature, Samuel G. Drake and John K. Wiggin.

" and strong as well as thick. He was, in all re-
" spects, exceedingly robust, and able to conquer
" such difficulties of diet and of travel, as would
" have killed most men alive ;" " he was well set,
" and he was therewithall of a very comely,
" though a very manly, countenance." He is described as of " a most incomparable generosity,"
" of a forgiving spirit." His faults are tenderly touched ; " upon certain affronts, he has made
" sudden returns, that have shewed choler enough ;
" and he has, by blow, as well as by word, chas-
" tised incivilities."

It is remarkable that Mather should have laid
himself out, to such an extent of preparation
and to such heights of eulogy, as this work exhibits. It is dedicated to the Earl of Bellamont,
just about to come over, as Phips's successor.
Mather held in his hand a talisman of favor, influence, and power. In the Elegy which concludes the *Life*, are lines like these :

" Phips, our great friend, our wonder, and our
   " glory,
" The terror of our foes, the world's rare story,
" Or but name Phips, more needs not be express-
   " ed,
" Both Englands, and next ages, tell the rest."

The writer of this *Life* had conferred the gift
of an immortal name upon one Governor of New
England, and might upon another.

But with all this panegyric, he does not seem
to have been careful to be just to the memory of
his hero. The reader is requested, at this point,
to turn back to pages 23, 24, of this article,
and examine the paragraph, quoted from the
Life of Phips, introducing the return of *Advice*
from the Ministers. I have shown, in that connection, how deceptive the expression " arriving
" to his Government is." In reporting the *Advice* of the Ministers, in the *Life of Phips*, Mather omits the paragraphs I have placed within
brackets [*p. 21, 22*]—the *first, second* and *eighth*.
The omission of these paragraphs renders the
document, as given by Mather, an absolute misrepresentation of the transaction, and places
Phips in the attitude of having disregarded the
advice of the Ministers, in suffering the trials to
proceed as they did ; throwing upon his memory
a load of infamy, outweighing all the florid and
extravagant eulogies showered upon him, in the
Life : verifying and fulfilling the apprehensions
he expressed in his letter of the fourteenth of October, 1692 : " I know my enemies are seeking to
" turn it all upon me."

The Reviewer says that " Mr. Mather did not
" profess to quote the whole *Advice*, but simply
" made extracts from it." He professed to give
what the Ministers " declared." I submit to every
honorable mind, whether what Mather printed,
omitting the *first, second* and *eighth* sections,

was a fair statement of what the Ministers " de-
" clared."

The paragraphs he selected, appear, on their
face, to urge caution and even delay, in the proceedings. They leave this impression on the
general reader, and have been so regarded from
that day to this. The artifice, by which the responsibility for what followed was shifted, from
the Ministers, upon Phips and the Court, has, in
a great measure, succeeded. I trust that I have
shown that the clauses and words that seem to
indicate caution, had very little force, in that direction ; but that, when the disguising veil of an
artful phraseology is removed, they give substantial
countenance to the proceedings of the Court,
throughout.

I desire, at this point, to ask the further attention of the reader to Mather's manner of referring
to the *Advice of the Ministers*. In his *Wonders*,
he quotes the *eighth* and *second* Articles of it (*Pages
12, 55*), in one instance, ascribing the *Advice* to
" Reverend persons," " men of God," " gracious
" men," and, in the other, characterizing it as
" gracious words." He also, in the same work,
quotes the *sixth* Article, *omitting the words I
have placed in brackets, without any indication
of an omission*. Writing, in 1692, when the
delusion was at its height, and for the purpose of keeping the public mind up to the work
of the prosecutions, he gloried chiefly in the
first, second, and *eighth* Articles, and brought
them alone forward, in full. The others he
passed over, with the exception of the *sixth*,
from which he struck out the central sentence—
that having the appearance of endorsing the
views of those opposed to spectral testimony.
But, in 1697, when the *Life of Phips* was written,
circumstances had changed. It was apparent,
then, to all, even those most unwilling to realize
the fact, that the whole transaction of the witchcraft prosecutions in Salem was doomed to perpetual condemnation : and it became expedient
to drop out of sight, forever, if possible, the
second and *eighth* articles, and reproduce the
sixth, entire.

Considering the unfair view of the import of
the *Advice*, in the *Life of Phips*, and embodied
in the *Magnalia*—a work, which, with all its de-
fects, inaccuracies, and absurdities, is sure of occupying a conspicuous place in our Colonial
literature—I said : " unfortunately for the reputa-
" tion of Cotton Mather, Hutchinson has pre-
" served the *Address of the Ministers, entire*."
Regarding the document published by Mather
in the light of a historical imposture, I expressed
satisfaction, that its exposure was provided in a
work, sure of circulation and preservation, equal-
ly, to say the least, with the *Life of Phips* or the
Magnalia. The Reviewer, availing himself of
the opportunity, hereupon pronounces me igno-

rant of the fact that the "*Advice, entire,*" was published by Increase Mather at the end of his *Cases of Conscience;* and, in his usual style—not, I think, usual, in the *North American Review*—speaks thus—it is a specimen of what is strown through the article : "Mr. Upham should have "been familiar enough with the original sources "of information on the subject, to have found "this *Advice* in print, seventy-four years before "Hutchinson's *History* appeared."

Of course, neither I, nor any one else, can be imagined to suppose that Hutchinson invented the document. It was pre-existent, and at his hand. It was not to the purpose to say where he found it. I wonder this Reviewer did not tell the public, that I had *never seen, read,* or *heard of* Calef; for, to adopt his habit of reasoning, if I had been acquainted with that writer, my ignorance would have been enlightened, as Calef would have informed me that "the whole "of the Minister's advice and answer is printed "in *Cases of Conscience,* the last pages."

That only which finds a place in works worthy to endure, and of standard value, is sure of perpetual preservation. Hutchinson's *History of Massachusetts* is a work of this description. Whatever is committed to its custody will stand the test of time. This cannot be expected of that class of tracts or books to which *Cases of Conscience* belongs, copies of which can hardly be found, and not likely to justify a separate republication. It has, indeed, not many years ago, been reprinted in England, in a series of *Old Authors,* tacked on to the *Wonders of the Invisible World.* But few copies have reached this country; and only persons of peculiar, it may almost be said, eccentric, tastes, would care to procure it. It will be impossible to awaken an interest in the general reading public for such works. They are forbidding in their matter, unintelligible in their style, obscure in their import and drift, and pervaded by superstitions and absurdities that have happily passed away, never, it is to be hoped, again to enter the realm of theology, philosophy, or popular belief; and will perish by the hand of time, and sink into oblivion. If this present discussion had not arisen, and the "*Advice,* entire," had not been given by Hutchinson, the *suppressio veri,* perpetrated by Cotton Mather, would, perhaps, have become permanent history.

In reference to the *Advice of the Ministers,* the Reviewer, in one part of his article, seems to complain thus: "Mr. Upham has never seen fit "to print this paper:" in other parts, he assails me from the opposite direction, and in a manner too serious, in the character of the assault, to be passed over. In my book, (ii. 267) I thus speak of the *Advice of the Ministers,* referring to it, in a note to p. 367, in similar terms: "The re-

sponse of the reverend gentlemen, while urg-"ing in general terms the importance of caution "and circumspection in the methods of examin-"ation, decidedly and earnestly recommended "that the proceedings should be vigorously car-"ried on."

It is a summary, in general and brief terms, in *my own language,* of the *import* of the whole document, covering both sets of its articles. Hutchinson condenses it in similar terms, as do Calef and Douglas. I repeat, and beg it to be marked, that I do *not quote it,* in *whole* or in *part,* but only give its import in my own words. I claim the judgment of the reader, whether I do not give the import of the articles Mather printed in the *Life of Phips*—those pretending to urge caution - as fairly as of the articles he omitted, applauding the Court, and encouraging it to go on.

Now, this writer in the *North American Review* represents to the readers of that journal and to the public, that I have *quoted* the *Advice of the Ministers,* and, in variety of phrase, rings the charge of unfair and false *quotation,* against me. He uses this language: "If it were such a heinous "crime for Cotton Mather, in writing the *Life of* "*Sir William Phips,* to omit three Sections, how "will Mr. Upham vindicate his own omissions, "when, writing the history of these very transac-"tions, and bringing the gravest charges against "the characters of the persons concerned, he "leaves out seven Sections?" I *quoted* no Section, and made no *omissions;* and it is therefore utterly unjustifiable to say that I *left out* any thing. I gave the substance of the Sections Cotton Mather left out, in language nearly identical with that used by Hutchinson and all others. In the same way, I gave the substance of the Sections Mather published, in the very sense he always claimed for them. What I said did not bear the form, nor profess the character, of a *quotation.*

In the *Wonders of the Invisible World,* written in 1692, when the prosecutions were in full blast and Mather was glorying in them, and for the purpose of prolonging them, the only Section he saw fit, in a particular connection, to quote, was the SECOND. He prefaced it thus: "They were "some of the Gracious Words inserted in the "*Advice,* which many of the neighboring Minis-"ters did this Summer humbly lay before our "Honorable Judges." Let it be noted, by the way, that when he thus praised the document, its authorship had not been avowed. Let it further be noted, that it is here let slip that the paper was *laid before the Judges,* not Phips; showing that it was a response to *them,* not him. Let it be still further noted, that the Section which he thus cited, in 1692, is one of those which, when the tide had turned, he left out, in 1697. .

The Reviewer, referring to Mather's quotation of the second Section of the *Advice*, in the *Wonders*, says: " he printed it in full, which Mr. Up- "ham has never done;" and following out the strange misrepresentation, he says: " Mr. Upham "does not print any part of the eighth Section, " as the Ministers adopted it. He suppresses the "essential portions, changes words, and, by in- "terpolation, states that the Ministers 'decided- "'ly,' 'earnestly,' and 'vehemently,' recom- "mended that the 'proceedings' should be vig- "orously carried on. He who quotes in this "manner needs other evidence than that produc- "ed by Mr. Upham to entitle him to impeach "Mr. Mather's integrity." In another place he says, pursuing the charge of quoting falsely, as to my using the word "proceedings," "the "word is not to be found in the *Advice*."

The eighth Section recommends "the speedy "and vigorous prosecutions of such as have ren- "dered themselves obnoxious." In a brief ref- erence to the subject, I use the words "speedily "and vigorously," marking them as quoted, al- though their form was changed by the structure of the sentence of my own in which they appear. Beyond this, I have made no *quotations*, in my book, of the *Advice*—not a Section, nor sen- tence, nor clause, nor line, is a quotation, nor pre- tends to be. Without characterising what the Reviewer has done, in charging me with *sup- pression of essential portions, interpolation*, and *not printing* in full, or correctly, what the Minis- ters or any body else said, my duty is discharged, by showing that there is no truth in the charge— no foundation or apology for it.

The last of the works of Cotton Mather I shall examine, in this scrutiny of his retrospective opin- ions and position, relating to the witchcraft pros- ecutions, is the *Magnalia*, printed at London, in 1702. He had become wise enough, at that time, not to commit himself more than he could help.

The Rev. John Hale, of Beverly, died in May, 1700. He had taken an active part in the pro- ceedings at Salem, in 1692, having, as he says, from his youth, been "trained up in the knowl- "edge and belief of most of the principles " up- on which the prosecutions were conducted, and had held them " with a kind of implicit faith." Towards the close of the Trials, his views under- went a change: and, after the lapse of five years, he prepared a treatise on the subject. It is a candid, able, learned, and every-way commend- able performance, adhering to the general be- lief in witchcraft, but pointing out the errors in the methods of procedu e in the Trials at Salem, showing that the principles there acted upon were fallacious. The book was not printed un- til 1702. Cotton Mather, having access to Mr. Hale's manuscript, professedly made up from it his account of the witchcraft transactions of

1692, inserted in the *Magnalia*, Book VI. Page 79. He adopts the narrative part of the work, sub- stantially, avoiding much discussion of the top- ics upon which Mr. Hale had laid himself out. He cites, indeed, some passages from the argu- mentative part, containing marvellous statements, but does not mention that Mr. Hale labored, throughout, to show that those and other like matters, which had been introduced at the Trials, as proofs of spectral agency, were easily resolva- ble into the visions and vagaries of a " deluded "imagination," " a phantasy in the brain," " phantasma before the eyes."

Mr. Hale limits the definition of a witch to the following: " Who is to be esteemed a capital "witch among Christians ? viz: Those that be- "ing brought up under the means of the knowl- "edge of the true God, yet, being in their right "mind or free use of their reason, do knowing- "ly and wittingly depart from the true God, so "as to devote themselves unto, and seek for "their help from, another God, or the Devil, as "did the Devil's Priests and Prophets of old, "that were magicians."—*Page 127*.

As he had refuted, and utterly discarded, the whole system of evidence connected with spec- tres of the living or ghosts of the dead, the above definition rescued all but openly profane, abandoned, and God-defying people from being prosecuted for witchcraft. Mather transcribes, as a quotation, what seems to be the foregoing definition, but puts it thus: "A person that, "having the free use of reason, doth knowingly "and willingly seek and obtain of the Devil, "or of any other God, besides the true God Jeho- "vah, an ability to do or know strange things, "or things which he cannot by his own humane "abilities arrive unto. This person is a witch."

The latter part of the definition thus trans- cribed, has no justification in Hale's language, but is in conflict with the positions in his book. Mather says, " the author spends whole Chapters "to prove that there yet is a witch." He omits to state, that he spends twice as many Chapters to prove that the evidence in the Salem cases was not suffi ient for that purpose. Upon the whole it can hardly be considered a fair tran- script of Mr. Hale's account. He dismisses the subject, once for all, in a curt and almost disre- spectful style—" But thus much for this manu- "script."

Whoever examines the manner in which he, in this way, gets rid of the subject, in the *Mag- nalia*, must be convinced, I think, that he felt no satisfaction in Mr. Hale's book, nor in the state of things that made it necessary for him to give the whole matter the go-by. If the public mind had retained its fanatical creduli- ty, or if Mather's own share in the delusion of 1692 had been agreeable in the retrospect, it cannot be doubted that it would have afforded THE GREAT THEME, of his great book. All the strange learning, passionate eloquence, and extravagant painting, of its author, would have been lavished upon it; and we should have had another separate Book, with a Hebrew, Greek, or Latin motto or title, which, interpreted, would read *Most Wonderful of Wonders*. In 1692, his language was: " Witchcraft is a business that " will not be shammed." In 1700, it was shoved off upon the memory of Mr. Hale, as a business not safe for him, Mather, to meddle with, any longer. It was dropped, as if it burned his fingers.

XV.

HISTORY OF OPINION AS TO COTTON MATHER'S CONNECTION WITH SALEM WITCHCRAFT. THOMAS BRATTLE. THE PEOPLE OF SALEM VILLAGE. JOHN HALL. JOHN HIGGINSON. MICHAEL WIGGLESWORTH.

Such passages as the following are found in the article of the *North American Review*: " These views, respecting Mr. Mather's connec- " tion with the Salem Trials, are to be found in " no publication of a date prior to 1831, when " Mr. Upham's *Lectures* were published." " These " charges have been repeated by Mr. Quincy, in " his *History of Harvard University*, by Mr. " Peabody, in his *Life of Cotton Mather*, by Mr. " Bancroft, and by nearly all historical writers, " since that date." " An examination of the his- " torical text-books, used in our schools, will " show when these ideas originated."

The position taken by the Reviewer, let it be noticed, is, that the idea of Cotton Mather's taking a leading part in the witchcraft prosecutions of 1692, "*originated*" with me, in a work printed in 1831; and that I have given "the " cue " to all subsequent writers on the subject. Now what are the facts?

Cotton Mather himself is a witness that the idea was entertained at the time. In his Diary, after endeavoring to explain away the admitted fact that he was t o eulogist and champion of the Judges, while the Trials were pending, he says: " Merely, as far as I can learn, for this rea- " son, the mad people through the country, " under a fascination on their spirits equal to " that which energumens had on their bodies, " reviled me as if I had been the doer of all the " hard things that were done in the prosecu- " tion of the witchcraft." He repeats the complaint, over and over again, in various forms and different writings. Indeed, it could not have been otherwise, than that such should have been the popular impression and conviction.

He was, at that time, bringing before the people, most conspicuously, the *second* and *eighth* Articles of the *Ministers' Advice*, urging on the prosecutions. His deportment and harangue at Witch-hill, at the execution of Burroughs and Proctor; his confident and eager endorsement, as related by Sewall, of the sentences of the Court, at the moment when all others were impressed with silent solemnity, by the spectacle of five persons, professing their innocency, just launched into eternity; his efforts to prolong the prosecutions, in preparing the book containing the trials of the "Malefactors" who had suffered; and his zeal, on all occasions, to " vindicate the Court" and applaud the Judges; all conspired in making it the belief of the whole people that he was, preëminently, answerable for the " hard things that were done " in the prosecutions of the witchcraft."

That it was the general opinion, at home and abroad, can be abundantly proved.

It must be borne in mind, as is explained in my book, that a general feeling prevailed, immediately, and for some years, after the witchcraft " judicial murders," that the whole subject was too horrible to be thought of, or ever mentioned; and as nearly the whole community, either by acting in favor of the proceedings or failing to act against them, had become more or less responsible for them, there was an almost universal understanding to avoid crimination or recrimination. Besides, so far as Cotton Mather was concerned, his professional and social position, great talents and learning, and capacity with a disposition for usefulness, joined to the reverence then felt for Ministers prevented his being assailed even by those who most disapproved his course. Increase Mather was President of the College and head of the Clergy. The prevalent impression that *he* had, to some extent, disapproved of the proceedings, made men unwilling to wound his feelings by severe criticisms upon his son; for, whatever differences might be supposed to exist between them, all well-minded persons respected their natural and honorable sensitiveness to each other's reputation. Reasons like these prevented open demonstrations against both of them. Nevertheless, it is easy to gather sufficient evidence to prove my point.

Thomas Brattle was a Boston merchant of great munificence and eminent talents and attainments. His name is perpetuated by " Brat- " tle-street Church," of which he was the chief founder. Dr. John Eliot, in his *Biographical Dictionary*, speaks of him thus—referring to his letter on the witchcraft of 1692, dated October 8, of that year: " Mr. Brattle wrote an account " of those transactions, which was too plain and " just to be published in those unhappy times, " but has been printed since; and which cannot " be read without feeling sentiments of esteem " for a man, who indulged a freedom of thought

"becoming a Christian and philosopher. He,
"from the beginning, opposed the prejudices of
"the people, the proceedings of the Court, and
"the perverse zeal of those Ministers of the Gos-
"pel, who, by their preaching and conduct,
"caused such real distress to the community.
"They, who called him an infidel, were obliged
"to acknowledge that his wisdom shone with
"uncommon lustre."

His brother, William Brattle, with whom he
seems to have been in entire harmony of opinion, on all subjects, was long an honored in-
structor and Fellow of Harvard College, and
Minister of the First Church, at Cambridge.
He was celebrated here and in England, for his
learning, and endeared to all men by his vir-
tues. He was a Fellow of the Royal Society of
London. Jeremiah Dummer, as well qualified
to pronounce such an opinion as any man of his
time, places him as a preacher above all his
contemporaries, in either Old or New England.

The Brattles were both politically opposed
to the Mathers. But, as matters then stood, in
view of the prevailing infatuation—particularly as the course upon which Phips had determined was not then known—caution and prudence were deemed necessary; and the letter was
confidential. Indeed, all expressions of criticism, on the conduct of the Government, were
required to be so. It is a valuable document,
justifying the reputation the writer had established in life and has borne ever since. Condemning the methods pursued in the Salem
Trials, he says: after stating that "several men,
"for understanding, judgment, and piety, infe-
"rior to few, if any, utterly condemn the pro-
"ceedings" at Salem, "I shall nominate some
"of these to you, viz.: the Hon. Simon Brad-
"street, Esq., our late Governor; the Hon.
"Thomas Danforth, our late Deputy-governor;
"the Rev. Mr. Increase Mather; and the Rev.
"Mr. Samuel Willard."

Bradstreet was ninety years of age, but in the
full possession of his mental faculties. In this
sense, "his eye was not dim, nor his natural
"force abated." Thirteen years before, when
Governor of the Colony, he had refused to
order to execution a woman who had been convicted of witchcraft, in a series of trials that
had gone through all the Courts, with concurring verdicts, confirmed at an adjudication by
the Board of Assistants—as President of which
body, it had been his official duty to pass upon
her the final sentence of death. Juries, Judges,
both branches of the Legislature, and the people,
clamored for her execution; but the brave old
Governor withstood them all, resolutely and in-
exorably: an innocent and good woman and
the honor of the Colony, at that time, were saved. Mr. Hale informs us that Bradstreet refus-

ed to allow the sentence to take effect, for these
reasons: that "a spectre doing mischief in
"her likeness, should not be imputed to her
"person, as a ground of guilt; and that one
"single witness to one fact and another single
"witness to another fact" were not to be esteemed "two witnesses in a matter capital."
No Executive Magistrate has left a record more
honorable to his name, than that of Bradstreet,
on this occasion. If his principles had been
heeded, not a conviction could have been obtained, in 1692. It was because of his known
opposition, that his two sons were cried out
upon and had to fly for their lives. That Brattle was justified in naming Danforth, in this
connection, the conversation of that person with
Sewall, on the fifteenth of October, proves. It
is understood, by many indications, that, although, in former years, inclined to the popular
delusions of the day, touching witchcraft, Willard was an opponent of the prosecutions; and
Brattle must be regarded as having had means
of judging of Increase Mather's views and feelings, on the eighth of October.

This singling out of the father, thereby dis-
tinguishing him from the son, must, I think, be
conclusive evidence, to every man who candid-
ly considers the circumstances of the case and
the purport of the document, that Brattle did
not consider Cotton Mather entitled to be named in the honored list.

Brattle further says: "Excepting Mr. Hale,
"Mr. Noyes, and Mr. Parris, the Rev. Elders,
"almost throughout the whole country, are very
"much dissatisfied." The word "almost,"
leaves room for others to be placed in the same
category with Hale, Noyes, and Parris. The
Reviewer argues that because Cotton Mather is
not named at all, in either list, therefore he must
be counted in the first!

The father and son were associate Ministers
of the same Church; they shared together a
great name, fame, and position; both men of the
highest note, here and abroad, conspicuous before all eyes, standing, hand in hand, in all the
associations and sentiments of the people, united by domestic ties, similar pursuits, and every
form of public action and observation—why did
Brattle, in so marked a manner, separate them,
holding the one up, in an honorable point of
view, and passing over the other, not ever mentioning his name, as the Reviewer observes?

If he really disapproved of the prosecutions
at Salem—if, as the Reviewer positively states,
he "denounced" them—is it not unaccountable
that Brattle did not name him with his father?

These questions press with especial force
upon the Reviewer, under the interpretation he
crowds upon the passage from Brattle, I am now
to cite. If that interpretation can be allowed,

it will, in the face of all that has come to us, make Brattle out to have had a most exalted opinion of Cotton Mather, and render it unaccountable indeed that he did not mention him, in honor, as he did his father and Mr. Willard. The passage is this: "I cannot but highly ap-
"plaud, and think it o r duty to be very thank-
"ful for, the endeavours of several Elders, whose
"lips, I think, should preserve knowledge, and
"whose counsel should, I think, have been more
"regarded, in a case of this nature, than as yet
"it has been: in particular, I cannot but think
"very honorably of the endeavours of a Rev.
"person in Boston, whose good affections to his
"country, in general, and spiritual relation to
"three of the Judges, in particular, has made
"him very solicitous and industrious in this
"matter; and I am fully persuaded, that had
"his notions and proposals been hearkened to
"and followed, when these troubles were in
"their birth, in an ordinary way, they would
"never have grown unto that height which now
"they have. He has, as yet, met with little
"but unkindness, abuse, and reproach, from
"many men; but, I trust, that in after times,
"his wisdom and service will find a more uni-
"versal acknowledgment; and if not, his re-
"ward is with the Lord."

The learned Editor of the Fifth Volume of the *Massachusetts Historical Collections*, First Series, in a note to this passage (*p. 76*), says: "Supposed to be Mr. Willard." Such has always been the supposition. The Reviewer has undertaken to make it out that Cotton Mather is the person referred to by Brattle. These two men were opposed to each other, in the politics of that period. The course of the Mathers, in connection with the loss of the old, and the establishment of the new, Charter, gave rise to much dissatisfaction; and party divisions were quite acrimonious. The language used by Brattle, applauding the public course of the person of whom he was speaking, would be utterly inexplicable, if applied to Mather. The "en-
"deavours, counsels, notions and proposals," to which he alludes, could not have referred to Mather's plans, which I have attempted to explain, because described by Brattle as being in "an ordinary way." "Unkindness, abuse, and "reproach" find an explanation in the fact, that Willard was "cried out upon" and brought into peril of reputation and life, by the creatures of the prosecution. The monstrousness of the supposition that Mather was referred to, would hardly be heightened if it should appear that Brattle supplied Calef with materials in his controversy with Mather.

The language, throughout, is in conformity with the political relations between Brattle and Willard. The side the latter had espoused was put beyond question by his appearing, on the fifteenth of November, at Elisha Cook's Thanksgiving; and that was the same occupied by Brattle. But the question is settled by the fact that *three of the Judges* belonged to Willard's Congregation and Church, whereas only *one* belonged to the Church of the Mathers. The Reviewer says: "We do not assert that this infer-
"ence is not the correct one." But, in spite of this substantial admission, with that strange propensity to overturn all the conclusions of history to glorify Cotton Mather, at the expense of others, and even, in this instance, against his own better judgment, he labors to make us believe—what he himself does not venture to "assert"—that the "spiritual relation" in which Mather stood to three of the Judges, was not, what, in those days and ever since, it has been understood to mean, that of a Pastor with his flock, but nothing more than intimate friendsh p. If this was what Brattle meant, he would have said at least *four* of the Judges, for, at that time, Sewall was in full accord with Mather. They took counsel together. It was at the house of Sewall that the preparation of the *Wonders of the Invisible World* was finally arranged with Mather; and he, alone, of all the side Judges, united with Stoughton, some days after the date of Brattle's letter, in endorsing and commending that work.

If the expression, "spiritual relations," is divorced from its proper sense, and made to mean sympathy of opinion or agreement in counsels, it ill becomes the Reviewer to try to make it out that Mather held that relation with *any of the Judges*. He represents him, throughout his article, as at sword's points with the Court. He says that he "denounced" its course, "as illegal, "uncharitable, and cruel." There is, indeed, not a shadow of foundation for this statement, as to Mather's relation to the Court; but it absolutely precludes the Reviewer from such an interpretation as he attempts, of the expression of Brattle.

The Reviewer says: "If Mr. Mather is not "alluded to, in this paragraph, he is omitted "altogether from the narrative, except as spiritual "adviser of the persons condemned."

This is an instance of the way in which this writer establishes history. Without any and against all evidence, in the license of his imagination alone, he had thrown out the suggestion that Mather attended the executions, as the ministerial comforter and counsellor of the sufferers. Then, by a sleight of hand, he transforms this "phantasy" of his own brain into an unquestionable fact.

If Mr. Mather is not alluded to in the following passage from Brattle's letter, who is! "I "cannot but admire, that any should go with

"their distempered friends and relatives to the
"afflicted children to know what these distem-
"pered friends ail; whether they are not be-
"witched; who it is that afflicts them · and the
"like. It is true, I know no reason why these
"afflicted may not be consulted as well as any
"other, if so be that it was only their natural
"and ordinary knowledge that was had recourse
"to; but it is not on this notion that these af-
"flicted children are sought unto; but as they
"have a supernatural knowledge—a knowledge
"which they obtain by their holding correspond-
"ence with spectres or evil spirits—as they them-
"selves grant. This consulting of these afflicted
"children, as abovesaid, seems to me a very gross
"evil, a real abomination, not fit to be known in
"New England, and yet is a thing practiced, not
"only by Tom and John—I mean the ruder and
"more ignorant sort—but by many who profess
"high, and pass among us for some of the better
"sort. This is that which aggravates the evil
"and makes it heinous and tremendous; and
"yet this is not the worst of it, for, as sure as I
"now write to you, even some of our civil lead-
"ers and spiritual teachers, who, I think, should
"punish and preach down such sorcery and
"wickedness, do yet allow of, encourage, yea,
"and practice, this very abomination.

"I know there are several worthy gentlemen,
"in Salem, who account this practice as an abom-
"ination; have trembled to see the methods of
"this nature which others have used; and have
"declared themselves to think the practice to be
"very evil and corrupt; but all avails little with
"the abettors of the said practice."

Does not this stern condemnation fall on the
head of the "spiritual teacher," who received
constant communications from the spectral world,
fastening the charge of diabolical confederacy
upon other persons, in confidential interviews
with confessing witches—not to mention the
Goodwin girls;—whose boast it was, "it may be
"no man living has had more people, under pre-
"ternatural and astonishing circumstances, cast
"by the Providence of God into his more par-
"ticular care than I have had:" and that he had
kept to himself information thus obtained, which,
if he had not suppressed it, would have led to
the conviction of "such witches as ought to
"die;" who sought to have the exclusive right
of receiving such communications conferred upon
him, "by the authority;" who, at that time, was
holding this intercourse with persons pretending
to spectral visions; and, the next year, held such
relations with Margaret Rule?

The next evidence in support of the opinion
that Cotton Mather was considered, at the time,
as identified with the proceedings at Salem, in
1692, although circumstantial, cannot, I think,
but be regarded as quite conclusive.

Immediately after the prosecutions terminated,
measures began to be developed to remove Mr.
Parris from his ministry. The reaction early took
effect where the outrages of the delusion had
been most flagrant; and the injured feelings of
the friends of those who had been so cruelly cut
off, and of all who had suffered in their characters and condition, found expression. A movement was made, directly and personally, upon Parris, in consequence of his conspicuous lead in the
prosecutions; showing itself, first, in the form of
litigation, in the Courts, of questions of salary
and the adjustment of accounts. Soon, it broke
out in the Church; and satisfaction was demanded, by aggrieved brethren, in the methods appropriate to ecclesiastical action. The charges here
made against him were exclusively in reference
to his course, at the Examinations and Trials, in
1692. The conflict, thus initiated, is one of the
most memorable in our Church History. Parris
and his adherents resisted, for a long time, the
rightful and orderly demands of his opponents
for a Mutual Council. At length, many of the
Ministers, who sympathized with the aggrieved
brethren, felt it their duty to interpose, and addressed a letter to Mr. Parris, giving him to understand that they were of opinion he ought to
comply with the demand for a Council. This letter, dated the fourteenth of June, 1694, was signed
by several of the neighboring Ministers, and by
James Allen, of the First, and Samuel Willard, of
the Old South, Churches, in Boston, *but not by the
Mathers.* On the tenth of September, a similar
letter was written to him, also signed by neighboring Ministers, and Mr. Allen, and Mr. Willard,
but not by the Mathers.

Not daring to refuse any longer, Parris, professedly yielding to the demand, consented to a
Mutual Council, but avoided it, in this way.
Each party was to select three Churches, to maintain its interests and give friendly protection to
its rights and feelings. The aggrieved brethren
selected the Churches of Rowley, Salisbury and
Ipswich. Parris undertook to object to the
Church of Ipswich; and refused to proceed, if it
was invited. Of course, the aggrieved brethren
persisted in their right to name the Churches on
their side. Knowing that they had the right so
to do, and that public opinion would sustain them
in it, Parris escaped the dilemma, by calling an
ex parte Council; and the Churches invited to it
were those of North Boston, Weymouth, Malden,
and Rowley. The first was that of the Mathers.
That Parris was right in relying upon the Rev.
Samuel Torrey of Weymouth, is rendered probable by the circumstance that, of the names of
the fourteen Ministers, including all those known
to have been opposed to the proceedings at Salem, attached to the recommendation of the
Cases of Conscience, his is not one; and may

be considered as made certain by the fact recorded by Sewall, that he was opposed to the discontinuance of the Trials. The Pastor of the Malden Church was the venerable Michael Wigglesworth, a gentleman of the highest repute; who had declined the Presidency of Harvard College; whose son and grand-son became Professors in that institution; and whose descendants still sustain the honor of their name and lineage. From the tone of his writings, it is quite probable that he favored the witchcraft proceedings, at the beginning; but the change of mind, afterwards strongly expressed, had, perhaps, then begun to be experienced, for he did not respond to the call, as his name does not appear in the record of the Council. The fact that Parris chiefly depended upon the Church at North Boston, of which Cotton Mather was Pastor, to sustain his cause, in a Council, whose whole business was to pass upon his conduct in the witchcraft prosecutions, is quite decisive. That Church was named by him, from the first to the last, and neither of the other Boston Churches. It shows that he turned to Cotton Mather, more than to any other Minister, to be his champion.

It is further decisively proved that the reaction had become strong among the Ministers, by the unusual steps they took to prevent that Council being under the sway of such men as Cotton Mather and Torrey, thereby prolonging the mischief. A meeting of the "Reverend Elders of "the Bay" was held; and Mr. Parris was given to understand that, in their judgment, the Churches of Messrs. Allen and Willard ought also to be invited. He bitterly resented this, and saw that it sealed his fate; but felt the necessity of yielding to it. The addition of those two Churches, with their Pastors, determined the character and result of the Council, and gave new strength to the aggrieved brethren, who soon succeeded in compelling Parris and his friends to agree to submit the whole matter to the arbitration of three men, mutually chosen, whose decision should be final.

The umpire selected in behalf of the opponents of Parris was no other than Elisha Cook, the head of the party arrayed against Mather. Wait Winthrop appears to have been selected by Parris; and Samuel Sewall was mutually agreed upon. Two of the three, who thus passed final judgment against the proceedings at the Salem Trials, sat on the Bench of the Special Court of Oyer and Terminer. The case of the aggrieved brethren was presented to the Arbitrators in a document, signed by four men, as "Attorneys of the "people of the Village," each one of whom had been struck at, in the time of the prosecutions. It *exclusively* refers to Mr. Parris's conduct, in the witchcraft prosecutions; to "his believing "the Devil's accusations;" and to his going to the

accusing girls, to know of them "who afflicted" them. For these reasons, and these alone, they "submit the whole" to the decision of the Arbitrators, concluding thus: "to determine wheth- "er we are, or ought to be, any ways obliged to "honor, respect, and support such an instrument "of our miseries." The Arbitrators decided that they *ought not*; fixed the sum to be paid to Parris, as a final settlement; and declared the ministerial relation, between him and the people of the Village, dissolved.

With this official statement of the grounds on which his dismission was demanded and obtained, before his eyes, as printed by Calef (*p. 65*), this Reviewer says that Parris remained the Minister of Salem Village, five years "after the "witchcraft excitement;" and further says, "the "immediate cause of his leaving, was his quar- "rel with the Parish, concerning thirty cords of "wood and the fee of the parsonage." He thus thinks, by a dash of his pen, to strike out the record of the fact that the main, in truth, the only, ground on which Parris was dismissed, was the part he bore in the witchcraft prosecutions. The salary question had been pending in the Courts; but it was wholly left out of view, by the the party demanding his dismission. It had nothing to do with *dismission;* was a question of *contract* and *debt;* and was absorbed in the "excitement," *which had never ceased,* about the witchcraft prosecutions. The Arbitrators did not decide those questions, about salary and the balance of accounts, except as incidental to the other question, of *dismission.*

The feeling among the inhabitants of Salem Village, that Cotton Mather was in sympathy with Mr. Parris, during the witchcraft prosecutions, is demonstrated by the facts I have adduced connected with the controversy between them and the latter, and most emphatically by their choice of Elisha Cook, as the Arbitrator, on their part. Surely no persons, of that day, understood the matter better than they did. Indeed, they could not have been mistaken about it. It remained the settled conviction of that community.

When the healing ministry of the successor of Parris, Joseph Green, was brought to a close, by the early death of that good man, in 1715, and the whole Parish, still feeling the dire effects of the great calamity of 1692, were mourning their bereavement, expressed in their own language: "the choicest flower, and greenest olive- "tree, in the garden of our God here, cut down "in its prime and flourishing estate," they passed a vote, earnestly soliciting the Rev. William Brattle of Cambridge, to visit them. He was always a known opponent of Cotton Mather. To have selected him to come to them, in their distress and destitution, indicates the views then prevalent in the Village. He went to them and guided them by his advice, until they obtained a new Minister.

The mention of the fact by Mr. Hale, already stated, that Cotton Mather's book, *Memorable Providences*, was used as an authority by the Judges at the Salem Trials, shows that the author of that work was regarded by Hale as, to that extent at least, responsibly connected with the prosecutions.

I pass over, for the present, the proceedings and writings of Robert Calef.

After the lapse of a few years, a feeling, which had been slowly, but steadily, rising among the people, that some general and public acknowledgment ought to be made by all who had been engaged in the proceedings of 1692, and especially by the authorities, of the wrongs committed in that dark day, became too strong to be safely disregarded. On the seventeenth of December, 1696, Stoughton, then acting as Governor, issued a Proclamation, ordaining, in his name and that of the Council and Assembly, a Public Fast, to be kept on the fourteenth of January, to implore that the anger of God might be turned away, and His hand, then stretched over the people in manifold judgments, lifted. After referring to the particular calamities they were suffering and to the many days that had been spent in solemn addresses to the throne of mercy, it expresses a fear that something was still wanting to accompany their supplications, and proceeds to refer, specially, to the witchcraft tragedy. It was on the occasion of this Fast, that Judge Sewall acted the part, in the public assembly of the old South Church, for which his name will ever be held in dear and honored memory.

The public mind was, no doubt, gratified and much relieved, but not satisfied, by this demonstration. The Proclamation did not, after all, meet its demands. Upon careful examination and deliberate reflection, it rather aggravated the prevalent feeling. Written, as was to be supposed, by Stoughton, it could not represent a reaction in which he took no part. It spoke of "mistakes on either hand," and used general forms, "wherein we have done amiss, to do so "no more." It endorsed, in a new utterance, the delusion, sheltering the proper agents of the mischief, by ascribing it all to "Satan and his "instruments, through the awful judgment of "God:" and no atonement, for the injuries to the good name and estates of the sufferers, not to speak of the lives that had been cut off, was suggested. The conviction was only deepened, in all good minds, that something more ought to be done. Mr. Hale, of Beverly, met the obligation pressing upon his sense of justice and appealing to him with especial force, by writing his book, from which the following passages are extracted: "I would come yet nearer to our own "times, and bewail the errors and mistakes that "have been, in the year 1692—by following such "traditions of our fathers, maxims of the com- "mon law, and precedents and principles, which "now we may see, weighed in the balance of "the sanctuary, are found too light—Such was "the darkness of that day, the tortures and "lamentations of the afflicted, and the power of "former precedents, that we walked in the "clouds and could not see our way—I would "humbly propose whether it be not expedient "that somewhat more should be publicly done "than yet hath, for clearing the good name and "reputation of some that have suffered upon this "account."

The Rev. John Higginson, Senior Pastor of the First Church in Salem, then eighty-two years of age, in a recommendatory *Epistle to the Reader*, prefixed to Mr. Hale's book, dated the twenty-third of March, 1698, after stating that, "under the in- "firmities of a decrepit old age, he stirred little "abroad, and was much disenabled (both in body "and mind) from knowing and judging of oc- "currents and transactions of that time," proceeds to say that he was "more willing to accompany" Mr. Hale "to the press," because he thought his "treatise needful and useful upon divers accounts;" among others specified by him, is the following: "That whatever errors or mistakes we fell into, "in the dark hour of temptation that was upon "us, may be (upon more light) so discovered, "acknowledged, and disowned by us, as that it "may be matter of warning and caution to those "that come after us, that they may not fall into "the like.—*I. Cor.* x, 11. *Felix quem faciunt "aliena pericula cautum.* I would also pro- "pound, and leave it as an object of considera- "tion, to our honored Magistrates and Reverend "Ministers, whether the equity of that law in "*Leviticus.* Chap. iv. for a sin-offering for the "Rulers and for the Congregation, in the case of "sins of ignorance, when they come to be known, "be not obliging, and for direction to us in a "Gospel way." The venerable man concludes by saying that "it shall be the prayer of him who "is daily waiting for his change and looking "for the mercy of the Lord Jesus Christ, unto "eternal life," that the "blessing of Heaven may "go along with this little treatise to attain the "good ends thereof."

Judge Sewall, too, and the Jury that had given the verdicts at the Trials, in 1692, publicly and emphatically acknowledged that they had been led into error.

All these things afford decisive and affecting evidence of a prevalent conviction that a great wrong had been committed. The vote passed by the Church at Salem Village, on the fourteenth of February, 1703—"We are, through

"God's mercy to us, convinced that we were,
"at that dark day, under the power of those
"errors which then prevailed in the land."
"We desire that this may be entered in our
"Church-book," "that so God may forgive our
"Sin, and may be atoned for the land; and we
"humbly pray that God will not leave us any
"more to such errors and sins"—affords striking proof that the right feeling had penetrated
the whole community. On the eighth of July,
of that same year, nearly the whole body of the
Clergy of Essex-county addressed a Memorial
to the General Court, in which they say, "There
"is great reason to fear that innocent persons
"then suffered, and that God may have a con-
"troversy with the land upon that account."

Nothing of the kind, however, was ever heard
from the Ministers of Boston and the vicinity.
Why did they not join their voices in this prayer, going up elsewhere, from all concerned, for
the divine forgiveness? We know that most
of them felt right Samuel Willard and James
Allen did; and so did William Brattle, of Cambridge. Their silence cannot, it seems to me,
be accounted for, but by considering the degree
to which they were embarrassed by the relation
of the Mathers to the affair. One brave-hearted
old man remonstrated against their failure to
meet the duty of the hour, and addressed his
remonstrance to the right quarter. The Rev.
Michael Wigglesworth, a Fellow of Harvard
College, and honored in all the Churches, wrote
a letter to Increase Mather, dated July 22,
1704 [*Mather Papers*, 647], couched in strong
and bold terms, beginning thus:

"REV. AND DEAR SR. I am right well assur-
"ed that both yourself, your son, and the rest of
"our brethren with you in Boston, have a deep
"sense upon your spirits of the awful symptoms
"of the Divine displeasure that we lie under
"at this day." After briefly enumerating the
public calamities of the period, he continues.
"I doubt not but you are all endeavouring to
"find out and discover to the people the caus-
"es of God's controversy, and how they are to
"be removed; to help forward this difficult and
"necessary work, give me leave to impart some
"of my serious and solemn thoughts. I fear
"(amongst our many other provocations) that
"God hath a controversy with us about what
"was done in the time of the Witchcraft. I
"fear that innocent blood hath been shed, and
"that *many have had their hands defiled there-
"with*." After expressing his belief that the
Judges acted conscientiously, and that the
persons concerned were deceived, he proceeds:
"Be it then that it was done ignorantly. Paul,
"a Pharisee, persecuted the Church of God,
"shed the blood of God's Saints, and yet obtain-
"ed mercy, because he did it in ignorance; but

"how doth he bewail it, and shame himself for it,
"before God and men afterwards. [*I. Tim. i. 13,
"16.*] I think, and am verily persuaded, God ex-
"pects that we do the like, in order to our obtain-
"ing his pardon: I mean by a Public and Sol-
"emn acknowledgment of it and humiliation
"for it; and the more particularly and person-
"ally it is done by all that have been actors, the
"more pleasing it will be to God, and more ef-
"fectual to turn away his judgments from the
"Land, and to prevent his wrath from falling
"upon the persons and families of such as have
"been most concerned.

"I know this is a *Noli Me tangere*, but what
"shall we do? Must we pine away in our in-
"iquities, rather than boldly declare the Counsel
"of God, who tells us, [*Isaie i. 15.*] 'When you
"'make many prayers, I will not hear you, your
"'hands are full of blood.'"

He further says that he believes that "the
"whole country lies under a curse to this day,
"and will do, till some effectual course be taken
"by our honored Governor and General Court to
"make amends and reparation" to the families
of such as were condemned "for supposed
"witchcraft," or have "been ruined by taking
"away and making havoc of their estates." After continuing the argument, disposing of the excuse that the country was too impoverished to
do any thing in that way, he charges his correspondent to communicate his thoughts to "the
"Rev. Samuel Willard and the rest of our breth-
"ren in the ministry," that action may be taken,
without delay. He concludes his plain and earnest appeal and remonstrance, in these words:
"I have, with a weak body and trembling hand,
"endeavoured to leave my testimony before I
"leave the world; and having left it with you
"(my Rev. Brethren) I hope I shall leave this
"life with more peace, when God seeth meet to
"call me hence."

He died within a year. When the tone of this
letter is carefully considered, and the pressure of
its forcible and bold reasoning, amounting to expostulation, is examined, it can hardly be questioned that it was addressed to the persons who
most needed to be appealed to. But no effect
appears to have been produced by it.

In introducing his report of the Trials, contained in the *Wonders of the Invisible World*,
Cotton Mather, alluding to the "surviving rela-
"tions" of those who had been executed, says:
"The Lord comfort them." It was poor consolation he gave them in that book—holding up
their parents, wives, and husbands, as "Malefac-
"tors." Neither he nor his father ever expressed a sentiment in harmony with those uttered by
Hale, Higginson, or Wigglesworth—on the contrary, Cotton Mather, writing a year after the Salem Tragedy, almost chuckles over it: "In the

"whole—the Devil got just nothing—but God
"got praises. Christ got subjects, the Holy
"Spirit got temples, the church got addition,
"and the souls of men got everlasting benefits."
"—*Calef, 12.*

Stoughton remained nearly the whole time, until his death, in May, 1702, in control of affairs. By his influence over the Government and that of the Mathers over the Clergy, nothing was done to remove the dark stigma from the honor of the Province, and no seasonable or adequate reparation ever made for the Great Wrong.

I am additionally indebted to the kindness of Dr. Moore for the following extracts from a Sermon to the General Assembly, delivered by Cotton Mather, in 1709, intitled *Theopolis America-* "*na. Pure Gold in the market place.*"

"In two or three too Memorable *Days of* "*Temptation*, that have been upon us, there "have been *Errors* Committed. You are always "ready to Declare unto all the World, 'That you "'disapprove those Errors.' You are willing to "inform all mankind with your *Declarations.*

"That no man may be Persecuted, because he "is Conscienciously not of the same Religious "Opinions, with those that are uppermost.

"And: That Persons are not to be judged "Confederates with Evil Spirits, merely because "the Evil Spirits do make Possessed People cry "out upon them.

"Could any thing be Proposed further, by "way of Reparation, [Besides the General Day "of Humiliation, which was appointed and ob- "served thro' the Province, to bewayl the Errors "of our Dark time, some years ago:] You would "be willing to hearken to it."

The suggestion thus made, not, it must be confessed, in very urgent terms, did not, it is probable, produce much impression. The preacher seemed to rest upon the Proclamation issued by Stoughton, some eleven years before. Coupling the two errors specified together, was not calculated to give effect to the recomendation. Public opinion was not, then, prepared to second such enlightened views as to religious liberty.

It is very noticable that Mather here must be considered as admiting that "in the Dark time," persons were judged "Confederates with Evil "Spirits," "merely" because of Spectral Evidence.

All that was said, on this occasion, does not amount to any thing, as an expression of *personal* opinion or feeling, relating to points on which Hale and Higginson uttered their deep sensibility, and Wigglesworth had addressed to the Mathers and other Ministers, his solemn and searching appeal. The duty of reparation for the great wrong was thrown off upon others, than those particularly and prominently responsible.

Nothing has led me to suppose that Cotton Mather was cruel or heartless, in his natural or

habitual disposition. He never had the wisdom or dignity to acknowledge, as an individual, or as *one of the Clergy*, or to propose specific reparation for, the fearful mischiefs, sufferings and horrors growing out of the witchcraft prosecutions. The extent to which he was at the time, and probably always continued to be, the victim of baleful superstitions, is his only apology, and we must allow it just weight.

A striking instance of the occasional ascendency of his better feelings, and of the singular methods in which he was accustomed to act, is presented in the following extract from his Diary, at a late period of his life. We may receive it as an indication that he was not insensible of his obligation to do good, where, with his participation, so much evil had been done: "There is a town "in this country, namely, Salem, which has many "poor and bad people in it, and such as are es- "pecially scandalous for staying at home on the "Lord's day. I wrapped up seven distinct par- "cels of money and annexed seven little books "about repentance, and seven of the monitory "letter against profane absence from the house "of God. I sent those things with a nameless "letter unto the Minister of that Town, and de- "sired and empowered him to dispense the char- "ity in his own name, hoping thereby the more "to ingratiate his ministry with the people. "Who can tell how far the good Angels of Heav- "en cooperate in these proceedings?"

XVI.

HISTORY OF OPINION AS TO COTTON MATHER, CONTINUED. FRANCIS HUTCHINSON. DANIEL NEAL. ISAAC WATTS. THOMAS HUTCHINSON. WILLIAM BENTLEY. JOHN ELIOT. JOSIAH QUINCY.

It was the common opinion in England, that the Mathers, particularly the younger, were pre-eminently responsible for the proceedings at Salem, in 1692. Francis Hutchinson, in the work from which I have quoted, speaks of the whole system of witchcraft doctrine, as "fantastic no- "tions," which are "so far from raising their "sickly visions into legal evidence, that they are "grounded upon the very dregs of Pagan and "Popish superstitions, and leave the lives of in- "nocent men naked, without defence against "them;" and in giving a list of books, written for upholding them, mentions, "Mr. Increase "and Mr. Cotton Mather's several tracts;" and, in his Chapter on Witchcraft in Massachusetts, in 1692, commends the book of "Mr. Calef, a Mer- "chant in that Plantation."

About the same time, the Rev. Daniel Neal, the celebrated author of the *History of the Puritans*, wrote a *History of New England*, in which he gives place to a brief, impartial, and just account of the witchcraft proceedings, in 1692. He abstains from personal criticisms, but expresses this general sentiment: "Strange were "the mistakes that some of the wisest and best "men of the country committed on this occa- "sion; which must have been fatal to the whole "Province, if God, in his Providence, had not "mercifully interposed." The only sentence that contains a stricture on Cotton Mather, partic- ularly, is that in which he thus refers to his statement that a certain confession was *freely* made. Neal quietly suggests, "whether the act "of a man in prison, and under apprehension of "death, may be called free. I leave others to "judge." Dr. Isaac Watts, having read Neal's book, thought it necessary to write a letter to Cotton Mather, dated, February 19, 1720; (*Mass- achusetts Historical Collections, I., s., 200*) and, describing a conversation he had just been having with Neal, says: "There is another "thing, wherein my brother is solicitous lest he "should have displeased you, and that is, the "Chapter on Witchcraft, but, as he has related "matters of fact, by comparison of several au- "thors, he hopes that you will forgive that he "has not fallen into your sentiments exactly." The anxiety felt by Neal and Watts, lest the feel- ings of Mather might be wounded, shows what they thought of his implication with the affair. This inference is rendered unavoidable, when we examine Neal's book and find that he quotes or refers to Calef, all along, without the slightest question as to his credibility, receiving his state- ments and fully recognizing his authority. In- deed, his references to Calef are about ten to one oftener than to Mather. The attempt of Neal and Watts to smoothe the matter down, by say- ing that the former had been led to his conclu- sions by "a comparison of several authors," could have given little satisfaction to Mather, as the authors whom he chiefly refers to, are Calef and Mather; and, comparing them with each other, he followed Calef.

The impression thus held in England, even by Mather's friends and correspondents, that he was unpleasantly connected with the Witchcraft of 1692, has been uniformly experienced, on both sides of the water, until this Reviewer's attempt to erase it from the minds of men.

Thomas Hutchinson was born in 1711, and brought up in the neighborhood of the Mathers; finishing his collegiate course and taking his Bach- elor's degree at Harvard College, in 1727, a year before the death of Cotton Mather. He had op- portunities to form a correct judgment about Sa- lem Witchcraft and the chief actors in the pro- ceedings, greater than any man of his day; but his close family connection with the Mathers imposed some restraint upon his expressions; not enough, however, to justify the statement of the

Reviewer that he does not mention the "agency" of Cotton Mather in that transaction. There are several very distinct references to Mather's "agency," in Hutchinson's account of the trans- actions connected with Salem Witchcraft, some of which I have cited. I ask to whom does the following passage refer?—ii., 63.—"One of the "Ministers, who, in the time of it, was fully "convinced that the complaining persons were "no impostors, and who vindicated his own con- "duct and that of the Court, in a Narrative he "published, remarks, not long after, in his Diary, "that many were of opinion that innocent blood "had been shed."

This shows that Hutchinson regarded Cotton Mather's agency in the light in which I have rep- resented it; that he considered him as wholly committed to the then prevalent delusion; as acting a part that identified him with the prose- cutions; and that the Narrative he published was a joint vindication of himself and the Court. Hutchinson fastens the passage upon Mather, by the reference to the Diary; and while he says that it contained a statement, that many believed the persons who suffered innocent, he avoids saying that such was the opinion of the author of the Diary.

Finally, his taking particular pains to do it, by giving a Note to the purpose of expressing his confidence in Calef, pronouncing him a "fair re- "lator"—ii, 56—proves that Governor Hutchin- son held the opinion about Mather's "agency," which has always heretofore been ascribed to him.

William Bentley, D. D., was born in Boston, and for a large part of the first half of his life, resid- ed, as his family had done for a long period, in the North part of that Town. He was of a turn of mind to gather all local traditions, and, through all his days, devoted to antiquarian pursuits. No one of his period paid more attention to the subject of the witchcraft delusion. For much of our information concerning it, we are indebted to his *History and Description of Salem*, printed in 1800—*Massachusetts Historical Collections, I., vi.*—After relating many of its incidents, he breaks forth in condemnation of those who, disapproving, at the time, of the proceed- ings, did not come out and denounce them. Holding the opinion, which had come down from the beginning, that Increase Mather disap- proved of the transaction, he indignantly repudi- ates the idea of giving him any credit therefor. "Increase Mather did not oppose Cotton Mather" —this is the utterance of a received, and, to him, unquestioned, opinion that Cotton Mather ap- proved of, and was a leading agent in, the pros- ecutions.

The views of Dr. John Eliot, are freely given, to the same effect, in his *Biographical Diction- ry*, as will presently be shown.

The late Josiah Quincy had studied the annals of Massachusetts with the thoroughness with which he grappled every subject to which he turned his thoughts. His ancestral associations covered the whole period of its history; and all the channels of the local traditions of Boston were open to his enquiring and earnest mind. His *History of Harvard University* is a monument that will stand forever. In that work, he speaks of the agreement of Stoughton's views with those of the Mathers; and, in connection with the witchcraft delusion, says that both of them "had "an efficient agency in producing and prolong- "ing that excitement." "The conduct of In- "crease Mather, in relation to it, was marked "with caution and political skill; but that "of his son, Cotton Mather, was headlong, zeal- "ous, and fearless, both as to character and con- "sequences. In its commencement and pro- "gress, his activity is every-where conspicuous."

The Reviewer represents Mr. Quincy as merely repeating what I had said in my Lectures. He makes the same reckless assertion in reference to Bancroft, the late William B. O. Peabody, D, D., and every one else, who has written upon the subject, since 1831. The idea that Josiah Quincy "took his cue" from me, is simply preposterous. He does not refer to me, nor give any indication that he had ever seen my *Lectures*, but cites Ca- lef, as his authority, over and over again. Dr. Peabody refers to Calef throughout, and draws upon him freely and with confidence, as every one else, who has written about the transaction, has probably done.

It may safely be said, that no historical fact has ever been more steadily recognized, than the action and, to a great degree, controlling agency, of Cotton Mather, in supporting and promoting the witchcraft proceedings of 1692. That it has, all along, been the established conviction of the public mind, is proved by the chronological series of names I have produced. Thomas Hutchinson, John Eliot, William Bentley, and Josiah Quincy, cover the whole period from Cotton Mather's day to this. They knew, as well as any other men that can be named, the current opinions, trans- mitted sentiments, and local and personal annals, of Boston. They reflect with certainty an assur- ance, running in an unbroken course over a cen- tury and a half. Their family connections, so- cial position, conversance with events, and famil- iar knowledge of what men thought, believed, and talked about, give to their concurrent and continuous testimony, a force and weight of au- thority that are decisive; and demonstrate that, instead of my having invented and originated the opinion of Cotton Mather's agency in the mat- ter now under consideration, I have done no more than to restate what has been believed and uttered from the beginning.

The writer in the *North American* says: "Within the last forty years, there has grown "up a fashion, among our historical writers, of "defaming his character and underrating his "productions. For a specimen of these attacks, "the reader is referred to a *Supposed Letter* "*from Rev. Cotton Mather, D. D., with com-* "*ments on the same by James Savage.*" The article mentioned consists of the "supposed let- "ter," and a very valuable communication from the late Rev. Samuel Sewall, with some items by Mr. Savage—[*Massachusetts Historical Collec- tions, IV., ii., 122.*] Neither of these enlightened, faithful, and indefatigable scholars is to be disposed of in this style. They followed no "fashion;" and their venerable names are held in honor by all true disciples of antiquarian and genealogical learning. The author of such works, in this department, as Mr. Savage has produced, cannot be thus set aside by a magiste- rial and supercilious waving of the hand of this Reviewer.

XVII.

THE EFFECT UPON THE POWER OF THE MATHERS, IN THE PUBLIC AFFAIRS OF THE PROVINCE, OF THEIR CONNECTION WITH WITCHCRAFT.

The Reviewer takes exception to my statement, that the connection of the Mathers with the witchcraft business, "broke down" their influ- ence in public affairs. What are the facts? It has been shown, that the administration of Sir William Phips, at its opening, was under their control, to an extent never equalled by that of private men over a Government. The prayers of Cotton Mather were fully answered; and if wise and cautious counsels had been given, what both father and son had so coveted, in the political management of the Province, would have been permanently realized. But, aiming to arm them- selves with terrific and overwhelming strength, by invoking the coöperation of forces from the spir- itual, invisible, and diabolical world, with rash "precipitancy," they hurried on the witchcraft prosecutions. The consequence was, that in six months, the whole machinery on which they had placed their reliance, was prostrate. At the very next election, Elisha Cook was chosen and Na- thaniel Saltonstall rechosen, to the Council; and, ever after, the Mathers were driven to the wall, in desperate and unavailing self-defence.

No party or faction could claim the Earl of Bellamont, during his brief administration, cov- ering but fourteen months. Although the only nobleman ever sent over as Governor of Massa- chusetts, more than all others, he conciliated the general good will. His short term of office and wise policy prevented any particular advantage to the Mathers from the dedication to him of the

Life of Phips. During the entire period, between 1692 and the arrival of Dudley to the Government, the opponents of the Mathers were steadily increasing their strength. Opposition to Increase Mather was soon developed in attempts to remove him from the Presidency of Harvard College. In 1701, an Order was passed by the General Court, "that no man should act as President "of the College, who did not reside at Cam-"bridge." This decided the matter. Increase Mather resigned, on the sixth of September following; and, the same day, the Rev. Samuel Willard took charge of the College, under the title of Vice-president, and acted as President, to the acceptance of the people and with the support of the Government of the Province, to his death, in 1707—all the while allowed to retain the pastoral connection with his Church, in Boston.

Joseph Dudley arrived from England, on the eleventh of June, 1702, with his Commission, as Captain-general and Governor of the Province. On the sixteenth, he made a call upon Cotton Mather, who relates the interview in his Diary. It seems that Mather made quite a speech to the new Governor, urging him "to carry an indiffer-"ent hand toward all parties," and explaining his meaning thus: "By no means, let any people "have cause to say that you take all your meas-"ures from the two Mr. Mathers." He then added: "By the same rule, I may say without of-"fence, by no means let any people say that "you go by no measures in your conduct but Mr. "Byfield's and Mr. Leverett's. This I speak, "not from any personal prejudice against the "gentlemen, but from a due consideration of "the disposition of the people, and as a service "to your Excellency."

Dudley—whether judging rightly or not is to be determined by taking into view his position, the then state of parties, and the principles of human nature—evidently regarded this as a trap. If he had followed the advice, and kept aloof from Byfield and Leverett, they would have been placed at a distance from him, and he would necessarily have fallen into the hands of the Mathers. He may have thought that the only way to avoid such a result, was for him to explain to those gentlemen his avoidance of them, by mentioning to them what Mather had said to him, thereby signifying to them, that, as a matter of policy, he thought it best to adopt the suggestion and stand aloof from both sides. Whether acting from this consideration or from resentment, he informed them of it; whereupon Mather inserted this in his Diary: "The WRETCH "went unto those men and told them that I had "advised him to be no ways directed by them, "and inflamed them into implacable rage against "me."

After this, the relations between Dudley and the Mathers must have been sufficiently awkward and uncomfortable; but no particular public demonstrations appear to have been made, on either side, for some time.

Mr. Willard died on the twelfth of September, 1707; and the great question again rose as to the proper person to be called to the head of the College. The extraordinary learning of Cotton Mather undoubtedly gave him commanding and preeminent claims in the public estimation; and he had reason to think that the favorite object of his ambition was about to be attained. But he was doomed to bitter disappointment. On the twenty-eighth of October, the Corporation, through its senior member, the Rev. James Allen of Boston, communicated to the Governor the vote of that body, appointing the "Honorable John Lev-"erett" to the Presidency; and, on the fourteenth of January, 1708, he was publicly inducted to office. The Mathers could stand it no longer; but, six days after, addressed, each, a letter to Dudley, couched in the bitterest and most abusive terms.—[*Massachusetts Historical Society's Collections, I., iii., 126.*] No explosions of disappointed politicians and defeated aspirants for office, in our day, surpass these letters. They show how deeply the writers were stung. They heap maledictions on the Governor, without any of the restraints of courtesy or propriety. They charge him with all sorts of malversation in office, bribery, peculation, extortion, falseness, hypocrisy, and even murder; imputing to him "the guilt of innocent blood," because, many years before, he had, as Chief-justice of New York, presided at the Trial of Leisler and Milburn; and averring that "those men were not "only murdered, but barbarously murdered."

It is observable that some of the heinous crimes charged upon Dudley, occurred before his arrival as Governor of Massachusetts, in 1702; and that, in these very letters, they remind him that it was, in part, by their influence that he was then appointed, and that a letter from Cotton Mather, in favor of his appointment, was read before "the late King William." Both the Mathers were remarkable for a lack of vision, in reference to the logical bearing of what they said. It did not occur to them, that the fact of their soliciting his appointment closed their mouths from making charges for public acts well known to them at the time.

Dudley says that he was assured by the Mathers, on his arrival, that he had the favor of all good men; and Cotton Mather, in his letter, reminds him that he signalized his friendly feelings, by giving to the public, on that occasion, the "portraiture of a good man." It is proved, therefore, by the evidence on both sides, that, well knowing all about the Leisler affair and other crimes alleged against him, they were ready, and most desirous, to secure his favor and friendship; and to identify themselves with his administration.

In alluding to these letters, Hutchinson (*History, ii, 194,*) says: "In times when party spirit "prevails, what will not a Governor's enemies "believe, however injurious and absurd? At "such a time, he was charged with dispensing "*summum jus* to Leisler and incurring an ag- "gravated guilt of blood beyond that of a "common murderer. The other party, no doubt, "would have charged the failure of justice up- "on him, if Leisler had been acquitted."

Dudley replied to both these extraordinary missives, in a letter dated the third of February, 1708. After rebuking, in stern and dignified language, the tone and style of their letters, reminding them, by apt citations from Scripture, of the "laws of wise and Christian reproof," which they had violated, and showing upon what false foundations their charges rested, he says: "Can you think it the most proper season to do "me good by your admonitions, when you have "taken care to let the world know you are out of "frame and filled with the last prejudice "against my person and Government?" "Every "one can see through the pretence, and is able "to account for the spring of these letters, and "how they would have been prevented, without "easing any grievances you complain of." He makes the following proposal: "After all "though I have reason to complain to heaven "and earth of your unchristain rashness, and "wrath, and injustice, I would yet maintain a "christain temper towards you. I do, therefore, "now assure you that I shall be ready to give "you all the satisfaction Christianity requires, in "those points which are proper for you to seek "to receive it in, when, with a proper temper "and spirit, giving me timely notice, you do see "meet to make me a visit for that end; and I "expect the same satisfaction from you." He offers this significant suggestion: "I desire you "will keep your station, and let fifty or sixty "good Ministers, your equals in the Province, "have a share in the Government of the College "and advise thereabouts, as well as yourselves, "and I hope all will be well." He concludes by claiming that he is sustained by the favor of the "Ministers of New England;" and char- acterises the issue between him and them thus: "The "College must be disposed against "the opinion of all the Ministers in New Eng- "land, except yourselves, or the Governor torn "in pieces. This is the view I have of your "inclination."

Dudley continued to administer the Govern- ment for eight years longer, until the infirmities of age compelled him to retire. Both Hutchin- son and Doctor John Eliot give us to under-

stand that he conducted the public affairs with great ability and success, with the general ap- proval of all classes, and particularly of the Clergy. His statement that he had the support of all the Ministers of New England, except the Mathers, was undoubtedly correct. It is certain- ly true of the Ministers of Boston. In his Di- ary, under the year 1709, Cotton Mather says: "The other Ministers of the Town are this day "feasting with our wicked Governor. I have, "by my provoking plainness and freedom, in "telling this Ahab of his wickedness, procured "myself to be left out of his invitations. I re- "joiced in my liberty from the temptations "wherewith they were encumbered." He set apart that day for fasting and prayer, the spec- ial interest of which, he says, "was to obtain "deliverance and protection" from his "ene- "mies," whose names, he informs us, he "men- "tioned unto the Lord, who had promised to be "my shield."

The bitterness with which Mather felt exclusion from power is strikingly illustrated in a letter addressed by him to Stephen Sewall, published by me in the Appendix to the edition of my *Lectures,* printed in 1831. I subjoin a few ex- tracts: "A couple of malignant fellows, a "while since, railing at me in the Bookseller's "shop, among other things they said, 'and his "'friend Noyes has cast him off,' at which they "set up a laughter." "No doubt, you under- "stand, how ridiculously things have been man- "aged in our late General Assembly; voting and "unvoting, the same day; and, at last, the "squirrels perpetually running into the mouth "open for them, though they had cried against "it wonderfully. And your neighbor, Sowgelder, "after his indefatigable pains at the castration "of all common honesty, rewarded, before the "Court broke up, with being made one of your "brother Justices; which the whole House, as "well as the apostate himself, had in view, all "along, as the expected wages of his iniquity." "If things continue in the present administra- "tion, there will shortly be not so much as a "shadow of justice left in the country. Bribery, "a crime capital among the Pagans, is already a "peccadillo among us. All officers are learning "it. And, if I should say, Judges will find the "way to it, some will say, there needs not the "future tense in the case." "Every thing is be- "trayed, and that we, on the top of our house, "may complete all, our very religion, with all "the Churches, is at last betrayed—the treachery "carried on with lies, and fallacious representa- "tions, and finished by the rash hands of our "Clergy."

That Cotton Mather continued all his subse- quent life to experience the dissatisfaction, and give way to the feelings, of a disappointed man, is evident from his Diary. I have quoted from it a few passages. The Reviewer says it "is full "of penitential confessions," and seems to liken him, in this respect, to the Apostle of the Gentiles. Speaking of my having cited the Diary, as historical evidence, he says: "Such a use of the "confessional, we believe, is not common with "historical writers." I do not remember anything like "penitential confessions," in the passages from the Diary given in my book. The reader is referred to them, in Volume II. Page 503. They belong to the year 1724, and are thus prefaced:

"DARK DISPENSATIONS, BUT LIGHT ARISING IN "DARKNESS."

"It may be of some use to me, to observe "some very dark dispensations, wherein the rec- "ompense of my poor essays at well-doing, in "this life, seem to look a little discouraging; and "then to express the triumph of my faith over "such and all discouragements." "Of the "things that look dark, I may touch of twice "seven instances."

The writer, in the *Christian Examiner*, November, 1831, from whom I took them, omitted two, "on account of their too personal or domes- "tic character."

I cannot find the slightest trace of a penitential tear on those I have quoted; and cite now but one of them, as pertinent to the point I am making: "What has a gracious Lord given me "to do for the good of the country? in appli- "cations without number for it, in all its inter- "ests, besides publications of things useful to it, "and for it. And, yet, there is no man whom "the country so loads with disrespect, and "calumnies, and manifold expressions of aver- "sion."

This is a specimen of the whole of them—one half recounting what he had done, the other complaining, sometimes almost scolding, at the poor requital he had received.

President Leverett died, on the third of May, 1724. His death was lamented by the country; and the most eminent men vied with each other in doing honor to his memory. The Rev. Benjamin Colman called him "our master," and pronounced his life as "great and good." "The "young men saw him and hid themselves, and "the aged arose and stood up." Dr. Appleton declared that he had been "an honored orna- "ment to his country. Verily, the breach is so "wide, that none but an all-sufficient God (with "whom is the residue of the Spirit) can repair "or heal it." The late Benjamin Peirce, in his *History of Harvard University*, says that "his "Presidency was successful and brilliant." He was honored abroad, as well as at home; and his name is inscribed on the rolls of the Royal Society of London. Mr. Peirce says: "He had a

"great and generous soul." His natural abilities were of a very high order. His attainments were profound and extensive. He was well acquainted with the learned languages, with the arts and "sciences, with history, philosophy, law, divin- "ity, politics." Such, we are told, were "the "majesty and marks of greatness, in his speech, "his behaviour, and his very countenance," that the students of the College were inspired with reverence and affection. In his earlier and later life, he had been connected with the College, as Tutor and as President; and in the intermediate period, he had filled the highest legislative and judicial stations, and been intrusted with the most important functions connected with the military service. I am inclined to think, all things con- sidered, a claim, in his behalf, might be put in for the distinction the Reviewer awards to Cotton Mather, as "doubtless the most brilliant man "of his day in New England."

President Leverett was buried on the sixth of May. Cotton Mather officiated as one of the Pall-bearers, and then went home, and made the following entry in his Diary, dated the seventh: "The sudden death of the unhappy man who "sustained the place of President in our College, "will open a door for my doing singular services "in the best of interests. I do not know "that the care of the College will now be cast "upon me; though I am told it is what is most "generally wished for. If it should be, I shall "be in abundance of distress about it; but, if it "should not, yet I may do many things for the "good of the College more quietly and more "hopefully than formerly."

As time wore away, and no choice of President was made, he became more and more sensible that an influence, hostile to him, was in the ascendency; and, on the first of July, he writes thus, in his Diary: "This day being our insipid, "ill-contrived anniversary, which we call Com- "mencement, I chose to spend it at home, in "supplications, partly on the behalf of the Col- "lege, that it may not be foolishly thrown away, "but that God may bestow such a President "upon it, as may prove a rich blessing unto it "and unto all our Churches."

In the meanwhile, he renewed his attendance at the meetings of the Overseers; having never occupied his seat, in that Body, with the excep- tion of a single Session, during the whole period of Leverett's presidency. The Board, at a meet- ing he attended, on the sixth of August, 1724, passed a vote advising and directing the speedy election of a President. On the eleventh, the Cor- poration chose the Rev. Joseph Sewall of the Old South Church; and Mather records the event in his Diary, as follows: "I am informed that, yes- "terday, the six men, who call themselves the "Corporation of the College, met, and, contrary

"to the epidemical expectation of the country,
"chose a modest young man, Sewall, of whose
"piety (and little else) every one gives a lauda-
"ble character."

"I always foretold these two things of the Cor-
"poration: First, that, if it were possible for
"them to steer clear of me, they will do so.
"Secondly, that, if it were possible for them to
"act foolishly, they will do so. The perpetual
"envy with which my essays to serve the king-
"dom of God are treated among them, and the
"dread that Satan has of my beating up his
"quarters at the College, led me into the former
"sentiment: the marvellous indiscretion, with
"which the affairs of the College are managed,
"led me into the latter."

Mr. Sewall declined the appointment. On the
eighteenth of November, the Rev. Benjamin Colman, of the Brattle street Church, was chosen. He
also declining, the Rev. Benjamin Wadsworth, of
the First Church, was elected. in June, 1725, and
inaugurated on the seventh of July.

It thus appears that Dr. Mather was pointedly
passed over; and every other Minister of Boston
successively chosen to that great office.

Of course he took. as Mr. Peirce informs us,
no further part in the management of the College. While he considered, as he expressed it,
the "senselessness" of those entrusted with its affairs, as threatening "little short of a dissolution
"of the College," yet he persuaded himself that
he had never desired the office. He had, he
says, "unspeakable cause to admire the compas-
"sion of Heaven, in saving him from the ap-
"pointment:" and that he had always had a
"dread of what the generality of sober men"
thought he desired—"dismal apprehension of the
"distresses which a call at Cambridge would
"bring" upon him.—He was sincere in those
declamations, no doubt; but they show how com-
pletely he could blind himself to the past and
even to the actual present. Mr. Peirce explains
why the Corporation were so resolute in with-
holding their suffrages from Mather: "His con-
"temporaries appear to have formed a very cor-
"rect estimate of his character." "They saw,
"what posterity sees, that he was a man of won-
"derful parts, of immense learning. and of em-
"inent piety and virtue." "They saw his weak-
"ness and eccentricities." "It is evident
"that his judgment was not equal to his other
"faculties: that his passions, which were natur-
"ally strong and violent, were not always under
"proper regulation; that he was weak. credulous,
"enthusiastic. and superstitious. His conversation
"is said to have been instructive and entertain-
"ing, in a high degree. though often marred by
"levity, vanity. imprudence and puns." For
these reasons, he was deemed an unsuitable person for the Presidency of the College.

XVIII.

COTTON MATHER'S WRITINGS AND CHARACTER.

While compelled—by the attempt of the writer in the *North American Review* to reverse the
just verdict of history in reference to Cotton
Mather's connection with Salem Witchcraft—to
show the unhappy part he acted and the terrible
responsibility he incurred, in bringing forward,
and carrying through its stages, that awful tragedy, and the unworthy means he used to throw
that responsibility, afterwards, on others, I am
not to be misled into a false position, in reference
to this extraordinary man. I endorse the language of Mr. Peirce: "He possessed great vigor
"and activity of mind, quickness of apprehen-
"sion, a lively imagination. a prodigious mem-
"ory, uncommon facility in acquiring and com-
"municating knowledge, with the most inde-
"fatigable application and industry; that he
"amassed an immense store of information on
"all subjects, human and divine." I follow Mr.
Peirce still further. in believing that his natural
temperament was pleasant and his sentiments of
a benevolent cast: "that he was an habitual
"promoter and doer of good. is evident, as well
"from his writings as from the various accounts
"that have been transmitted respecting him."

If the question is asked, as it naturally will
be. how these admissions can be reconciled with
the views and statements respecting him. contained in this article and in my book on witchcraft, the answer is: that mankind is not divided
into two absolutely distinct and entirely sepa-
rated portions—one good and the other evil.
The good are liable to, and the bad are capable
of, each receiving much into their own lives and
characters, that belongs to the other. This inter-
fusion universally occurs. The great errors and
the great wrongs imputable to Cotton Mather do
not make it impracticable to discern what was
commendable in him. They may be accounted
for without throwing him out of the pale of humanity or our having to shut our eyes to traits
and merits other ways exhibited.

The extraordinary precocity of his intellect—
itself always a peril. often a life-long misfortune—awakened vanity and subjected him to the
flattery by which it is fed. All ancestral associations and family influences pampered it. Such
a speech as that made to him, at his graduation,
by President Oakes, could not have failed to
have inflated it to exaggerated dimensions. Clerical and political ambition was natural, all but
instinctive, to one, whose father. and both whose
grandfathers, had been powers, in the State as
well as Church. The religious ideas, if they can
be so called, in which he had been trained from
childhood, in a form bearing upon him with more
weight than upon any other person in all history,

inasmuch, as they constituted the prominent feature of his father's reading, talk, thoughts, and writings, gave a rapid and overshadowing growth to credulity and superstition. A defect in his education, perhaps, in part, a natural defect, left him without any true logical culture, so that he seems, in his productions and conduct, not to discern the sequences of statements, the coherence of propositions, nor the consistency of actions, thereby entangling him in expressions and declarations that have the aspect of untruthfulness—his language often actually bearing that character, without his discerning it. His writings present many instances of this infirmity. Some have already been incidentally adduced. In his *Life of Phips*, avowing himself the author of the document known as the *Advice of the Ministers*, he uses this language: "By Mr. Mather the "younger, as I have been informed." He had, in fact, never been *so informed*. He knew it by consciousness. Of course he had no thought of deceiving; but merely followed a habit he had got, of such modes of expression. So, also, when he sent a present of money and tracts to " poor "and bad people," in Salem, with an anonymous letter to the Minister of the place, "desiring and "empowering him to dispense the charity, *in his* "*own name*, hoping thereby the *more to ingra-* "*tiate his ministry with the people*," he looked only on one side of the proposal, and saw it in no other light than a benevolent and friendly transaction. It never occurred to him that he was suggesting a deceptive procedure and drawing the Minister into a false position and practice.

When, in addition, we consider to what he was exposed by his proclivity to, and aspirations for, political power, the expedients, schemes, contrivances, and appliances, in which he thereby became involved in the then state of things in the Colony, and the connection which leading Ministers, although not admitted to what are strictly speaking political offices, had with the course of public affairs—his father, to an extent never equalled by any other Clergyman, before or since—we begin to estimate the influences that disastrously swayed the mind of Cotton Mather.

Vanity, flattery, credulity, want of logical discernment, and the struggles between political factions, in the unsettled, uncertain, transition period, between the old and new Charters, are enough to account for much that was wrong, in one of Mather's temperament and passions, without questioning his real mental qualities, or, I am disposed to think, his conscious integrity, or the sincerity of his religious experiences or professions.

But his chief apology, after all, is to be found in the same sphere in which his chief offences were committed. Certain topics and notions, in reference to the invisible, spiritual, and diabolical world, whether of reality or fancy it matters not, had, all his life long, been the ordinary diet, the daily bread, of his mind.

It may, perhaps, be said with truth, that the theological imagery and speculations of that day, particularly as developed in the writings of the two Mathers, were more adapted to mislead the mind and shroud its moral sense in darkness, than any system, even of mythology, that ever existed. It was a mythology. It may be spoken of with freedom, now, as it has probably passed away, in all enlightened communities in Christendom. Satan was the great central character, in what was, in reality, a Pantheon. He was surrounded with hosts of infernal spirits, disembodied and embodied, invisible demons, and confederate human agents. He was seen in everything, everywhere. His steps were traced in extraordinary occurrences and in the ordinary operations of nature. He was hovering over the heads of all, and lying in wait along every daily path. The affrighted imagination, in every scene and mode of life, was conversant with ghosts, apparitions, spectres, devils. This prevalent, all but universal, exercise of credulous fancy, exalted into the most imposing dignity of theology and faith, must have had a demoralizing effect upon the rational condition and faculties of men, and upon all discrimination and healthfulness of thought. When error, in its most extravagant forms, had driven the simplicity of the Gospel out of the Church and the world, it is not to be wondered at that the mind was led to the most shocking perversions, and the conscience ensnared to the most indefensible actions.

The superstition of that day was foreshadowed in the ferocious cannibal of classic mythology—a monster, horrific, hideous in mein, and gigantic in stature. It involved the same fate. The eye of the intellect was burned out, the light of reason extinguished—*cui lumen ademptum*.

Having always given himself up to the contemplation of diabolical imaginations, Cotton Mather was led to take the part he did, in the witchcraft proceedings; and it cannot be hidden from the light of history. The greater his talents, the more earnestly he may, in other matters, have aimed to be useful, the more weighty is the lesson his course teaches, of the baleful effects of bewildering and darkening superstition.

There is another, and a special, explanation to be given of the disingenuousness that appears in his writings. He was a master of language. He could express, with marvelous facility, any shade of thought. He could also make language conceal thought. No one ever handled words with more adroitness. He could mould them to suit his purposes, at will, and with ease. This faculty was called in requisition by the special circumstances of his times. It was necessary to preserve, at least, the appearance of unity among the Churches, while there was as great a tendency, then, as ever, to diversity of speculations, touching points of casuistical divinity or ministerial policy. The talent to express in formulas, sentiments that really differed, so as to obscure the difference, was needed; and he had it. He knew how to frame a document that would suit both sides, but, in effect, answer the purposes of one of them, as in the *Advice of the Ministers*. He could assert a proposition and connect with it what appeared to be only a judicious modification or amplification, but which, in reality, was susceptible of being interpreted as either more or less corroborating or contradicting it, as occasion might require. This was a sort of sleight of hand, in the use of words; and was noticed, at the time, as "legerdemain." He practised it so long that it became a feature of his style; and he actually, in this way, deceived himself as well as others. It is a danger to which ingenious and hair-splitting writers are liable. I am inclined to think that what we cannot but regard as patent misstatements, were felt by him to be all right, in consequence, as just intimated, of this acquired habit.

His style is sprightly, and often entertaining. Neal, the author of the *History of the Puritans*, in a letter to the Rev. Benjamin Colman, after speaking with commendation of one of Cotton Mather's productions, says: "It were only to be "wished that it had been freed from those puns "and jingles that attend all his writings, before "it had been made public."—*Massachusetts Historical Collections*, I., v., 199.—Mr. Peirce, it has been observed, speaks of his "puns," in conversation. It is not certain, but that, to a reader now, these very things constitute a redeeming attraction of his writings and relieve the mind of the unpleasant effects of his credulity and vanity, pedantic and often far-fetched references, palpable absurdities, and, sometimes, the repulsiveness of his topics and matter.

The Reviewer represents me as prejudiced against Cotton Mather. Far from it. Forty-three years ago before my attention had been particularly called to his connection with alleged witchcrafts or with the political affairs of his times, I eulogized his "learning and liberality," in warm terms.—*Sermon at the Dedication of the House of Worship of the First Church, in Salem, Massachusetts, 48.*

I do not retract what I then said. Cotton Mather was in advance of his times, in liberality of feeling, in reference to sectarian and denominational matters. He was, undoubtedly, a great student, and had read all that an American scholar could then lay his hands on. Marvellous stories were told of the rapidity of his reading. He was a devourer of books. At the same time,

I vindicated him, without reserve, from the charge of pedantry. This I cannot do now. Observation and reflection have modified my views. He made a display, over all his pages, of references and quotations from authors then, as now, rarely read, and of anecdotes, biographical incidents, and critical comments relating to scholars and eminent persons, of whom others have but little information, and of many of whom but few have ever heard. This filled his contemporaries with wonder; led to most extravagant statements, in funeral discourses, by Benjamin Colman, Joshua Gee, and others; and made the general impression that has come down to our day. Without detracting from his learning, which was truly great, it cannot be denied that this superfluous display of it subjects him, justly, to the imputation of pedantry. It may be affected where, unlike the case of Cotton Mather, there is, in reality, no very extraordinary amount of learning. It is a trick of authorship easily practised.

Any one reading Latin with facility, having a good memory, and keeping a well-arranged scrap-book, needs less than half a dozen such books as the following, to make a show of learning and to astonish the world by his references and citations—the six folio volumes of Petavius, on Dogmatic Theology, and his smaller work, *Rationarium Temporum*, a sort of compendium or schedule of universal history; and a volume printed, in the latter half of the seventeenth century, at Amsterdam, compiled by Limborch, consisting of an extensive collection of letters to and from the most eminent men of that and the preceding century, such as Arminius, Vossius, Episcopius, Grotius, and many others, embracing a vast variety of literary history, criticism, biography, theology, philosophy, and ecclesiastical matters—I have before me the copy of this work, owned by that prodigy of learning, Dr. Samuel Parr, who pronounced it "a precious "book;" and it may have contributed much to give to his productions, that air of rare learning that astonished his contemporaries. To complete the compendious apparatus, and give the means of exhibiting any quantity of learning, in fields frequented by few, the only other book needed is Melchior Adams's *Lives of Literati*, including all most prominently connected with Divinity, Philosophy, and the progress of learning and culture, during the fifteenth and sixteenth centuries, and down to its date, 1615. I have before me, the copy of this last work, owned by Richard Mather, and probably brought over with him, in his perilous voyage, in 1635. It was, successively, in the libraries of his son, Increase, and his grandson, Cotton Mather. At a corner of one of the blank leaves, it is noted, apparently in the hand of Increase Mather: "began Mar. 1, fin-

"ished April 30, 1676." According to the popular tradition, Cotton would have read it, in a day or two. It contains interesting items of all sorts—personal anecdotes, critical comments, and striking passages of the lives and writings of more than one hundred and fifty distinguished men, such as Erasmus, Fabricius, Faustus, Cranmer, Tremellius, Peter Martyr, Beza, and John Knox. Whether Mather had access to either of the above-named works, except the last, is uncertain; but, as his library was very extensive, he sparing no pains nor expense in furnishing it, and these books were severally then in print and precisely of the kind to attract him and suit his fancy, it is not unlikely that he had them all. They would have placed in easy reach, much of the mass of amazing erudition with which he "entertained" his readers and hearers.

Cotton Mather died on the thirteenth of February, 1728, at the close of his sixty-fifth year.

Thirty-six years had elapsed since the fatal imbroglio of Salem witchcraft. He had probably long been convinced that it was vain to attempt to shake the general conviction, expressed by Calef, that he had been "the most active and "forward of any Minister in the country in "those matters," and acquiesced in the general disposition to let that matter rest. It must be pleasing to all, to think that his very last years were freed from the influences that had destroyed the peace of his life and left such a shade over his name. Having met with nothing but disaster from attempting to manage the visible as well as the invisible world, he probably left them both in the hands of Providence; and experienced, as he had never done, a brief period of tranquillity, before finally leaving the scene. His aspiration to control the Province had ceased, The object of his life-long pursuit, the Presidency of the College, was forever baffled. Nothing but mischief and misery to himself and others had followed his attempt to lead the great combat against the Devil and his hosts. It had fired his early zeal and ambition; but that fire was extinguished. The two ties, which more than all others, had bound him, by his good affections and his unhappy passions, to what was going on around him, were severed, nearly at the same time, by the death of his father, in 1723, and of his great and successful rival, Leverett, in 1724. Severe domestic trials and bereavements completed the work of weaning him from the world; and it is stated that, in his very last years, the resentments of his life were buried and the ties of broken friendships restored. The pleasantest intercourse took place between him and Benjamin Colman; men of all parties sought his company and listened to the conversation, which was always one of his shining gifts; he had written kindly about Dudley; and his end was as peaceful as his whole life would have been, but for the malign influences I have endeavored to describe, leading him to the errors and wrongs which, while faithful history records them, men must regard with considerate candor, as God will with infinite mercy.

It is a curious circumstance, that the two great public funerals, in those early times, of which we have any particular accounts left, were of the men who, in life, had been so bitterly opposed to each other. When Leverett was buried, the cavalcade, official bodies, students, and people, "were fain to proceed near as far as Hastings' "before they returned," so great was the length of the procession: the funeral of Mather was attended by the greatest concourse that had ever been witnessed in Boston.

XIX.

I approach the close of this protracted discussion with what has been purposely reserved. The article in the *North American Review* rests, throughout, upon a repudiation of the authority of Robert Calef. Its writer says, "his faculties "appear to us to have been of an inferior order." "He had a very feeble conception of what credible testimony is." "If he had not intentionally lied, he had a very imperfect appreciation "of truth." He speaks of "Calef's disqualifications as a witness." He seeks to discredit him, by suggesting the idea that, in his original movements against Mather, he was instigated by pre-existing enmity—"Robert Calef, between "whom and Mr. Mather a personal quarrel existed." "His personal enemy, Calef."

There is no evidence of any difficulty, nor of any thing that can be called "enmity," between these two persons, prior to their dealings with each other, in the Margaret Rule case, commencing on the thirteenth of September, 1693. Mather himself states, in his Diary, that the enmity between them arose out of Calef's opposition to his, Mather's, views relating to the "existence and "influences of the invisible world." So far as we have any knowledge, their acquaintance began at the date just mentioned. The suggestion of pre-existing enmity, therefore, gives an unfair and unjust impression.

Robert Calef was a native of England, a young man, residing, first in Roxbury, and afterwards at Boston. He was reputed a person of good sense; and, from the manner in which Mather alludes to him, in one instance, of considerable means: he had, probably, been prosperous in his business, which was that of a merchant. Not a syllable is on record against his character, outside of his controversy with the Mathers; all that is known of him, on the contrary, indicates that he was an honorable and excellent person. He enjoyed the confidence of the people; and was called to municipal trusts, for which only reliable, discreet, vigilant, and honest citizens were selected, receiving the thanks of the Town for his services, as Overseer of the Poor. (As he encountered the madness and violence of the people, when they were led by Cotton Mather, in the witchcraft delusion, it is a singular circumstance, constituting an honorable distinction, in which they shared, that, in a later period of their lives, they stood, shoulder to shoulder, breasting bravely together, another storm of popular fanaticism, by publicly favoring inocculation for the small pox.) He offered several of his children to be treated, at the hands of Dr. Boylston, in 1721. His family continued to bear up the respectability of the name, and is honorably mentioned in the municipal records. A vessel, named *London*, was a regular Packet-ship, between that port and Boston, and probably one of the largest class then built in America. She was commanded by " Robert Calef;" and, in the Boston *Evening Post*, of the second of May, 1774, " Dr. Calef of Ipswich " is mentioned among the passengers just arrived in her. Under his own, and other names, the descendants of the family of Calef are probably as numerous and respectable as those of the Mathers; and on that, as all other higher accounts, there is an equal demand for justice to their respective ancestors.

. It is related by Mather, that a young woman, named Margaret Rule, belonging to the North part of Boston, " many months after the General " Storm of the late enchantments, was over," " when the country had long lain pretty quiet," was " seized by the Evil Angels, both as to mo- " lestations and accusations from the Invisible " World". On the Lord's Day, the tenth of September, 1693, " after some hours of previous " disturbance of the public assembly, she fell " into odd fits," and had to be taken out of the congregation and carried home, " where her fits " in a few hours, grew into a figure that satisfied " the spectators of their being supernatural." He further says, that, " from the 10th of September " to the 18th, she kept an entire fast, and yet, " she was to all appearance as fresh, as lively, as " hearty, at the nine days end, as before they " began. In all this time she had a very eager " hunger upon her stomach, yet if any refresh- " ment were brought unto her, her teeth would " be set, and she would be thrown into many " miseries. Indeed, once, or twice, or so, in all " this time, her tormentors permitted her to swal- " low a mouthful of somewhat that might in- " crease her miseries, whereof a spoonful of rum " was the most considerable."

The affair, of course, was noised abroad. It reached the ears of Robert Calef. On the thir-

teenth, after sunset, accompanied by some others, he went to the house, "drawn," as he says, " by " curiosity to see Margaret Rule, and so much " the rather, because it was reported Mr. Mather " would be there, that night." They were taken into the chamber where she was in bed. They found her of a healthy countenance. She was about seventeen years of age. Increase and Cotton Mather came in, shortly afterwards, with others. Altogether, there were between thirty and forty persons in the room. Calef drew up Minutes of what was said and done. He repeated his visit, on the evening of the nineteenth. Cotton Mather had been with Margaret half an hour; and had gone before his arrival. Each night, Calef made written minutes of what was said and done, the accuracy of which was affirmed by the signatures of two persons, which they were ready to confirm with their oaths, He showed them to some of Mather's particular friends. Whereupon Mather preached about him; sent word that he should have him arrested for slander; and called him " one of the worst of liars." Calef wrote him a letter, on the twenty-ninth of September; and, in reference to the complaints and charges Mather was making, proposed that they should meet, in either of two places he mentioned, each accompanied by a friend, at which time he, Calef, would read to him the minutes he had taken, of what had occurred on the evenings of the thirteenth and nineteenth. Mather sent a long letter, not to be delivered, but read to him, in which he agreed to meet him, as proposed, at one of the places; but, in the mean time, on the complaint of the Mathers, for scandalous libels upon Cotton Mather, Calef was brought before " their Majes- " ties Justice, and bound over to answer at Ses- " sions." Mather, of course, failed to give him the meeting for conference, as agreed upon. On the twenty-fourth of November, Calef wrote to him again, referring to his failure to meet him and to the legal proceedings he had instituted; and, as the time for appearance in Court was drawing near, he " he thought it not amiss to " give a summary " of his views on the " great " concern," as to which they were at issue. He states, at the outset, " that there are witches, is not " the doubt." The Reviewer seizes upon this expression, to convey the idea that Calef was trying to conciliate Mather, and induce him to desist from the prosecution. Whoever reads the letter will see how unfair and untrue this is. Calef keeps to the point, which was not whether there were, or could be, witches; but whether the methods Mather was attempting, in the case of Margaret Rule, and which had been used in Salem, the year before, were legitimate or defensible. He was determined not to suffer the issue to be shifted.

Upon receiving this letter, Mather, who had

probably, upon reflection, begun to doubt about the expediency of a public prosecution, signified that he had no desire to press the prosecution; and renewed the proposal for a conference. Calef "waited on Sessions;" but no one appearing against him, was dismissed. The affair seemed, at this crisis, to be tending toward an amicable conclusion. But Mather failed to meet him; and, on the eleventh of January, 1694, Calef addressed him again, recapitulating what had occurred, sending him copies of his previous letters and also of the Minutes he had taken of what occurred on the evenings of the thirteenth and nineteenth of September, with these words: "Reverend Sir: Finding it necessary, on many accounts, I here present you with the copy of "that Paper, which has been so much misrepre- "sented, to the end, that what shall be found "defective or not fairly represented, if any such "shall appear, they may be set right."

This letter concludes in terms which show that, in that stage of the affair, Calef was disposed to treat Mather with great respect; and that he sincerely and earnestly desired and trusted that satisfaction might be given and taken, in the interview he so presistently sought—not merely in reference to the case of Margaret Rule, but to the general subject of witchcraft, on which they had different apprehensions: "I have rea- "son to hope for a satisfactory answer to him, "who is one that reverences your person and of- "fice."

This language strikingly illustrates the estimate in which Ministers were held. Reverence for their office and for them, as a body, pervaded all classes.

On the fifteenth of January, Mather replied, complaining, in general terms, of the narrative contained in Calef's Minutes, as follows: "I do "scarcely find any one thing, in the whole pa- "per, whether respecting my father or myself, "either fairly or truly represented." "The nar- "rative contains a number of mistakes and false- "hoods which, were they wilful and designed, "might justly be termed great lies." He then goes into a specification of a few particulars, in which he maintains that the Minutes are incorrect.

On the eighteenth of January, Calef replied, reminding him that he had taken scarcely any notice of the general subject of diabolical agency; but that almost the whole of his letter referred to the Minutes of the meetings, on the thirteenth and nineteenth of September; and he maintains their substantial accuracy and shows that some of Mather's strictures were founded upon an incorrect reading of them. In regard to Mather's different recollection of some points, he express- es his belief that if his account, in the Minutes, "be not fully exact, it was as near as memory

"could bear away." He notices the fact that he finds in Mather's letter no objection to what relat- ed to matters of greatest concern. Mather had complained that the Minutes reported certain statements made by Rule, which had been used to his disadvantage; and Calef suggests, "What "can be expected less from the father of lies, by "whom, you judge, she was possest?"

Appended to Mather's letter, are some docu- ments, signed by several persons, declaring that they had seen Rule lifted up by an invisible force from the bed to the top of the room, while a strong person threw his whole weight across her, and several others were trying with all their might to hold her down or pull her back. Up- on these certificates, Calef remarks: "Upon the "whole, I suppose you expect I should believe "it; and if so, the only advantage gained is, "that what has been so long controverted be- "tween Protestants and Papists, whether mira- "cles are ceased, will hereby seem to be decided "for the latter; it being, for ought I can see, if "so, as true a miracle as for iron to swim; and "the Devil can work such miracles."

Calef wrote to him again, on the nineteenth of February, once more praying that he would so far oblige him, as to give him his views, on the important subjects, for a right understanding of which he had so repeatedly sought a conference and written so many letters; and expressing his earnest desire to be corrected, if in error, to which end, if Mather would not, he indulged a hope that some others would, afford him relief and satisfaction. On the sixteenth of April, he wrote still another letter. In all of them, he touched upon the points at issue between them, and importuned Mather to communicate his views, fully, as to one seeking light. On the first of March, he wrote to a gentleman, an acknowledg- ment of having received, through his hands, "af- "ter more than a year's waiting," from Cotton Mather, four sheets of paper, not to be copied, and to be returned in a fortnight. Upon return- ing them, with comments, he desires the gentle- man to request Mr. Mather not to send him any more such papers, unless he could be allowed to copy and use them. It seems that, in answer to a subsequent letter, Mather sent to him a copy of Richard Baxter's *Certainty of the World of Spirits*, to which, after some time, Calef found leisure to reply, expressing his dissent from the views given in that book, and treating the sub- ject somewhat at large. In this letter, which closes his correspondence with Mather, he makes this solemn and severe appeal: "Though there is "reason to hope that these diabolical principles "have not so far prevailed (with multitudes of "Christains), as that they ascribe to a witch and a "devil the attributes peculiar to the Almighty; "yet how few are willing to be found opposing

"such a torrent, as knowing that in so doing they
"shall be sure to meet with opposition to the ut-
"most, from the many, both of Magistrates,
"Ministers, and people : and the name of Saddu-
"cee, atheist, and perhaps witch too, cast upon
"them, most liberally, by men of the highest
"profession in godliness ; and, if not so learned as
"some of themselves, then accounted only fit to
"be trampled on, and their arguments (though
"both rational and scriptural) as fit only for con-
"tempt. But though this be the deplorable di-
"lemma, yet some have dared, from time to time,
"(for the glory of God and the good and safety
"of men's lives, etc,) to run all these risks. And,
"that God who has said, 'My glory I will not
"'give to another,' is able to protect those that
"are found doing their duty herein against all
"opposers ; and, however otherwise contempti-
"ble, car make them useful in his own hand,
"who has sometimes chosen the weakest instru-
"ments that His power may be the more illustri-
"ous.

"And now, Reverend Sir, if you are con-
"scious to yourself, that you have, in your prin-
"ciples or practices, been abetting to such grand
"errors, I cannot see how it can consist with sin-
"cerity, to be so convinced, in matters so nearly
"relating to the glory of God and lives of in-
"nocents, and, at the same time, so much to
"fear disparagement among men, as to trifle with
"conscience and dissemble an approving of
"former sentiments. You know that word, 'He
"'that honoreth me I will honor, and he that
"'despiseth me shall be lightly esteemed.' But,
"if you think that, in these matters, you have
"done your duty, and taught the people theirs ;
"and that the doctrines cited from the above
"mentioned book [*Baxter's*] are ungainsayable ;
"I shall conclude in almost his words. He that
"teaches such a doctrine, if through ignorance
"he believes not what he saith, may be a Chris-
"tain : but if he believes them, he is in the
"broad path to heathenism, devilism, popery,
"or atheism. It is a solemn caution (*Gal. i, 8*):
"'But though we, or an angel from heaven,
"'preach any other gospel unto you than That
"'which we have preached unto you, let him be
"'accursed.' I hope you will not misconstrue
"my intentions herein, who am, Reverend Sir,
"yours to command, in what I may."

Resolute in his purpose to bring the Ministers,
if possible, to meet the questions he felt it his duty
to have considered and settled, and careful to
leave nothing undone that he could do, to this
end, he sought the satisfaction from others, he
had tried, in vain, to obtain from Mather. On the
eighteenth of March, 1695, he addressed a letter
"To the Ministers, whether English, French, or
"Dutch," calling their attention to "the myster-
"ious doctrines" relating to the "power of the

"Devil," and to the subject of Witchcraft. On
the twentieth of September, he wrote to the Rev.
Samuel Willard, invoking his attention to the
"great concern," and his aid in having it
fairly discussed. On the twelfth of January,
1696, he addressed "The Ministers in and near
"Boston," for the same purpose ; and wrote a
seperate letter to the Rev. Benjamin Wadsworth.

These documents were all composed with great
earnestness, frankness, and ability ; and are most
creditable to his intelligence, courage, and sense of
public duty. I have given this minute account of
his proceedings with Mather and the Clergy generally, because I am impressed with a conviction
that no instance can be found, in which a great
question has been managed with more caution,
deliberation, patience, manly openness and up-
rightness, and heroic steadiness and prowess, than
this young merchant displayed, in compelling all
concerned to submit to a thorough investigation
and over-hauling of opinions and practices, established by the authority of great names and
prevalent passions and prejudices, and hedged in
by the powers and terrors of Church and State.

It seems to be evident that he must have received aid, in some quarter, from persons conversant
with topics of learning and methods of treating such subjects, to an extent beyond the reach
of a mere man of business. In the First Volume
of the *Proceedings of the Massachusetts Historical Society*, Page 288, a Memorandum, from which
I make an extract, is given, as found in Doctor
Belknap's hand-writing, in his copy of Calef's
book, in the collection, from the library of that
eminent historian, presented by his heirs to that institution : "A young man of good sense, and free
"from superstition ; a merchant in Boston. He
"was furnished with materials for his work, by
"Mr. Brattle of Cambridge, and his brother of
"Boston, and other gentlemen, who were oppos-
"ed to the Salem proceedings.—E. P."

The fact that Belknap endorsed this statement,
gives it sufficient credibility. Who the "E. P."
was, from whom it was derived, is not known.
If it were either of the Ebenezer Pembertons,
father or son, no higher authority could be adduced. But whatever aid Calef received, he so
thoroughly digested and appropriated, as to make
him ready to meet Mather or any, or all, the other
Ministers, for conference and debate ; and his title
to the authorship of the papers remains complete.

The Ministers did not give him the satisfaction
he sought. They were paralyzed by the influence or the fear of the Mathers. Perhaps they
were shocked, if not indignant, at a layman's daring to make such a movement against a Minister.
It was an instance of the laying of unsanctified
hands on the horns of the altar, such as had not
been equalled in audacity, since the days of Anne
Hutchinson, by any but Quakers. Calef, how-

ever, was determined to compel the attention of the world, if he could not that of the Ministers of Boston, to the subject; and he prepared, and sent to England, to be printed. a book, containing all that had passed, and more to the same purpose. It consists of several parts.

PART I. is *An account of the afflictions of Margaret Rule*, written by Cotton Mather, under the title of *Another Brand plucked out of the Burning, or more Wonders of the Invisible World*. In my book, the case of Margaret Rule is spoken of as having occurred the next "Summer" after the witchcraft delusion in Salem. This gives the Reviewer a chance to strike at me, in his usual style, as follows : "The case did not occur in "the Summer; the date is patent to any one who "will look for it." Cotton Mather says that she "first found herself to be formally besieged by "the spectres," on the tenth of September. From the preceding clauses of the same paragraph, it might be inferred that she had had fits before. He speaks of those, on the tenth, as "the first I'll "mention." The word "formally," too, almost implies the same. This, however, must be allowed to be the smallest kind of criticism, although uttered by the Reviewer in the style of a petulant pedagogue. If Summer is not allowed to borrow a little of September, it will sometimes not have much to show, in our climate. The tenth of September is, after all, fairly within the astronomical Summer.

The Reviewer says it will be "difficult for me "to prove" that Margaret Rule belonged to Mr. Mather's Congregation, before September, 1693. Mather vindicates his taking such an interest in her case, on the ground that she was one of his "poor flock." The Reviewer raises a question on this point; and his controversy is with Mather, not with me. If Rule did not belong to the Congregation of North Boston, when Mather first visited her, his language is deceptive, and his apology, for meddling with the case, founded in falsehood. I make no such charge, and have no such belief. The Reviewer seems to have been led to place Cotton Mather in his own light—in fact, to falsify his language—on this point, by what is said of another Minister's having visited her, to whose flock she belonged, and whom she called, "Father." This was Increase Mather. We know he visited her; and it was as proper for him to do so, as for Cotton. They were associate Ministers of the same Congregation—that to which the girl belonged—and it was natural that she should have distinguished the elder, by calling him "Father."

In contradiction of another of my statements, the Reviewer says : "Mr. Mather did not pub-"lish an account of the long-continued fastings, "or any other account of the case of Margaret "Rule." He seems to think that "published"

means "printed." It does not necessarily mean, and is not defined as exclusively meaning, to put to press. To be "published," a document does not need, now, to be printed. Much less then. Mather wrote it, as he says, with a view to its being printed, and put it into open and free circulation. Calef publicly declared that he received it from "a gentleman, who had it of the author, "and communicated it to me, with his express "consent." Mather says, in a prefatory note: "I now lay before you a very entertaining story," "of one who had been prodigiously handled by "the evil Angels." "I do not write it with a "design of throwing it presently into the press, "but only to preserve the memory of such mem-"orable things, the forgetting whereof would "neither be pleasing to God, nor useful to men." The unrestricted circulation of a work of this kind, with such a design, was *publishing it*. It was the form in which almost every thing was published in those days. If Calef had omitted it, in a book professing to give a true and full account of his dealings with Mather, in the Margaret Rule case, he would have been charged with having withheld Mather's carefully prepared view of that case. Mather himself considered the circulation of his "account," as a publication, for in speaking of his design of ultimately printing it himself, he calls it a "farther publi-"cation."

PART II. embraces the correspondence between Calef, Mather, and others, which I have particularly described.

PART III. is a brief account of the Parish troubles, at Salem Village.

PART IV. is a correspondence between Calef and a gentleman, whose name is not given, on the subject of witchcraft, the latter maintaining the views then prevalent.

PART V. is *An impartial account of the most memorable matters of fact, touching the supposed witchcraft in New England*, including the "Re-"port" of the Trials given by Mather in his *Wonders of the Invisible World*.

The work is prefaced by an *Epistle to the Reader*, couched in plain but pungent language, in which he says : "It is a great pity that the matters of "fact, and indeed the whole, had not been done "by some abler hand, better accomplished, and "with the advantages of both natural and ac-"quired judgment; but, others not appearing, I "have enforced myself to do what is done. My "other occasions will not admit any further scru-"tiny therein." A Postcript contains some strictures on the *Life of Sir Wm. Phips*, then recently printed. "which book," Calef says, "though it "bear not the author's name, yet the style, man-"ner. and matter are such, that, were there no "other demonstration or token to know him by, "it were no witchcraft to determine that Mr.

"Cotton Mather is the author of it." The real agency of Sir William Phips, in demolishing, with one stern blow, the Court of Oyer and Terminer, and treading out the witchcraft prosecutions, has never, until recently, been known. The Records of the Council, of that time, were obtained from England, not long since. They, with the General Court Records, Phips's letter to the Home Government—copied in this article—and the Diary of Judge Sewall, reveal to us the action of the brave Governor, and show how much that generation and subsequent times are indebted to him, for stopping, what, if he had allowed it to go on, would have come, no man can tell "where at last."

Calef speaks of Sir William, kindly: "It is "not doubted but that he aimed at the good of "the people ; and great pity it is that his Govern- "ment was so sullied (for want of better inform- "ation and advice from those whose duty it "was to have given it) by the hobgoblin Monster, "Witchcraft, whereby this country was night- "mared and harassed, at such a rate as is not "easily imagined."

Such were the contents, and such the tone, of Calef's book. The course he pursued, his careful- ness to do right and to keep his position fortified as he advanced, and the deliberate courage with which he encountered the responsibilities, con- nected with his movement to rid the country of a baleful superstition, are worthy of grateful re- membrance.

Mather received intelligence that Calef had sent his book to England, to be printed ; and his mind was vehemently exercised in reference to it. He set apart the tenth of June, 1698, for a private Fast on the occasion ; and he commenced the ex- ercise of the day, by, "first of all, declaring unto "the Lord" that he freely forgave Calef, and praying "the Lord also to forgive him." He "pleaded with the Lord," saying that the design of this man was to hurt his "precious opportu- "nities of glorifying" his "glorious Lord Jesus "Christ." He earnestly besought that those op- portunities might not be "damnified" by Calef's book. And he finished by imploring deliverance from his calumnies. So "I put over my calum- "nious adversary into the hands of the righteous "God."

On the fifth of November, Calef's book having been received in Boston, Mather again made it the occasion of Fasting and Praying. His friends also spent a day of prayer, as he expresses it, "to complain unto God," against Calef, he, Mather, meeting with them. On the twenty-fifth of November, he writes thus, in his Diary: "The "Lord hath permitted Satan to raise an extraor- "dinary Storm upon my father and myself. All "the rage of Satan, against the holy churches of "the Lord, falls upon us. First Calf's and then

"Colman's, do set the people into a mighty fer- "ment."

The entries in his Diary, at this time, show that he was exasperated, to the highest degree, against Calef, to whom he applies such terms as, "a "liar," "vile," "infamous," imputing to him diabolical wickedness. He speaks of him as "a "weaver ; " and, in a pointed manner calls him *Calf*, a mode of spelling his name sometimes practised, but then generally going out of use. The probability is that the vowel *a*, formerly, as in most words, had its broad sound, so that the pronunciation was scarcely perceptibly different, when used as a dissyllable or monosyllable. As the broad sound became disused, to a great ex- tent, about this time, the name was spoken, as well as spelled, as a dyssyllable, the vowel hav- ing its long sound. It was written, *Calef*, and thus printed, in the title-page of his book ; so that Mather's variation of it was unjustifiable, and an unworthy taunt.

It is unnecessary to say that a fling at a person's previous occupation, or that of his parents—an attempt to discredit him, in consequence of his having, at some period of his life, been a me- chanic or manufacturer—or dropping, or altering a letter in his name, does not amount to much, as an impeachment of his character and credi- bility, as a man or an author. Hard words, too, in a heated controversy, are of no account what- ever. In this case, particularly, it was a vain and empty charge, for Mather to call Calef *a liar*. In the matter of the account, the latter drew up, of what took place in the chamber of Margaret Rule : as he sent it to Mather for correction, and as Mather specified some items which he deemed erroneous, his declaration that all the rest was a tissue of falsehoods, was utterly futile ; and can only be taken as an unmeaning and ineffectual expression of temper. So far as the truthfulness of Calef's statements, generally, is regarded, there is no room left for question.

In his Diary for February, 1700, Mather says, speaking of the "calumnies that Satan, by his in- "strument, *Calf*, had cast upon " him and his father, "the Lord put it into the hearts of a con- "siderable number of our flock, who are, in "their temporal condition, more equal unto our "adversary, to appear in our vindication." A Committee of seven, including John Goodwin, was appointed for this purpose. They called up- on their Pastors to furnish them with materials ; which they both did. The Committee drew up, as Mather informs us, in his Diary, a "hand- "some answer unto the slanders and libels of "our slanderous adversary," which was forth- with printed, with the names of the members of the Committee signed to it. The pamphlet was entitled, *Some Few Remarks*, &c. Mather says of "it: The Lord blesses it, for the illumination of

"his people in many points of our endeavour to
"serve them, whereof they had been ignorant;
"and there is also set before all the Churches a
"very laudable example of a people appearing
"to vindicate their injured Pastors, when a storm
"of persecution is raised against them."

This vindication is mainly devoted to the case
of the Goodwin children, twelve years before, and
to a defence of the course of Increase Mather, in
England, in reference to the Old and New Charters. No serious attempt was made to controvert
material points in Calef's book, relating to Salem
Witchcraft. As it would have been perfectly
easy, by certificates without number, to have exposed any error, touching that matter, and as no
attempt of the kind was made, on this or any
other occasion, the only alternative left is to ac-
cept Hutchinson's conviction, that "Calef was a
"fair relator" of that passage in our history.

His book has, therefore, come down to us, hearing the ineffaceable stamp of truth.

It was so regarded, at the time, in England, as
shown in the manner in which it was referred to
by Francis Hutchinson and Daniel Neal; and in
America, in the way in which Thomas Hutchinson speaks of Calef, and alludes to matters as
stated by him. I present, entire, the judgment of
Dr. John Eliot, as given in his *Biographical
Dictionary.* Bearing in mind that Eliot's work
was published in 1806, the reader is left to make
his own comments on the statement, in the *North
American Review,* that I originated, in 1831, the
unfavorable estimate of Cotton Mather's agency
in the witchcraft delusion of 1692. It is safe
to say that no higher authority can be cited than
that of John Eliot : "CALEF, ROBERT, merchant,
"in the town of Boston, rendered himself fa-
"mous by his book against Witchcraft, when
"the people of Massachusetts were under the
"most strange kind of delusion. The nature of
"this crime, so opposite to all common sense,
"has been said to exempt the accusers from ob-
"serving the rules of common sense. This was
"evident from the trials of witches, at Salem, in
"1692. Mr. Calef opposed facts, in the simple
"garb of truth, to fanciful representations; yet
"he offended men of the greatest learning and
"influence. He was obliged to enter into a con-
"troversy, which he managed with great bold-
"ness and address. His letters and defence were
"printed, in a volume, in London, in 1700. Dr.
"Increase Mather was then President of Har-
"vard College; he ordered the wicked book to
"be burnt in the College yard; and the members
"of the Old North Church published a defence
"of their Pastors, the Rev. Increase and Cotton
"Mather. The pamphlet, printed on this occa-
"sion, has this title-page: *Remarks upon a scan-
"dalous book, against the Government and Min-
"istry of New England, written by Robert*

"*Calef,* &c. Their motto was, *Truth will come
"off conqueror,* which proved a satire upon them-
"selves, because Calef obtained a complete tri-
"umph. The Judges of the Court and the Jury
"confessed their errors; the people were aston-
"ished at their own delusion; reason and com-
"mon sense were evidently on Calef's side; and
"even the present generation read his book with
"mingled sentiments of pleasure and admira-
"tion."

Calef's book continues, to this day, the recognized authority on the subject. Its statements of
matters of fact, not disputed nor specifically denied by the parties affected, living at the time,
nor attempted to be confuted, then, and by them,
never can be. The current of nearly two centuries
has borne them beyond all question. No assault
can now reach them. No writings of Mather
have ever received more evidence of public interest or favor. First printed in London, Calef's
volume has gone through four American editions, the last, in 1861, edited by Samuel P. Fowl-
er, is presented in such eligible type and so read-
able a form, as to commend it to favorable notice.

It may be safely said that few publications
have produced more immediate or more lasting
effects. It killed off the whole business of Margaret Rule. Mather abandoned it altogether.
In 1694, he said "the forgetting thereof would
"neither be pleasing to God nor useful to men."
Before Calef had done with him, he had dropped it forever.

Calef's book put a stop to all such things, in
New and Old England. It struck a blow at the
whole system of popular superstition, relating to
the diabolical world, under which it reels to this
day. It drove the Devil out of the preaching,
the literature, and the popular sentiments of the
world. The traces of his footsteps, as controlling the affairs of men and interfering with the
Providence of God, are only found in the dark
recesses of ignorance, the vulgar profanities of
the low, and a few flash-expressions and thought-
less forms of speech.

No one can appreciate the value of his service.
If this one brave man had not squarely and defiantly met the follies and madness, the priestcraft
and fanaticism, of his day; if they had been allowed to continue to sway Courts and Juries; if
the pulpit and the press had continued to throw
combustibles through society, and, in every way,
inflame the public imaginations and passions,
what limit can be assigned to the disastrous consequences?

Boston Merchants glory in the names, on their
proud roll of public benefactors, of men whose
wisdom, patriotism, and munificence have up-
held, adorned, and blessed society; but there is
no one of their number who encountered more

danger, showed more moral and intellectual prowess, or rendered more noble service to his fellow citizens and fellow men, every where, than ROBERT CALEF.

I again ask attention to the language used in the *North American Review*, for April, 1869. "These views, respecting Mr. Mather's connec- "tion with the Salem trials, are to be found in "NO PUBLICATION OF A DATE PRIOR TO 1831, when "Mr. Upham's *Lectures* were published."

Great as may be the power of critical journals, they cannot strike into non-existence, the record- ed and printed sentiments of Brattle, the Hutch- insons, Neal, Watts, Bentley, Eliot, Quincy, and Calef.

XX.

MISCELLANEOUS REMARKS. CONCLUSION.

There are one or two minor points, where the Reviewer finds occasion to indulge in his pe- culiar vein of criticism on my book, which it is necessary to notice before closing, in order to prevent wrong impressions being made by his ar- ticle, touching the truth of history.

A pamphlet, entitled, *Some Miscellany Observa- tions on our present debates respecting Witch- craft, in a Dialogue between S and B*, has been referred to. It was published in Philadelphia, in 1692. Its printing was procured by Hezekiah Usher, a leading citizen of Boston, who, at the later stages of the prosecution, had been cried out upon, by the accusing girls, and put under arrest. Its author was understood to be the Rev. Samuel Willard. The Reviewer claims for its writer precedence over the Rev. John Wise, of Ipswich, and Robert Pike, of Salisbury. as hav- ing earlier opposed the proceedings. Wise head- ed a Memorial, in favor of John Proctor and against the use of spectral evidence, before the trials that took place on the fifth of August; and Pike's second letter to Judge Corwin was dated the eighth of August.

The pamphlet attributed to Willard is a spirit- ed and able performance; but seems to allow the use of spectral evidence, when bearing against persons of "ill-fame."

Pike concedes all that believers in the general doctrines of witchcraft demanded, particularly the ground taken in the pamphlet attributed to Willard, and then proceeds, by the most acute technical logic, based upon solid common sense, to overturn all the conclusions to which the Court had been led. It was sent, by special messenger, to a Judge on the Bench, who was also an asso- ciate with Pike at the Council Board of the Province. Wise's paper was addressed to the Court of Assistants, the Supreme tribunal of the Province. The *Miscellany Observations*, appear to have been written after the trials. There is nothing, however, absolutely to determine the pre-

cise date; and they were published anonymously, in Philadelphia. The right of Wise and Pike to the credit of having first, by written remon- strance, opposed the proceedings, on the spot, cannot, I think, be taken away.

The Reviewer charges me, in reference to one point, with not having thought it necessary to "pore over musty manuscripts, in the obscure "chirography of two centuries ago." So far as my proper subject could be elucidated by it, I am constrained to claim, that this labor was encoun- tered, to an extent not often attempted. The files of Courts, and State, County, Town, and Church records, were very extensively and thoroughly studied out. So far as the Court papers, belong- ing to the witchcraft Examinations and Trials, are regarded, much aid was derived from *Records of Salem Witchcraft, copied from the origi- nal documents*, printed in 1864, by W. Eliot Woodward. But such difficulty had been ex- perienced in deciphering them, that the originals were all subjected to a minute re-examination. The same necessity existed in the use of the *An- nals of Salem*, prepared and published by that most indefatigable antiquary, the late Rev. Joseph B. Felt, LL. D. In writing a work for which so little aid could be derived from legislative rec- ords or printed sources, bringing back to life a generation long since departed. and reproducing a community and transaction so nearly buried in oblivion, covering a wide field of genealogy, top- ography and chronology, embracing an indefinite variety of municipal, parochial, political, social, local, and family matters, and of things, names, and dates without number. it was, after all, im- possible to avoid feeling that many errors and oversights might have been committed; and, as my only object was to construct a true and ade- quate history, I coveted. and kept myself in a frame gratefully to receive all corrections and suggestions, with a view of making the work as perfect as possible. in a reprint. As I was rea- sonably confident that the ground under me could stand, at all important points, any assaults of criticism, made in the ordinary way, it gave me satisfaction to hear, as I did, in voices of ru- mor reaching me from many quarters, that an ar- ticle was about to appear in the *North American Review* that would "demolish" my book. I flattered myself that, whether it did or not, much valuable information would, at least, be receiv- ed, that would enable me to make my book more to my purpose, by making it more true to history.

After the publication of the article, and before I could extricate myself from other engagements so far as to look into it, I read, in editorials, from week to week, in newspapers and journals, that I had been demolished. Surely, I thought. some great errors have been discovered, some precious "original sources" opened, some lost records ex-up the Complaint. In the hurry and horrors of the moment, the error in the names was not discovered: *Jonathan* and *Hannah* were sent forthwith to prison, from which they broke, and escaped to New York. The girls, thinking they had got *Mrs. Elizabeth Carey* in prison, said no more about it. As Jonathan and his wife were safe, and beyond reach, the whole matter dropped out of the public mind; and Mrs. Elizabeth remained undisturbed. This is the only way in which I can account for the strange incongruity of the statements, as found in the "Complaint," Calef, and Hutchinson. The letter of Jonathan Carey is decisive of the point that it was "Hannah," his wife, that was arrested, and escaped. The error in Calef was not discovered by him, as his book was printed in London; and, under the general disposition to let the subject pass into oblivion, if possible, no explanation was ever given.

I cannot let the letter of Jonathan Carey pass, without calling to notice his statement that, upon reaching New York, they found "His Excellency, Benjamin Fletcher, Esq. very courteous" to them. Whatever multiplies pleasant historical reminiscences and bonds of association between different States, ought to be gathered up and kept fresh in the minds of all. The fact that when Massachusetts was suffering from a fiery and bloody, but brief, persecution by its own Government, New York opened so kind and secure a shelter for those fortunate enough to escape to it, ought to be forever held in grateful remembrance by the people of the old Bay State, and constitutes a part of the history of the Empire State, of which she may well be proud. If the historians and antiquaries of the latter State can find any traces, in their municipal or other archives, or in any quarter, of the refuge which the Careys and others found among them, in 1692, they would be welcome contributions to our history, and strengthen the bonds of friendly union.

The Reviewer seems to imagine that, by a stroke of his pen, he can, at any time, make history. Referring to Governor Winthrop, in connection with the case of Margaret Jones, forty-two years before, he says that he "presided at her Trial; "signed her Death-warrant; and wrote the report of the case in his journal." The fact that, in his private journal, he has a paragraph relating to it, hardly justifies the expression "wrote the report of the case." Where did he, our Reviewer, find authority for the positive statement that Winthrop "signed the Death-"warrant?" We have no information, I think, as to the use of Death-warrants, as we understand such documents to be, in those days; and especially are we ignorant as to the official who drew and signed the Order for the execution of a capital convict. Sir William Phips, although present, did not sign the Death-warrant of Bridget Bishop.

The Reviewer expresses, over and over again, his great surprise at the view given in my book of Cotton Mather's connection with Salem witchcraft. It is quite noticeable that his language, to this effect, was echoed through that portion of the Press committed to his statements. My sentiments were spoken of as "sur- "prising errors." What I had said was, as I have shown, a mere continuation of an ever-received opinion; and it was singular that it gave such a widespread simultaneous shock of "surprise." But that shock went all around. I was surprised at their surprise; and may be allowed, as well as the Reviewer, to express and explain that sensation. It was awakened deeply and forcibly by the whole tenor of his article. He was the first reader of my book, it having been furnished him by the Publishers before going to the binder. He wrote an elaborate, extended, and friendly notice of it, in a leading paper of New York city, kindly calling it "a monument "of historical and antiquarian research;" "a "narrative as fascinating as the latest novel;" and concluding thus: "Mr. Upham deserves the "thanks of the many persons interested in "psychological inquiries, for the minute details he has "given of these transactions." Some criticisms were suggested, in reference to matters of form in the work; *but not one word was said about Cotton Mather.* The change that has come over the spirit of his dream is more than surprising.

The reference, in the foregoing citation, to "psychological enquiries," suggests to me to allude, before closing, to remarks made by some other critics. I did not go into the discussion, with any particularity, of the connection, if any, between the witchcraft developments of 1692 and modern spiritualism, in any of its forms. A fair and candid writer observes that "the facts "and occurrences," as I state them, involve difficulties which I "have not solved. There are "depths," he continues, "in this melancholy ep- "isode, which his plummet has not sounded, by "a great deal." This is perfectly true.

With a full conviction that the events and circumstances I was endeavoring to relate, afforded more material for suggestions, in reference to the mysteries of our spiritual nature, than any other chapter in history, I carefully abstained, with the exception of a few cautionary considerations hinting at the difficulties that encompass the subject, from attempting to follow facts to conclusions, in that direction. My sole object was to bring to view, as truthfully, thoroughly, and minutely, as I could, the phenomena of the case, as bare historical facts, from which others were left to make their own deductions. This was the extent of the service I desired to render, in aid of such as may attempt to advance the boundaries of the spiritual department of science. I was content, and careful, to st y my steps. Feeling that the story I was telling led me along the outer edge of what is now knowledge—that I was treading the shores of the *ultima Thule*, of the yet discovered world of truth—I did. not venture upon the ocean beyond. My only hope was to afford some data to guide the course of those who may attempt to traverse it. Other hands are to drop the plummet into its depths, and other voyagers feel their way over its surface to continents that are waiting, as did this Western Hemisphere, for ages upon ages, to be revealed. The belief that fields of science may yet be reached, by exploring the connection between the corporeal and spiritual spheres of our being, in which explorations the facts presented in the witchcraft Delusion may be serviceab'e, suggested one of the motives that led me to dedicate my volumes to the Professor of Physiology in Harvard University.

The Reviewer concludes his article by saying that the " History of Sa'em witchcraft is as yet " unwritten," but. that I must write it; and he tells me how to write it. He advises a more concise form, although his whole article consists of complaints because I avoided discussions and condensed documents, which, if fully gone into and spread out at length, would have swelled the dimensions of the work, as well as broken the thread of the narrative. It must be borne in mind, that a reader can only be held to the line of a subject, by an occasional retrospection and reiteration of what must be constantly kept in view. The traveler needs, at certain points and suitable stages, to turn and survey the ground over which he has passed. A condensation that would strike out such recapitulations and repetitions, might impair the effect of a work of any kind, particularly, of one embracing complicated materials.

The Reviewer says that, " by all means, I must " give references to authorities," when I quote. This. as a general thing, is good advice. But it must be remembered that my work consists of three divisions. The History of Salem Village constitutes the First. This is drawn, almost wholly, from papers in the offices of registry, and from judicial files of the County, to which references would be of little use, and serve only to cumber and deform the pages. Everything can be verified by inspection of the originals, and not otherwise. The Second Part is a cursory, general, abbreviated sketch or survey of the history of opinions, not designed as an authoritative treatise for special students, but to prepare the reader for the Third Part, the authorities for which are, almost wholly, Court files.

As to the remaining suggestion, that I must divide the work into Chapters, with headings, there is something to be said. When the nature of an historical work admits of its being invested with a dramatic interest—and all history is capable, more or less, of having that attraction—where minute details can fill up the whole outline of characters, events, and scenes, all bearing the impress of truth and certainty, real history, being often stranger than fiction, may be, and ought to be, so written as to bring to bear upon the reader, the charm, and work the spell, of what is called romance. The same solicitude, suspense, and sensibilities, which the parties, described, experienced, can be imparted to the reader; and his feelings and affections keep pace with the developments of the story, as they arise, with the progress of time and events. Headings to Chapters, in historical works, capable of this dramatic element, would be as out of place, and as much mar and defeat the effect. as in a novel.

As for division into Chapters. This was much thought of and desired; but the nature of the subject presented obstacles that seem insurmountable. One topic necessarily ran into, or over lapped, another. No chronological unity, if the work had been thus cut up, could have been preserved; and much of the ground would have had to be gone over and over again. Examinations, Trials, Executions were, often, all going on at once.

There is danger of a diminution of the continuous interest of some works, thus severed into fragments. There are, indeed, animals that will bear to be chopped up indefinitely, and each parcel retain its life: not so with others. The most important of all documents have suffered injury, not to be calculated, in their attractiveness and impressiveness, by being divided into Chapter and Verse, in many instances without reference to the unity of topics, or coherence of passages; dislocating the frame of narratives, and breaking the structure of sentences. We all know to what a ridiculous extent this practice was, for a long period, carried in Sermons, which were " divided " to a degree of artificial and elaborate dissection into " heads," that tasked to the utmost the ingenuity of the preacher, and overwhelmed the discernment and memory of the hearer. He, in fact, was thought the ablest sermonizer, who could stretch the longest string of divisions, up to the " nineteenthly, " and beyond. This fashion has a prominent place among *The Grounds and Occasions of the Contempt of the Clergy and Religion*, by John Eachard, D. D., a work published in London, near the commencement of the last century—one of the few books, like Calef's, which have turned the tide, and arrested the follies, of their times. In bold, free. forcible satire, Eachard's book stands alone. Founded on great learning, inspired by genuine wit, its style is plain even to homeliness. It struck at the highest, and was felt and appreciated by the lowest. It reformed the pulpit, simplified the literature. eradicated absurdities of diction and construction, and removed many of the ecclesiactic abuses, of its day. No work of the kind ever met with a more enthusiastic reception. I quote from the Eleventh Edition, printed in 1705: " We must observe, that there " is a great difference in texts. For all texts " come not asunder. alike; for sometimes the " words naturally fall asunder; sometimes they " drop asunder; sometimes they melt; some- " times they untwist; and there be some words " so willing to be parted, that they divide them- " selves, to the great ease and rejoicing of the " Minister. But if they will not easily come in " pieces, then he falls to hacking and hewing, " as if he would make all fly into shivers. The " truth of it is, I have known, now and then, " some knotty texts, that have been divided " seven or eight times over, before they could " make them split handsomely, according to " their mind."

An apology to those critics who have complained of my not dividing my book into Chapters, is found in the foregoing passage. I tried to do it, but found it a " knotty " subject, and, like the texts Eachard speaks of, " would not " easily come in pieces." With all my efforts, it it could not be made to " split handsomely."

This, and all other suggestions of criticism, are gratefully received and respectfully considered. But, after all, it will not be well to establish any canons, to be, in all cases. implicitly obeyed, by all writers. Much must be left to individual judgment. Regard must be had to the nature of subjects. Instead of servile uniformity, variety and diversity must be encouraged. In this way, only, can we have a free. natural, living literature.

In passing, I would say, that in meeting the demand made upon me by the Reviewer, to rewrite the history of Salem witchcraft, I shall avail myself of the opportunity to correct the single error he has mentioned, In a re-issue of the work, I shall endeavor to make it as accurate as possible. Anything that is found to be wrong shall be rectified. The work, in the different forms in which it was published, is nearly out of print. When issued again, it will be in a less costly style and more within the reach of all. From the result of my own continued researches and the suggestions of others, I feel inclined to the opinion that no very considerable alterations will be made; and that subsequent editions, will not impair the authority or value of the work, as originally published. in 1867.

In preparing the statement, now brought to a close, the only object has been to get at, and present, the real facts of history. Nothing, merely personal, affecting the writer in the *North American Review* or myself, can be considered as of comparative moment. Many of the expressions used by that writer, as to what I have "seen" or "read" and the like, are, it must be confessed, rather peculiar; but of very little interest to the public. Any notice, taken of them, has been incidental, and such as naturally arose in the treatment of the subject.

In parting. with the reader, I venture so far further to tax his patience, as to ask to take a retrospective glance, together, over the outlines of the road we have travelled.

In connection with some preliminary observations, the first step in the argument was to show the relation of the Mathers, father and son, to the superstitions of their times culminating in the Witchcraft Delusion of 1692, and their share of responsibility therefor. The several successive stages of the discussion were as follows:—The connection of Cotton Mather with alleged cases of Witchcraft in the family of John Goodwin of Boston, in 1688; and said Goodwin's certificates disposed of: Mather's idea of Witchcraft, as a war waged by the Devil against the Church; and his use of prayer: The connection between the cases, at Boston in 1688, and at Salem in 1692: The relation of the Mathers to the Government of Massachusetts, in 1692: The arrival of Sir William Phips; the impression made upon him by those whom he first met; his letter to the Government in England: The circumstances attending the establishment of the Special Court of Oyer and Terminer, and the precipitance with which it was put into operation: Its proceedings, conducted by persons in the interest of the Mathers: Spectral Testimony; and the extent to which it was authorized by them to be received at the Trials, as affording grounds of enquiry and matter of presumption: Letter of Cotton Mather to one of the Judges: The Advice of the Ministers: Cotton Mather's probable plan for dealing with spectral evidence: His views on that subject, as gathered from his writings and declarations: The question of his connection with the Examinations before the Magistrates: His connection with the Trials and Executions: His Report of five of the Trials: His book entitled *The Wonders of the Invisible World;* its designs; the circumstances attending its preparation for the press; and the views, feelings, and expectations of its author, exhibited in extracts from it: Increase Mather's *Cases of Conscience:* The suppression of the Court of Oyer and Terminer, by

Sir William Phips: Cotton Mather's views subsequent to 1692, as gathered from his writings.

In traversing the field thus marked out, I submit that it has become demonstrated that, while Cotton Mather professed concurrence in the generally-received judgment of certain writers against the reception of spectral evidence, he approved of the manner in which it had been received by the Judges, at the Salem Trials, and eulogized them throughout, from the beginning to the end of the prosecutions, and ever after. He vindicated, as a general principle, the *admission* of that species of testimony, on the ground of its being a sufficient basis of enquiry and presumption, and needing only some additional evidence, —his own Report and papers on file show how little was required—to justify conviction and execution. This has been proved, at large, by an examination of his writings and actions, and is fully admitted by him, in various forms of language, on several occasions—substantially, in his statement, that Spectral Testimony was the "chief" ground upon which "divers" were condemned and executed, and, explicitly, in his letter to Foster, in which he says that " a very " great use is to be made " of it, in the manner and to the extent just mentioned; and that, when thus used, the " use for which the Great God in-" tended it," will be made. In the same passage, he commends the Judges for having admitted it; and declares they had the divine blessing thereupon, inasmuch as " God strangely sent other " convincing testimony," to corroborate, and thereby render it sufficient to convict. In his Address to the General Assembly, years afterward, he fully admits that the Judges, in 1692, whose course he applauded at the time, allowed persons to be adjudged guilty, " merely because" of Spectral Testimony.

My main purpose and duty, in preparing this article, have been to disprove the absolute and unlimited assertions made by the contributor to the *North American Review*, that Cotton Mather was opposed to the *admission* of Spectral Evidence; " denounced it as illegal, uncharitable, " and cruel ;" and " ever testified against it, both " publicly and privately ; " and that the *Advice of the Ministers*, drawn up by him, " was *very* " *specific* in *excluding* Spectral Testimony."

It has been thought proper, also, to vindicate the truth of history against the statements of this Reviewer, on some other points: as, for instance, by showing that the opinion of Cotton Mather's particular responsibility for the Witchcraft Tragedy, instead of originating with me, was held at the time, at home and abroad, and has come down, through an unbroken series of the most accredited writers, to our day; and that the influence of the Mathers never recovered from the shock given it, by the catastrophe of 1692.

The apology for the great length of this article is, that the high authority justly accorded to the *North American Review*, demanded, in controverting any position taken in its columns, a thorough and patient investigation, and the production, in full, of the documents belonging to the question. It has further been necessary, in order to get at the predominating tendency and import of Cotton Mather's writings, to cite them, in extended quotations and numerous extracts. To avoid the error into which the Reviewer has fallen, the peculiarity of Mather's style must be borne in mind. Opposite drifts of expression appear in different writings and in different parts of the same writing ; and, not infrequently, the clauses of the same passage have contrary bearings. He often palters, with himself as well as others, in a double sense.

Quotations, to any amount, from the writings of either of the Mathers, of passages having the appearance of discountenancing spectral evidence, can be of no avail in sustaining the positions taken by the Reviewer, because they are qualified by the admission, that evidence of that sort might and ought, notwithstanding, to be received as a basis for enquiry and ground of presumption, and, if supported by other ordinary testimony, was sufficient for conviction. That other testimony, when adduced, was, as represented by Mather, clothed with a divine authority ; having, as he says, been supplied by a special Providence, and been justly regarded, by the " excellent " Judges," as " an encouraging presence of God, " strangely sent in." It could, indeed, in the then state of the public mind, always be readily obtained. No matter how small in quantity or utterly irrelevant, it was sufficient for conviction, coming after the Spectral Evidence. To minds thus subdued and overwhelmed with " awe," trifles light as air were confirmation strong.

It is to be presumed that his warmest admirers would not think of comparing Cotton Mather with his transatlantic correspondent and coadjutor, as to force of character, power of mind, or the moral and religious value of their writings. Yet there were some striking similarities between them. They were men of undoubted genius and great learning. They were all their lives awake to whatever was going on around them. Earnestly interested, and actively engaging, in all questions of theology and government, they both rushed forthwith and incontinently to the press, until their publications became too voluminous and numerous to be patiently read or easily counted. Of course, what they printed was imbued with the changing aspects of the questions they handled and open to the imputation of inconsistency, of which Baxter was generally disregardful and Mather mostly unconscious.

Sir Roger L'Estrange was one of the great

wits and satirists of his age. His style was rough and reckless. A vehement and fierce upholder of the doctrines of arbitrary government, he was knighted by James the Second. His controversial writings, having all the attractions of unscrupulous invective and homely but cutting sarcasm, were much patronized by the great, and extensively read by the people. All Nonconformists and Dissenters were the objects of his coarse abuse. He issued an ingenious pamphlet with this title: *The Casuist uncased; in a Dialogue betwixt Richard and Baxter, with a moderator between them, for quietness sake.* The two disputants range over a variety of subjects, and are quite vehement against each other; the Moderator interposing to keep them to the point, preserve order in the debate, and, as occasion required, reduce them to "quietness." At one stage of the altercation, he exclaimed: "If an "Angel from Heaven, I perceive, were employed "to bring you two to an agreement, he should lose "his labour." Great was the amusement of all classes to find that the language uttered by the combatants, on each side, was taken from one or another of writings published by Richard Baxter, during his diversified controversial life.

If any skilful and painstaking humorist of our day, should feel so disposed, he might, by wading through the sea of Cotton Mather's writings, pick up material enough for the purpose; and, by cutting in halves paragraphs and sentences, entertain us in the same way, by giving to the public, through the Press, "*A Dialogue betwixt* "Cotton and Mather. *with a Moderator be-* "*tween them for quietness sake.*"